Nikki Turner

PRESENTS

A Woman's Work

STREET CHRONICLES

ONE WORLD TRADE PAPERBACKS

BALLANTINE BOOKS NEW YORK

A One World Books Trade Paperback Original

Copyright © 2011 by Nikki Turner

Published in the United States by One World Books, an imprint of The Random House Publishing Group, a division of Random House, Inc., New York.

ONE WORLD is a registered trademark and the One World colophon is a trademark of Random House, Inc.

Title-page photograph: iStockphoto

ISBN 978-0-345-50430-2
eBook ISBN 978-0-345-52630-4

Printed in the United States of America

www.oneworldbooks.net

2 4 6 8 9 7 5 3

Book design by Laurie Jewell

To all the people who have uplifted us,
who have always pushed us toward our best

I know you've got a little life in you yet
I know you've got a lot of strength left.

—*This Woman's Work*,
Kate Bush, as sung by Maxwell

Special Message from Nikki Turner to Her Readers

Dear Loyal Readers,

Back in the day, James Brown said this is a man's world, but it wouldn't be "nothing without a woman or a girl." Today, Beyoncé makes it known, girls, we run the world. I couldn't agree with them more.

Today's woman is juggling a 9-to-5, a part-time job, *and* selling Avon on the side while being a room mother to her child's class. She's the CEO of a multimillion-dollar corporation by day and pumping breast milk from her tired body at night for her newborn baby. She's the student cramming for finals in the college library (or not) and working the pole after hours in an off-campus bar to pay tuition, and the woman squeezing the most out of the measly handouts the state gives, turning nothing into something. Whether she's in the office, the classroom, or the boardroom, she's doing more than her share to make it happen.

Today's girl is no longer waiting for that dream to come true, where Prince Charming rolls up on his white horse to sweep her off her feet, take her away from all her troubles, and make everything all right. The white horse in this fantasy may have evolved into a white Bentley or white-on-white Air Force Ones, but beyond all that, women have taken their dreams—and realities—to a brand-new level. We aren't sitting around picking our fingernails waiting for that proverbial knight in shining armor anymore. We're taking matters into our own hands, tightening our boot straps, rolling up our sleeves, getting creative and paving our own way, blazing trails for other women to follow.

I've been one of those women trying to juggle it all, and I know a lot of you know my plight personally: being a single mother of two children, having a larger-than-life nontraditional career, trying to maintain a graceful balance of everything from kids to friendships, relationships, bills, pressing deadlines, and my own sanity. And that's one of the reasons why I wanted to do another Street Chronicles collection for the ladies: because *A Woman's Work* is *never* done!

Another reason for this edition is that although all my Street Chronicles books have been well received—thank you—Girls in the Game was the most popular in the series. Getting together another stellar team of women writers to take my loyal readers to the next level in urban fiction wasn't hard at all. As a matter of fact, it only took a couple of emails and text messages for my girls to come through. Tysha and LaKesa Cox were natural fits—their work appeared in *Girls in the Game*. I'd met Monique S. Hall at BookExpo America (BEA) a few years back, and the way she told me about some crazy drama she had going on at the time, I knew she could definitely put a fire story on paper. Keisha Starr and I had been trying to work together for a long time, and this was the perfect opportunity. Each story from this colorful and talented cast of writers fit to create this fantabulous collaboration. I enjoyed each and every one of their stories, and I hope you will, too.

Last, I would like to say, from the depths of my heart, thank you to my loyal, do-or-die readers. You all have supported all of my work from day one, and I appreciate you rolling with me one mo' time for another edition of my original urban lit smorgasbord: Street Chronicles. And if this is your first time—maybe you were referred by a friend, or you're just curious and trying something new—I thank you and welcome you to a riveting and gritty literary experience.

Much love,
Nikki Turner

Contents

KEISHA STARR

Dying to Be a Star

The Preacher's Daughter

I walked through my front door at 11:15 p.m. and headed straight to my bedroom because I was exhausted and damn near drained from tonight's performance, but I knew that I wasn't going to reach my destination before checking in with my parents, who were still up waiting for me to come home. Week after week, it was the same fucking routine: I would come home late, they would be in the living room waiting for me to give them an explanation, and I would tell them the same bullshit!

"Melissa, why didn't you make curfew tonight? You are supposed to be in the house by ten p.m. sharp, and even that's too late. I'm getting sick and tired of you strolling through these doors after hours like your name is written on the deed. You know people look up to us, and you're not setting a good example for the kids in the neighborhood."

Growing up in a strict Christian household can do some serious damage to a girl's social life. I never got the chance to go to any parties or social gatherings with other kids my age. As far as my parents were concerned, Bible study, choir rehearsal, and the children's ministry group were all the social gatherings that a sixteen-year-old needed. You see, my father is Pastor Earl T. Booker James, and trust me, he always said his entire name wherever he went because it rang bells in our community. He loved the attention and praise that everyone gave him, but my mother, Sister Patricia James, loved it even more. Because my father's pastor of one of the biggest churches in Harrisburg, Pennsylvania, he and my mother always seemed to focus their attention on impressing others, and I for one was becoming very tired of it all.

"Melissa, you live in a Christian household, and you are going to walk in the right path, young lady. How do you think it looks when someone drives past the house and sees the pastor's daughter living like she doesn't have any rules to follow? What kind of example are you setting?"

First of all, no one should be driving past here minding my fucking business in the first place, so if they see me doing anything that hurts their precious feelings, then it serves them right. But of course I wasn't stupid enough to say that shit. "Ma, you knew that I had a game today in Wilmington, Delaware. It's not my fault that the bus came back to the school late. The game ran into overtime, and I couldn't just pick up and leave."

"When you asked us to join the volleyball team I didn't know that it was going to cause such a problem. You come home from practice late in the afternoons, and you've missed dinner almost every night since we allowed you to join that team. You know how important it is to your father for us to sit and eat dinner together. That's our special time for ourselves without anyone intervening. You even missed Bible study tonight, and last week you missed choir rehearsal. Now, this can't continue much longer because the church depends on you to do certain things."

My mother was making my head hurt to the point that it felt like I had a migraine giving birth to another migraine. Every time the subject of church came up, I could actually feel the tension running through my body. "You can't serve two masters, you know."

"I hate it when you say things like that. It's bad enough that you won't let me join the school choir but you also stopped me from joining one of the hottest R&B groups out in Pennsylvania. Tiffany and Jasmine have been trying to get me to join their group Pretty in Pink for over a year now but you and Daddy keep shutting down the idea without even listening. I joined the volleyball team and now that's starting to be a problem as well. I never get to do anything I want to do."

"Don't tell me about those fast girls. I can't tell you the last time Tiffany's mother was able to get her to come to church, and I won't even talk about Jasmine's mother. She wants to live her life through her daughter, and she's not raising her with morals, might I add. She allows Jasmine to have boyfriends, and I can almost bet my right eye that your friend is far from a virgin, just like her mother, if you know what I mean."

My mother had some nerve talking about Jasmine's mother like she's better than her or something. At least Mrs. Tarsha has enough faith in her daughter to manage her singing career. Jasmine and her mother have an excellent relationship. It's like they were more sisters than mother and daughter. Shit, sometimes I wish she was my mother; if she was, I would probably be signed to a major label by now.

"You say you want to sing; well, we've put you in the choir at church. You have solos every single Sunday. What's the difference between you singing in that group and you singing for the Lord? Either way, you're singing, aren't you?"

"Yes, I'm singing, but not the kind of music I love. Ma, I eat, sleep, and breathe R&B. I want to be the next Mary J. Blige, and you're trying to turn me into the next Mary Mary. I'm not saying anything is wrong with them but it's just not right for me. I'm sixteen years old. I should be allowed to make my own decisions."

"I told you before that you have to be an example to others. I will not allow you to bring shame to this family. We worked long and hard to build up our sterling reputation, and no one will ever get the satisfaction of talking bad about the James family—at least not while I'm alive."

"But Ma, can't you at least talk to Mrs. Tarsha and ask her questions about the group? They're not singing about sex, drugs, or murder. They're singing good music."

My mother laughed as if I'd said something funny. "And what is good music?" Before I got a chance, she answered her own question. "Good music is music that uplifts God's holy name. Good music is not music that leads to sinful engagement. If you sing about being in love, then sooner or later you'll be singing about making love, and one day you're going to be tempted to do it. R&B and hip-hop music ain't nothing more than the devil's way of getting God's children to commit sin. They have hidden messages behind the lyrics, and you are not allowed to sing those songs while living under this roof, and if I *ever* find out that you are, then you will be out of here!"

"But, Ma . . ."

"Goodnight, Melissa. This discussion is over, and I suggest you stop while you're ahead."

And there you have it, folks: a typical one-on-one with my mother. It was like someone picked up a remote control and pressed the MUTE button every time I talked about pursuing my dreams. Music is my sole purpose in life. Not one day goes by without me writing a song or performing in front of the mirror behind closed doors. I know that one day I am going to be a superstar, so I will do anything, and I mean *anything* I need to do to make sure that happens.

After realizing that this conversation wasn't going where I wanted it to, I walked into my bedroom, slammed the door, and called Jasmine to make sure she'd made it home safely. "What's up, girl?" she answered. "Were your parents tripping about you coming home late again? I know they were," she said, giggling.

"Yeah but I told her that our game went into overtime and blah, blah, blah. I told her what she needed to hear."

"So when are you going to tell her that you joined the group, Melissa? Sooner or later you're going to graduate from high school and then you can't use the volleyball team as an alibi."

I walked over, slightly opened the door, and peeked out because my mother was known to stick her ear in a couple of cracks around the house. "Girl, I tried to talk to her about the group tonight but she started to talk fucking crazy. Basically, she said if I sing R&B then I'm going to be tempted to fuck." Jasmine burst out laughing so loud that I had to move the receiver from my ear to avoid a busted eardrum.

"Little does she know, huh," she replied while still laughing. "She still thinks that her precious Melissa is a virgin. She would really like to know the business."

Since I was an only child on top of being a preacher's kid, I was sheltered and overprotected. And on top of that, it didn't help that my body started developing early. I had a figure that was any parent's nightmare—especially a pastor. People always ranted and raved over my beauty, which assured me that I was born to be a star. I'm 5'7", with a smooth, light-skinned complexion and hazel eyes. My curves could put Pam Grier to shame. I have more hips, ass, and tits than the average bitch. My cinnamon-colored hair flowed like I was in a Revlon perm commercial. I was stunning—I knew it, my parents knew it, and everyone else did too.

As I said earlier, I'm no saint and I don't want to be anyone's savior. My parents were so worried about preventing me from fucking that they couldn't see that I have been giving it up for over a year now. As a matter of fact, I lost my virginity in the church's parking lot to Charles Manley, the boy who played drums in our youth choir. Come to think of it, I was giving Charles head for about three months before we actually had sex, and every single sexual episode took place somewhere on the church grounds.

And just in case you're wondering, I don't feel bad about it because the majority of the kids at church were fucking each other. For me, having sex in my father's sanctuary was a way of balancing the stress that my parents threw in my lap from day to day. It was my way of rebelling against them for being my shadow's shadow.

"I can't wait to turn eighteen years old. Then they won't have any say-so in my life. I tell you, when that day comes, we're moving to Atlanta, Georgia, and striking it big, girl."

"Atlanta," Jasmine repeated. "What's in Atlanta?"

"Everything is there, Jasmine. Haven't you noticed that all the latest R&B singers are coming out of Atlanta? Usher, Monica, and 112 are all from Atlanta, and that's where we need to be to get exposed."

"Well, as soon as you turn eighteen, we're moving to the A," Jasmine said, giggling again.

"Mark that date on your calendar," I advised her, knowing good and well that I was going to do it. Jasmine might think it was a joke, but I'm dead-ass serious about moving to Atlanta. I know there are plenty of opportunities out there waiting for me.

Jasmine and I then talked for a few minutes about concepts for a track that I had to write for the group. A couple of times I could have sworn I saw someone's shadow outside my door, so I decided to end the call before I got caught. "Well, let me get off this phone before my mother comes in here and asks me who I'm talking to this late. I'll see you in school tomorrow. Bye-bye."

"Okay, girl, and don't forget that we have practice tomorrow after school, so tell your mother something believable, okay? We need you in this group, and we've come too far for you to get caught now. Just make up a good lie."

"I always do," I reassured her before hanging up. And I damn sure always do!

For months I continued to juggle my two very separate worlds like a pro without my parents catching on. I came close to getting caught once or twice but, overall I held my own. At times, I felt like I was suffering from multiple personality disorder. In the presence of my parents, I was the churchgoing teenager who sang her heart out each and every Sunday and moved the congregation like any adult who stood at the pulpit. Everyone would praise me and tell me how talented I was. "Your voice is a gift from God," they would say. I made sure to hit very powerful notes from my diaphragm and put on an Oscar-worthy performance when singing, just to get the crowd moving. In my eyes, singing at church each Sunday was no different from the shows that I did throughout the week with the group. My main goal was to give the people what they wanted.

On the other hand, when my parents weren't around, I transformed into a sassy member of the group Pretty in Pink. Every moment I could spare to sneak into the studio with the group, I was there. And whenever we had a show to do, I always managed to trick my parents into believing that I was doing something productive after school. Likewise, I found time to sneak around with my new boyfriend, Shawn, who I might add was two years older than I.

I had the game down pat, and no one played it quite like me. Jasmine's mother, Mrs. Tarsha, was very cool and down-to-earth. Shit, she was young herself. She had Jasmine when she was only fourteen years old, so she was more in tune with our generation than the average parent. She understood how it felt to be young, in love, and in need. She didn't mind when Jasmine, Tiffany, and I had company over to her house. She even allowed Jasmine's boyfriend to sleep over. She said she knew we were fucking already, so it made no sense to try to stop us. Her way of dealing with the situation was to give us condoms and say, "Wrap it up and don't make any babies like I did, because it will interrupt the flow of the group." I thought she was the perfect mother, and I can't stress enough how much I loved and admired her.

Mrs. Tarsha was the manager of Pretty in Pink and her husband, Mr. George, was our entertainment lawyer. Together, they were a force to be reckoned with. Mr. George spoiled Mrs. Tarsha rotten like she was his own child, which is understandable, considering that he was nearly sixty-five years old. She'd had about five plastic surgeries so far, drove three sports cars, and lived in a phat-ass crib. Jasmine was one lucky girl, I tell you.

We had just finished our fifth song on the album when my boo called and asked if I could stop over at his house because his roommate was gone for the night. From the moment he told me that we were going to be alone, I knew it was on. My pussy began to moisten the crotch of my panties from the thought of how good he made my body feel. "What a perfect way to end a perfect day," I mumbled to myself as I grabbed my pocketbook and headed out the door. I just wrote and recorded a very hot song and now I'm going to get some dick; bing-bang, life is grand!

It was 8:00 p.m., which was perfect because I had two hours to spend with Shawn and head home without my parents suspecting a thing. On my way over, I sprayed on perfume, touched up my makeup, and fixed my hair. All of this would be in vain, because all Shawn was going to do was mess it up as usual. Still, I had to be cute as a button.

My boo was cute and sexy, and had a nice flow of dough coming in from hustling for his cousin, Rex, who owned the studio that we were recording in. He drove a Black Tahoe, and always gave me money whenever we hooked up, so it's safe to say that I enjoyed hooking up with him as much as possible. The dick was good, the head was marvelous, but the best part of dating Shawn, or should I say Shawn-Da-Don, was that he was a dynamic producer. As a matter of fact, that's how we met.

Mrs. Tarsha took us to Rex's studio to listen to some instrumentals and he was down there making a very hot track for this rap group called Black Out. She kept telling me how pretty Shawn thought I was and gave me the okay to go over and formally intro- duce myself. Then she made us exchange numbers and suggested that we go upstairs to the bedroom to talk more privately. To make a long story short, I fucked him not even an hour after that, and from then on, Shawn began to give the group free tracks, which saved Mrs. Tarsha a lot of money. The way I saw it, I was investing in my career.

Shawn knew the drill about me lying to my parents to spend time with him, so we never wasted time on foreplay when we hooked up. It was always a strong, hot physical chemistry that pulled our bodies together like magnets.

I knocked on the basement door and within seconds, my boo opened up wearing nothing but a pair of Polo boxer shorts. Damn, this brother looked like a scrumptious Snickers bar, and I was feeling mighty hungry.

"Hello, baby," he greeted as he opened the door and looked me up and down like I was a buffet table and he didn't know where to begin. "What's up with you tonight?" Very much aware that I was pressed for time, I simply reached into my pocketbook, pulled out a red nylon cloth, and stuffed it directly into his mouth.

"That's what's up with me tonight," I replied as I made my way over to the couch and began removing the rest of my clothes. I was racing the clock and wasn't going to spend a minute engaging in small talk. For me, there was nothing to talk about.

Shawn pulled the cloth out of his mouth, looked at it, and saw that he was holding my thong. Being the freak that he is, he slowly rubbed it across his face and sniffed it.

"Oh, so you're ready for this dick, huh? Well, bend that phat ass over and let me see that juicy pussy." Before turning around and assuming the position, I stood up, stuck my tongue deeply into his mouth, and stole a big kiss. The texture and deep stroke of his tongue sent bolts of friction to my clitoris.

The way I passionately sucked his tongue only made me yearn to put other parts of him into my mouth, so I kneeled down and removed his boxers. His big cock stood up in front of my eyes as if it was standing to sing our national anthem. As a matter of fact, I was damn near saluting that shit in my mind; that's how official it looked. *I pledge allegiance to this dick of the United Dick Suckers of America.*

I wasted no time sticking Shawn's love stick deeply into the back of my throat as he began thrusting back and forth. As soon as he felt the first stroke, he grabbed a handful of my hair and let out a loud moan. The sound of his baritone voice going up two pitches like he was singing falsetto gave me confidence that I was doing a very good job.

"Damn, damn, shit, baby. You suck this dick so fucking good. Oh yeah, suck that shit, bitch." The dirtier he talked to me, the more turned on I got. I began to switch up the flow of my head game while wrapping my lips deeper and deeper around his dick until the entire thing became shiny and hard. I then took his balls in my hands and massaged them while sucking his luscious pole.

"Wait, baby, stop, stop before I cum. Please don't drain me, Melissa. I want some of that good, wet pussy." A bitch knows she's bad when her man has to beg her not to make him erupt. That right there shows me that I'm in total control when a dick is between these strong jaws.

"Do you really want me to stop?" I asked, looking straight into his eyes, with his dick still plunging to the back of my throat. Nothing turns a man on more than a pretty bitch sucking his dick while looking him dead in his eyes. It's the thrill of that forbidden innocence being displayed in a sexual environment that gets him. And if you really want to add sparks to the room, let one teardrop fall down your cheek. Sounds crazy, huh? Try that shit and watch how fast that dick erupts.

"Melissa, stop! Baby, you're about to make me cum; stop!"

"Okay, I'm going to be a good girl tonight. I'm not going to take it from you," I arrogantly replied as I walked back to the couch, planted my face in the cushion, and bent over. You know, giving him the facedown, ass-up position.

"Come on and fuck me then, Shawn." I knew that I was in charge, and I loved every second of it.

I didn't get my last word out before he put one of his legs up on the couch, pulled me closer to him, and inserted every inch of his dick inside me. The first stab is always the most painful. I screamed because it felt like it went straight into my back.

My pussy was drenched to the point that my juices were running down my legs. Shawn tried his best to work me out, but the truth is, I was just too damn good and wet. I knew he was going to cum any minute now because his strokes slowed while his heavy breathing increased.

"Oh, oh, shit . . . I'm cumming, baby. I'm cumming." Shawn pushed himself to the limit to get every drop of this good-good wet-wet before pulling out and creaming on my lower back and ass. Let's just say that for about ten minutes we both laid down on the couch speechless 'cause I needed to regain my strength before going home.

After getting ourselves together, I quickly washed up to remove any sexual scent that might still be lingering on me. As usual, Shawn hit me with a couple of hundreds, handed me a few tracks for the group, and sent me on my merry way. True, we didn't have love, but we had a lot of lust for each other, which made our relationship more than perfect. I didn't need his love; all I needed was those blazing-ass tracks anyhow.

In my head I practiced the lies I was going to tell my parents when I got home. I wasn't late because I still had a whole half hour before curfew; however, I did miss Bible study, which was like missing your own wedding in my parents' eyes. *Let's see, tonight I think I'll tell them I failed a math test and went over to Kimberly Mat-*

thews's house to study. My parents were very fond of her 'cause she was smart as hell and her mother sat on the board at church. Also, Kimberly was my friend, so I knew she'd definitely back up any story I gave.

Both of my parents were sitting in the living room when I walked through the door, which wasn't uncommon. My father had a stern look on his face, and my mother looked upset. *Here we go again. They're about to grill me about going to church.*

"Hello," I nonchalantly said as I headed toward the kitchen to get a cold drink. My father barely looked my way, as if I hadn't just said hello to him. The expression on his face never changed, and I knew he was pissed off about something. My mother, however, walked over, grabbed me by the arm, and forcefully demanded that I take a seat.

"Wait just a minute, young lady. We have something to talk to you about, and depending on your decisions tonight, you may not need to go into the kitchen because you'll need to go to your room and pack your things."

Oh brother, what the hell is going on? I've come into this house late many times before, and the one night I'm on time, she's talking about putting me out. That sounded totally backward to me. Not one for wasting time, I asked them straight up what was going on, because I wasn't going to sit and play charades, especially while I was still on the high that Shawn just gave me. "What do y'all have to talk to me about? What did I do now?" I asked in a bored tone.

My father, who I guess was the good cop, continued to sit and ignore me while "Mother Commando" played the bad cop. "So you missed Bible study?"

"I told you before that I can't control what time the games are over," I interrupted. "Do you want me to quit the team? Because I'm tired of having the same conversation every time we have a game or late practice." My mother looked at my father and smirked as he turned toward me and shook his head. That was the only time he displayed any emotion, and I didn't like it because it seemed like they had something over me. "What do you want me to do?" I asked.

My father jumped from his seat and yelled, "What we want you to do is stop lying in this house! Stop lying to your mother! Stop lying to me! Stop lying to yourself! And stop trying to lie to God when he knows the truth! Stop it, stop it, *stop it*!" I've heard my father scream and holler over the years, particularly on Sundays, when he's at the peak of his sermon, but this was something new. He was furious with me and why, I didn't know. I'd been so careful about covering my tracks that I couldn't imagine my parents knowing anything about the group or Shawn.

"I'm not lying," I replied, feeling confused about what was really going on. "I went over to Kimberly's house after volleyball practice to study for a math test. I didn't call because—"

"Oh, just shut your mouth, Melissa. We know you're not on the volleyball team. As a matter of fact, volleyball season ended months ago, and from what Mrs. Clifford, the volleyball coach, said you were never on the team to begin with. So I met with your teachers, who told me your grades have dropped drastically since you joined that R&B group. They said you've missed days of school, and when you do show up, you're barely awake." *Oh, shit, I'm dead.* I knew I was backed against the wall, but I kept my composure.

"Your math teacher said the only things you're focused on are music and boys. He said you sit in his class writing songs, and you've failed every test he gave this year. When I asked him why he didn't contact us a long time ago, he showed me the progress report, which to my surprise had my signature on it, which is confusing, since I never saw that paper before." My father was so upset his hands were trembling. I was speechless, and it didn't make any sense to lie anymore.

As my parents both took turns grilling me, it became clear that someone from church had dropped a dime on me. Turns out that one of my stupid friends was talking on the phone about me and their mother overheard. She in turn called my parents, who then went to the school to verify what they'd heard. It was so unfair. I didn't mind getting caught because I knew that was one of the consequences of lying; you win some, and you lose some. What I did find disturbing was that I was going down because of someone else's big mouth. I'm on the chopping board because some bitch decided to be all up in my business and let her meddling mother snitch on my ass.

"Look, I'm sorry, okay, but you guys put too much pressure on me, and I have to live my life. I'm sixteen years old but you treat me like I'm six. It's no secret how much I love music; not the type of music that you force me to sing, but the music I actually love. Daddy, you wanted to be a preacher, and you followed your heart and became a preacher. Well, I did the same except I chose R&B over gospel. I'm not saying I'll never sing gospel music because it's uplifting and I enjoy singing lots of it; but I'll be the next big R&B star. Why can't I just have your support?"

"Look, young lady!" Mother Commando yelled. "I've warned you on numerous occasions about the dangers of that music and forbade you to join that group. It's apparent to me that you respect neither me nor your father, and I will not tolerate that. After coming back from your school, your father and I went to your room to see what else you may have been hiding. Let's just say we found some things that brought tears to our eyes. I saw your love letters and pictures, and even found and listened to the CDs you had stashed under your mattress. Melissa, you are sexually active. You've given away a precious gift that God gave you to save for your husband." My mother began to cry, and I could see the pain in her eyes. At that moment, I realized how serious the situation was for me. Then my father took over.

"I'm going to cut to the chase because I'm embarrassed beyond imagination, and your mother can't take any more of this.
Do you know how it feels to have someone tell you your daughter
is not worthy to stand in your own pulpit?" I didn't answer because I was too busy thinking of ways to get out of this situation.
"*Do you?*" my father yelled louder than the first time.

"No, sir, I don't," I replied under my breath. I was scared. I
truly didn't expect that this day would come so soon. I was hoping
to at least hold on to these secrets until I turned eighteen.

"Well, it's not a good feeling when you're the pastor of the
church and hear that kind of news from a member. It's even worse
when you have to stand up and hear every teacher in the school
say nothing but bad things about your child. I don't know where
we went wrong, Melissa, but I can tell you that I'm going to make
it right tonight!" he yelled as he banged his fist on our coffee
table. "You have two choices at this point. You can ask God for for-
giveness, quit that group, and turn your life around before it's too
late, or you can go upstairs, pack your things, and go. Those are
the two options that I'm giving you, and you must choose one *tonight!*"

Quit the group? Were they fucking insane? Being a part of
Pretty in Pink meant the world to me, and I wasn't going to give
that shit up anytime soon. I would promise to quit fucking Shawn
before I promised to quit the group. I couldn't believe that those
were the only two choices for me. On top of it all, I couldn't believe that my parents were so wrapped up in upholding their
image that they were actually considering putting me out on the
street. They were so hypocritical. It's got to be a sin to put your
underage child out of the only home she's known, just for being
true to herself.

We argued back and forth, and at the end of the day, I had to
make a decision, so I did. "Mom and dad, I love you both to
death and I know that I've hurt you. Please believe me when I

say that wasn't my intention, but I have to follow my heart, and my heart is leading me to be in that group. I cannot and will not quit Pretty in Pink because we're a team and we're very close to getting a recording deal. So if you want me to leave, then I'll go. I don't want to, but if I have to choose my warm bed over singing for the group, then I'll say goodbye to that bed without thinking twice."

"Okay, Miss Melissa James," my father sarcastically said. "Get your things and leave my home tonight." I looked over at my mother to see if this was what she really wanted and she turned away from me as if I were already dead to her. Then she said, "I will pray for you, my child, and ask God to show you the light. One day you will look back and understand where I'm coming from. I declare that one day God will truly touch your heart, and on that day, if my eyes are still open, then these doors will be too. However, if you can't abide by our rules—no, I take that back—if you can't abide by God's rules, then you have to go. I will not allow the devil to destroy my home, and that's what's going to happen if I let you stay here and continue living the sinful life that you're living."

I couldn't believe what I was hearing, but it became very clear to me that this was real as I packed my clothes and left the only home I'd ever known. My mother had threatened me before, but I never in a million years actually thought they'd abandon me. Since they were so-called Christians, I just never thought they had it in them to really put me out on the street, all because I "chose music over God," as my father so bluntly put it.

I called Shawn and told him what happened, and he had the nerve to ask me, "So where are you going to stay?" Apparently he had no intention of helping me, so I went down the list, calling other dudes who I was dealing with, but they all said the same stupid shit, "So where are you going to stay?" I couldn't believe that I was in this predicament. It still hadn't registered that I no longer had a roof over my head. Besides that, all this pussy I gave up to these niggas and none of them was making a move to at least come and get me from the side of the road; oh, hell no! I couldn't believe this shit.

After calling about a million no-good niggas, I decided to call some bitches for help. The first person I called was Jasmine. As soon as she picked up, I began crying and telling her what went down at home word for word. She told me to calm down, then handed her mom the phone. When she came on the line, I repeated my story, except this time around, I made sure to pile it on for sympathy. "Mrs. Tarsha, I have to leave the group because I don't have anywhere to live. My parents somehow found out what's been going on and they basically told me to quit the group or move out. I couldn't do that to Jasmine and Tiffany after all we've been through. I begged and pleaded with them but they wouldn't listen and kicked me out." I let out a big cry loud enough to be heard in Japan. "I feel like I'm going to die. I want to kill myself."

"Just calm down and tell us where you are, Melissa. I'm on my way for you right now." Bingo! That's what I'd been waiting to hear all night long. Those were the fucking words that Shawn should have said over an hour ago.

"I'm on Division Street, across from the McDonald's."

"All right, I'm on my way. Don't panic. We'll work this out together. You can't quit the group now after we've worked so hard and come this far."

I stood on the corner for twenty minutes, but when you're distraught and feeling beside yourself, every second feels like an eternity. When Mrs. Tarsha's white-on-white BMW pulled to the curb, I felt a load of worries drop off my shoulders. She beeped the horn to grab my attention and opened her trunk for me to put my things in. Jasmine got out of the car to help.

"Damn, girl, I can't believe your peoples really put you out just for singing. You've done some sneaky shit in your life, but to be punished like this just for joining a singing group is plain ridiculous." I loaded my bags in the trunk, closed it, and took a seat in the back. I purposely didn't respond to Jasmine's comment because I wasn't in the mood, and she was making me feel worse. However, the very second Jasmine sat back down in the car she continued to speak her mind. "You joined a group, not a cult. What's the problem?"

Being the smart chick that I was, I decided to kill two birds with one stone. I could smash my mother for putting me out while grabbing Mrs. Tarsha's attention so that she could help fix the situation. "Everything that's not their way is the wrong way. My mother once told me that your mom is not a good mother and that you're going to get pregnant at a young age just like she did. She said your brothers are going to be in jail before they're twenty-one just like their fathers. They're so phony because they always have something negative to say about people yet smile in their face at church on Sunday mornings." I knew what I was doing by saying that. I wanted Mrs. Tarsha to get mad and go against my mother.

"Wait a minute!" Mrs. Tarsha yelled as she slammed on her brakes and stopped the car in the middle of the street. "Your mother said that I'm not a good mother? I'm not a good mother, huh? Then why is it that my child is in my possession and she threw hers out on the street? That fake-ass righteous bitch better keep my name out of her fucking mouth before I go to church and whip her ass in front of the entire congregation." Mrs. Tarsha was furious. She began calling her million and one friends and telling them what my mother had said about her and her kids. Inside, I was laughing my heart out at some of the things she was saying.

"I tell you what, I bet I'll be a better mother to you than she was. Melissa, you can stay with us as long as you want, baby. Fuck your fake-ass mother."

"Thank you so much," I replied, feeling a sense of joy running through every inch of my body. Maybe, just maybe, this could be a blessing in disguise. I had always asked God to make my mother more down-to-earth like Mrs. Tarsha. At times, I had flat-out asked God why Mrs. Tarsha wasn't my mother, and now I would actually get the chance to live with her. With my parents off my back and out of my business, nothing can stop me from accomplishing my goal of being a big star. I have the talent, an excellent manager, and now the freedom. Goodbye and so long choir rehearsal. Melissa James is on her way to Hollywood!

Now that all the secrets were finally out of the bag, I was free to go after my music career full force. I began to do things that I had always wanted to do, like join the hip-hop dance class at school. The majority of R&B singers are also dancers, so I made it my business to learn the fundamentals of choreography. I also went full steam ahead with my writing. I wrote at least one song per day for the group, and with Shawn still pushing us tracks, our album was done in no time. Mrs. Tarsha and her husband began to shop our demo around like crackheads selling a hot TV. Pretty in Pink soon became very popular in Pennsylvania and many surrounding states. Our songs were even playing on all the local radio stations, and for the first time in my life, my dreams were within my reach.

Mrs. Tarsha's only rule in the house was "Thou shall not steal." As long as you didn't steal from her pocketbook or closet, she pretty much turned a blind eye to everything else and did her own thing. Half the time, she wasn't even home. Although I had lost my virginity before I moved in, I had many first-time experiences while living in that house. I had my first threesome and then some with Jasmine's two brothers, Dylan and Michael. Shit, I had my first bisexual experience with Jasmine, which might I add was very hot. That girl taught me things that I never knew existed. I was still sleeping with Shawn, but with Jasmine joining in; he pretty much took care of all my production and financial needs.

My list of sexual partners soon climbed into the double digits. It was more about rebelling against my parents than anything. I had my first, second, and third abortions, and probably would have been on my fourth if someone hadn't put me on to birth control pills. I didn't know what to do with my newfound freedom, so I chose to do it all. I was certainly living a life that would have caused my parents to die of shame if they found out about it. The way I looked at it was, if they hadn't put me out, I would still have had a drop of innocence somewhere left in my body. But as you can see, my innocence became nonexistent after moving in with Jasmine.

Before I knew it, two years had passed and I was still on my grind. I graduated from high school and enrolled in "Fuck 'Em University." Rather than attend college, I continued to focus on my music career. I even saved up some money Shawn gave me and bought a little Honda. It was nothing fancy, but it got me where I wanted to go, and for once in my life I felt like an adult.

Mrs. Tarsha and her husband, George, walked into the studio one night on cloud nine and told everyone to gather in the waiting room area. I was wondering what the hell was going on because they were very excited and pumped up. After Tiffany, Jasmine, and I walked in and sat down she said, "Girls, I have some news that's going to knock your socks off. As you know, I've been shopping your demos like crazy and it finally paid off. Next week we're flying out to New York to meet with some A&R executives from Sony Music Group."

I was hearing her words in real time but it took a minute for them to register in my brain. Did she just say that we were going to New York to meet A&Rs from Sony? Oh, my God, is it finally going to happen for me? All my hard work and sacrifice were finally going to pay off. We were all so happy that night. I remember us just hugging each other and falling to the floor with tears in our eyes. It was a feeling I'll always remember.

Then Mrs. Tarsha said, "There have to be some changes made before we meet with them next week, though. You girls have to get your styles together and make some minor adjustments to the album."

She then went into details of all the changes, which I found very interesting. Right away, when she discussed the direction she wanted us to go in regard to our looks, I noticed that Tiffany and I were going to have average styles while Jasmine's sounded flashy and hot. "Melissa and Tiffany, we're going to give you both new looks. I think you both need to cut your hair and rock nice short hairdos. Jasmine, I think you would look nice wearing something more dramatic, like a full lace-front weave down your back. That would be hot!" I stood there not saying a word but I had a lot to say. Next she was removing songs from the CD that featured all of us and adding songs where Jasmine sang a majority of the leads. Then she dropped a bomb on us, saying that the group's name would change from Pretty in Pink to Jazzy Girls. "Pretty in Pink sounds too innocent, and I want you girls to target a more mature audience. Jazzy Girls sounds better, and will grab much more attention!"

The more she talked, the more I heard Jasmine's name being mentioned and ours being taken away. She even said that we had a photo shoot in the morning and told us that the CD cover was being changed. And, as you might have guessed, she stressed that we were going to take many pictures with Jasmine standing in the middle because it would look better for the group "*heightwise.*" "Jasmine needs to stand in the middle when you guys are taking pictures because it looks better when everyone is positioned according to their height." I was thinking, how could it look better for the group heightwise when I was taller than the other two girls? So it made perfect sense for me to be in the middle if anything.

"Oh, and by the way, Melissa, Jasmine is going to share some of the writing credits with you because I want them to see that you can all write." What the fuck? If that's the case, then why wasn't she adding Tiffany to the credits too? I wrote every song that we recorded all by myself, and I didn't see why I should share my writer's credits with someone who couldn't write a decent song to save her fucking life. Not only did I write every song, but I also did our background vocals because I had the strongest voice. Without me, this group wouldn't have taken its music to the level where it was, and I didn't think these changes were fair. I didn't want to cut my hair, and I didn't want to share my writer's credits.

I looked over at the other girls and Jasmine had this huge smile on her face. Of course she would be happy as shit; the ball was in her corner. Tiffany, however, looked tense and uneasy, just like I was feeling, but she had this awkward half smile on her face. I could tell she was faking being happy, and I for one wasn't going to do that. I haven't spoken to my parents in two years just to get an opportunity like this, and I wasn't going to let Jasmine and her mother take it away from me.

"Excuse me, Mrs. Tarsha, can I talk to you in private?" I politely asked.

"No, you can talk to me right here in front of everyone, if it's in regard to the group." She was instantly on the defensive and I suspected that she knew exactly what I wanted to talk about.

"I was wondering why we have to change anything. If they like us enough to fly us out to New York, then they must like what they see. I don't want to cut my hair, and I don't have a problem with helping anyone out, but if Jasmine wants writer's credits, then she should write some songs. I put in hard work writing, arranging, and recording all these songs, and I don't think it's fair that Jasmine gets to take credit for them."

"Is that correct?" she casually asked while looking over at her husband. "You feel that I'm being unfair, huh?"

"Well, sort of," I replied.

"Was I being unfair when I allowed you to join the group? Was I being unfair when I bought your clothes for the shows? Or better yet, was I being unfair when I took you in when you had nowhere to live? Let me tell you something, Melissa, you need to kiss the ground that not only I but my daughter walk on. If it wasn't for us, you would be out on the street somewhere." I couldn't believe what I was hearing. Mrs. Tarsha had this evil look on her face that I'd never seen before. "You know, I figured you'd do something like this. That's why I covered my ass from the start."

"What do you mean?" I asked.

She smiled as she looked over at Jasmine and her husband, who both had big grins on their faces. Mr. George then opened his briefcase, pulled out some papers that I had signed years ago, and handed me a copy. "That's what I mean, little girl. You're under a seven-year contract with me, and it basically says that I own rights to every song, which means that I can make any changes that I deem fit. You were paid for hire, and have no rights or claims to anything over here."

"But I wrote everything and recorded the majority of the leads and background vocals. Shawn gave those tracks to me, not the group. You haven't paid for anything in over three years except studio time. Why would you make me sign something like that? I would never have signed that if I knew what it meant."

"Well, you should have had a lawyer look it over before you signed it," Mrs. Tarsha said.

"But Mr. George is our lawyer, and when he explained the contract to me, he didn't say anything about me signing over my rights. You knew what you were doing all along, didn't you? You all used me to get a deal because you knew you wouldn't get one without me. That's why y'all insisted that I lie to my parents every day. That's some fucked-up shady shit!"

Jasmine pushed her mother out of the way and forcefully jumped into my face. "Wait a minute, bitch, you can't talk to my mother like that!" I was amazed at how fast she turned on me. We were just in here recording and having fun and now that she saw that money was involved, she called me "bitch" like I was just going to take it? Forget that. I wasn't taking this lying down.

"*Bitch,* I'm going to talk to you and your conniving mother any fucking way I please, because y'all are trying to rob me, and that's not going to fly with me. I'm going to take you to court."

"Well, we'll be ready for that," Mr. George said. "It's going to cost you thousands of dollars that you don't have just to draw up a case against us, and with this contract you signed, you might as well save yourself the time and money."

"Then I refuse to be in this group. Let's see what you're going to do now. Who's going to write and record the lead and background vocals from now on, huh?"

Again, the family began to laugh at me like I was doing stand-up comedy or something. "Well, we thought about this day coming, so we had a girl practicing every song that you recorded just in case you walked out of the group. As a matter of fact, it's my niece Lisa, who's more than ready to join Jazzy Girls, so you can leave the group tonight. And please leave our house as well."

"With pleasure!" I yelled. "Fuck you all. You can have those stupid songs. I can write a million more, fifty times better. I'll do my own solo thing, and when I make it, I'm going to tell the world about you bitches." The only thing I heard was laughter as I stormed out. They were laughing at me!

I left the studio and headed over to Shawn's house to tell him what had happened, but when I got there he had already heard Jasmine's side of the story. They had called him and told him everything, and I mean *everything*! She told him about me having sex with her brothers and his homeboy Trey. She told him about the abortions that I had because I didn't know who the fathers were. Shawn didn't even open the door for me. He simply yelled through it and told me to get the fuck off his porch before he shot me. I couldn't believe this shit was happening to me tonight. Shawn was the only person besides Mrs. Tarsha whom I could turn to, and now I had neither one in my corner.

I drove back to Jasmine's house to get my things, but when I pulled up I noticed my clothes and undergarments hanging on a post. The bitches had thrown everything I owned up and down the block. I wanted to kill them all but I was alone and knew it was a battle I couldn't win so, humiliated, I got out of my car and retrieved my belongings, most of which were cut up and bleached. Why was this happening to me? What was I going to do from here on? I had no one to turn to. I was alone and homeless again. All I had was this unreliable car, the clothes on my back, and $300. My only valuable possession was my God-given talent and a dream of being successful, and I knew I had to use them both to survive.

I couldn't let life get the best of me because I've sacrificed enough. *I may not be where I want to be right now, but I won't sit here for long. There's nothing in Pennsylvania for me anymore, and I knew exactly where I needed to go.* I packed everything I owned into the back of my car, even the cut-up and bleached clothes, and set out on a do-or-die road trip. God forbid my car got stolen or towed because everything in my whole life was in it. I had made this promise to Jasmine years ago, and I'm a woman of my word. Since Pennsylvania was not working out for me, I now have to make moves. Atlanta, Georgia, I sure hope you're ready for Melissa James, because I'm on my way and I'm coming full force!

Success Is a Journey, not a Destination!

I drove on I-95 for hours with my mind completely filled with thoughts of uncertainty. It was frightening to drive into an unknown future, and I felt like, no matter how long I drove, I would never reach my destination simply because I had none. I didn't have anywhere to go, no one to call, and nothing to look forward to. My family was gone, my friends were gone, and worst of all, my music and hard work were back in Pennsylvania with Pretty in Pink, which I bet by now had changed its name to Jazzy Girls. Most of my clothes were wrecked and drenched in bleach to the point that I had to wind my window down to avoid passing out from the strong fumes that filled my car, but they were all I had, so I couldn't afford to throw them away. I was starving but wouldn't even buy a value meal from McDonald's because I needed to save my money for a rainy day, which could be anytime soon. I was living like a bum on the street, and for the first time in my life, I was completely alone with no one to turn to.

I cried until my eyes were puffy and bloodshot but I continued to drive. The only time I stopped was to fill up the tank and get snacks and soda. I was truly living on the edge and when I realized that it was me against the world it took no time to jump into survival mode. I drove for nearly eighteen hours until I saw a billboard that read, "Welcome to Georgia . . . Home of the Sweet Peach!" Instantly tears began to pour from my eyes like a waterfall. However, this time around I wasn't crying because I was depressed, but because I felt proud of myself for actually accomplishing at least one dream in my life. It's true that I had nothing but the clothes on my back and wishful thinking; however, it was those two factors that gave me the confidence and determination to go on.

I drove and drove until finally spotting a street name that sounded familiar to me: Martin Luther King, Jr. Drive SE. With nothing to lose, I exited 28A and said a quick prayer to the man above. "Lord, please guide and protect me as I enter into this unfamiliar state. May the doors of opportunity open for me so that I may be in a better predicament than I am now. Amen!" Hopefully this was the beginning of a new life.

I drove around the neighborhoods, admiring this amazing city filled with countless opportunities. I began to size people up as they walked or drove past in their luxurious cars and wondered if they were famous producers, up-and-coming artists, or people with the connections that I needed to get my foot in the door. Someone once told me that Atlanta is to music as Hollywood is to acting, and if that's true, then it shouldn't take much time to get into the mix. I was already prepared to do exactly what I did with Shawn to get my jump start into the industry until I had the cash to hold my own. Then I'd be able to afford quality music tracks and studio time. All I needed to do was meet one or two prominent producers so I could fuck their brains out, get money, a hot ass track, and studio time. I had made that sacrifice for Pretty in Pink, so doing it for my own damn self wouldn't be a problem for me at all.

For three hours, I walked up and down various blocks to the point that my feet began to ache. But it wasn't in vain. Dudes were hollering at my fine ass from left and right, and I gave out my number to more men than I ever have in my whole life. Let's just say that I was extra friendly to everyone, including dudes whom I wouldn't even throw piss on. They would ask me, "So where are you from?" and I would tell them a big fat lie, something I've been doing all my life. Lying became as natural to me as breathing.

"Oh, I'm in town visiting a friend and checking out the city because I may relocate here to pursue my music career. Do you have any suggestions or recommendations?"

It didn't take me long to realize that everyone and their mamas were trying to strike it big in this city. Ain't nothing sadder than seeing people in their late forties and fifties handing over business cards and CDs, claiming they were *about* to get signed. It started to discourage me at times, but I had to keep reminding myself that I was not going to end up like them because I was young and talented. Although the situation was dispiriting, I did walk away with some valuable information. I was told by many aspiring artists to contact all the local record labels, radio stations, and DJs to get people familiar with my name. They said that people out here were always looking for that next big star to break and represent Atlanta. I was also told that the fastest way to get my music heard was to have it playing in the strip clubs. It seemed that gentlemen's clubs were very popular out here and could introduce my music to a vast number of male and female listeners, including some very famous producers and musicians. I took note of every drop of information that I got, big or small, and planned on using it right away.

I was strolling the block like a prostitute when I literally bumped heads with this very heavy guy who was dressed to kill and iced-out from head to toe. His big ass nearly knocked me to the ground, but he looked like he had serious paper, and somehow I knew that he would be valuable to me. It may sound a bit crazy, but I had a strange feeling that he was going to change my life.

"Excuse me, sweetheart. I didn't mean to knock down a pretty sexy thing like you."

I smiled and replied, "It's okay, Big Daddy, you're cool." I regained my balance, straightened out my tight-ass skirt, and kept the conversation going. "So where are you in a rush to on this fine evening? I want to holler at you, but it seems that you're way too busy for me." Yeah, you would have thought I was a man the way I was spitting game and macking this nigga, but hey, time was against me, and I had to move quickly.

"Well, I have some business to attend to tonight, but if you call me tomorrow then I promise I won't be as busy." He then began to check out all my assets. Men are always so predictable, especially when they're trying to hold a conversation with you while scoping out your breasts, thighs, and ass at the same time. "So are you from around here? I've never seen you before, and I know just about everybody out here."

Those words were music to my ears. If he knew everyone, then I needed to know him so that I could know everyone too. I had to get in good with this guy so he could help me out any way he possibly could. "I'm not from Atlanta. I'm out here on vacation. However, I plan to move here very soon to pursue my music career. Do you have any suggestions on what a girl needs to do to find a manager and hook up with some hot producers?"

"Are you serious?" he asked. "I know tons of producers, and as far as management is concerned, baby, you're speaking to the best of them right now. I manage Sha Diamond and Jay'Son, who are two R&B singers, as well as a rap group called Dash. I also have tons and tons of producers under my belt." He then lifted the platinum necklaces that hung over his chest to show me the words written on his T-shirt. "See, the name of my record label is Never Broke Entertainment—NBE all day, every day, shawty."

"So will you manage me?" I eagerly asked, feeling quite enthused. "I was in a group back in Pennsylvania and we did very well. I wrote, arranged, and sang just about ninety-nine percent of the songs on our album. However, I had some problems with my previous manager, who was also the mother of one of the girls in the group. Her husband was our crooked-ass entertainment lawyer and the rest is history."

"So basically they fucked you over, huh? That right there was a conflict of interest from the jump. You should have found yourself a lawyer who had no other ties to or interest in the group except you."

"Fucked me over? Fucked ain't even the word. Fuck insinuates that it was consensual. Those motherfuckers raped me and took everything I owned. So I'm back at square one looking for a manager and ready to get back into the studio to do it all over again. Anyway, that's all in the past, and I'm looking into the future now. My name is Melissa, and you are?"

He rubbed his big belly and replied, "Just call me Fatz; everyone does." He began to laugh so I joined in.

"So Fatz, can you add me to the roster of clients you're representing? I write my own lyrics and could sing bells around anyone you put in front of me, even Sha Diamond and Jay'Son. I'm not afraid of competition, so I'll fight and do just about anything to defend my talent."

"You're a feisty one, aren't you? Listen, my truck is parked over in that garage across the street. I have some instrumental tracks inside. If you can sing over one of those tracks and convince me to take you on, then you got a new manager, and trust me, your name will flood these streets like a rainstorm."

"Oh, that's not a problem. Let me listen to those tracks. I bet they just might be my first singles on the album." I was aggressive but I knew I had to impress this man. I was not leaving this situation without knowing that I gave it my all. We walked into the garage and he hit the alarm on his black Cadillac Escalade. The rims on that truck were damn near taller then me; they were huge, I tell you. As soon as we got inside he popped in the CD and a banging-ass track began to play. The beat was sick as hell, and I knew that it had to be mine right away. Knowing that Atlanta loves that dirty south sound, I quickly began to think of lyrics that would make the crowd want to jump to their feet and dance. I listened for less than one minute and began to freestyle to the beat. "Boy, the way you got me krunking on the floor, no joke, I'm craving more. After the club, tell me where you wanna go: my place, your place, maybe the mo." I was singing my heart out and getting into the track as if it was already mine.

"Damn! Shawty, you can really sing. No lie, at first I thought you were all looks and no talent because we see a lot of that out here. But you, you can really sing and you're gifted. Did you just make that up or was it already written?"

"No, I just thought of the melody and lyrics now. See, I told you I could sing. All I need is a trustworthy and dedicated manager. If you're loyal to me, then I promise I will be extra loyal to you, if you know what I mean."

Fatz sat back in his seat and looked deeply into my eyes. "Well, I think I know what you mean but you can get more in depth so that both of us can be on the same page, *if you know what I mean.*" To be honest, I knew the game pretty well because I'd been playing it for a while now. Fatz seemed like a very confident dude. But I knew my skills. If I gave a little, then I could play my cards right to get a lot out of him. I needed at least one friend out here, even if it was someone who considered me a freak. I had to grab his attention, so I did it the way I knew best.

"I can show you better than I can tell you," I said as I reached over and began to passionately kiss and rub my tongue all over his fat-ass neck. He smelled intoxicatingly good, which made my job a lot easier; his scent was driving me through the roof. I ran my tongue across his ear and whispered, "I'm official, baby. You can have all of me as long as I get fifty percent of you. I don't need *all* your time; I just need enough to get me tracks, a studio to record in, and some gigs to perform." I then unbuttoned his jeans, pulled out his fat juicy dick, and began giving him some serious tongue action, the type I would typically give Shawn. His dick was very thick and it had a curve, which made it shift down my throat with ease. As soon as I took him in my mouth, he began to cry like a bitch.

"Shit . . . what the fuck! Damn, sweetheart, you're sucking this dick so fucking good. Ohh, baby, don't stop until I bust, all right."

"Okay, Big Daddy. I'm going to suck this fat-ass dick until it erupts like a volcano." I took it that Fatz loved dirty talk because he forcefully grabbed my head and began to push it down as he pounded inside my mouth. His dick was hitting the back of my throat, but I was persistent with my thrust and strokes. I held that dick inside my mouth like I was seasoning and marinating it with my saliva. I was literally hungry too, so I pretended his dick was a sausage and went to work on it. "Fuck my mouth, baby. Fuck the words back down my throat," I said.

Fatz closed his eyes tightly as he released his tasty cum into my throat. Not a single drop of his semen reached the surface; I swallowed him up. "I'm cumming. Open your mouth wide. Oh shit!" I leaned up and licked my lips to show him how yummy it was, which must have lit a fire under him because he grabbed me sternly and moaned, "Jump over in the backseat, pull your skirt up, and open those sexy-ass legs."

And that's exactly what I did, jumped over, pulled up my skirt, and opened my legs wider than the Pacific Ocean. Fatz climbed over, pulled my thong aside, and without warning plunged his thick dick into my wet, dripping pussy. I was wet to the point that it was making a splashing sound, which turned both of us on. He felt so good as he lay down on top of me and began to move inside me while passionately kissing me as if we were old-time lovers.

Words can't explain how good this sex felt. I don't know if it was because we were fucking in public or because I knew he was going to get me some tracks and pay for studio time; whatever the case, it just felt damn good to me. Before I knew it, I was climaxing. "Fatz . . . Fatz . . . I'm cumming. Fuck it, baby. Fuck the cum out of me."

Then all of a sudden Fatz started to moan in ecstasy too. "Oh, baby girl, I'm cumming too. Damn, you got some bomb-ass pussy. Here go some more cum for you." I knew it was wrong, but I didn't want Fatz to stop, so when he rose to pull out, I squeezed my arms and legs tightly around his waistline.

"Cum inside my pussy just like you did my mouth. I want to feel that warm nut. Don't worry, I'm on the pill." Fatz didn't hesitate to bust inside me, and yes, his warm nut felt soothing to my walls. At that very moment, I knew that I had sealed the deal with him. I had myself a new manager from Atlanta, Georgia, baby!

We exchanged numbers and made plans to hook up the next day so we could meet some of his producer friends. It was nothing to me, because, as I always say, fucking a dude for tracks is an investment for my career. Yes, I walked away from this deal still homeless, damn near broke, and exceptionally hungry, but I'd be recording in a day or two. I just got a new dirty-south track plus some good dick out of the deal; what more could a girl ask for?

After surrendering to my sexual appetite, I decided to treat myself to a real meal to ease my hunger pangs. My body couldn't go another hour without putting something hearty inside. After all, I was not used to this kind of deprived living, and it was beginning to take a toll on me. I remembered someone telling me that Peachtree Avenue was the place to be and even mentioning that P. Diddy had a soul-food restaurant named Justin's on the block. That was right up my alley because I could get something good to eat and possibly run into Diddy himself.

I walked back to the garage, got in my car, and asked the parking attendant for directions to Peachtree Avenue. I followed his directions until I pulled up in front of the restaurant.

When I got there, I parked my car about fifty miles away from the restaurant. I couldn't afford to pay for parking because my money was getting low and I had to preserve it. So I sucked it up and hiked to my destination.

Before walking into Justin's I stopped, straightened out my one and only outfit, and reapplied my makeup and perfume so that no one would guess that my fly dirty ass was a pauper beneath all this beauty.

I walked through the front entrance of the restaurant in complete amazement at how elaborate it was. Chandeliers hung from the ceiling, and chic furniture and flat-screen televisions were displayed throughout. From the very moment I entered, I knew this was what you call fine dining, which frightened the fuck out of me because I would probably spend my life's savings in here on a glass of water. Feeling overwhelmed and out of place, I turned to walk back out just as the hostess arrived to seat me.

"Table for one?" she politely asked. I felt like Florida Evans from *Good Times* because although I was smiling, in my mind I was screaming *damn, damn, damn!* God knows I wanted to walk out, but the captivating aroma of all those lovely soul-food meals was holding my stomach hostage. I guess I could just order something from the appetizer menu and drink a glass of water.

"Yes, I'll be eating alone, thank you," I replied as I followed her to my seat.

"Here's your table, ma'am." She walked over, stood in front of the table, and pointed at my seat. "Okay, ma'am, your waitress, Amanda, will be over shortly. If you need any assistance before she arrives, just let me know. Enjoy your stay here at Justin's." I smiled and thanked her for the hospitality.

Although I didn't really want to be there, I found comfort in my surroundings. As I looked around at everyone eating their meals, seemingly without any cares or worries, I kept telling myself that I would be in that state of mind very soon.

"Hello, welcome to Justin's. I'm Amanda. Can I start you out with an appetizer and a drink?" Start me out with an appetizer and a drink? I wanted to tell the bitch that's all I'd be eating, so she could start me out and finish me up with an appetizer and some water, to be exact.

I looked down at my menu and saw that the cheapest appetizer was the Caribbean egg roll, which was seven dollars. To be honest, the prices were extremely reasonable, but I didn't have room to splurge, and on my fixed income $7.00 was over the top. I had plenty of time to come back here and eat lavishly after I got my record deal. I couldn't afford any appetizer, so I simply ordered a side order. "Yes, I'll have an order of rice and peas with any kind of gravy on top and a glass of water without ice."

"You want an order of rice and peas with gravy and nothing else?" she sarcastically asked while looking at me as if she was waiting for the punch line of a joke. After waiting for a moment and seeing the self-conscious look on my face, I think she caught on that I was dead serious. "Will that be all tonight, ma'am?"

"Yes, I just ate about an hour ago. I'm just trying to kill time before meeting some friends. I heard the rice and peas and gravy is to die for."

"Is that right?" Amanda replied with a look on her face that assured me that she knew I was lying my ass off. "So that's one order of rice and peas with gravy and a glass of water with no ice? Would you like some lemon with your water?"

"Yes," I replied, feeling extremely embarrassed about my situation. I felt lower than the belly of a pregnant worm.

I sat at the table for about ten minutes stressing over my situation and was about to just swallow my pride and walk out when Amanda returned with my order. She had placed my plate on the table and started to walk away when I noticed that she had messed up *big*-time.

"Umm, excuse me, Amanda," I softly called out. "This isn't what I ordered. Remember I ordered . . ."

"You ordered the rice and peas with gravy," she interjected. "There's rice and peas with gravy on your plate."

"Yes, but there's also fried chicken, macaroni and cheese, and collard greens on there. Plus, I ordered water and this looks like iced tea." How could someone fuck up an order so simple? If she thinks she's going to trick me into eating this shit and then being stuck with the bill, she had another think coming.

"Look, sweetie, I've been working here long enough to know that no one orders off the side menu *alone* unless they can't afford what they really want. Try that chicken. It's very popular here."

"But Amanda, I can't afford any of this," I replied with tears in my eyes. "I barely have money for the rice and peas and water."

"I figured that much. Don't worry about the bill. I got you covered. Eat up. It's on the house." She winked and walked over to another table as I sat speechless and utterly thankful. I hadn't eaten in almost two days, and I didn't know where to dig in first. If I'd had the power to stuff the entire plate into my mouth, believe me, I would have. Amanda just didn't know what she'd done for me tonight. She was truly a lifesaver.

What should have taken me thirty minutes to eat I consumed in less than fifteen. I even chewed the chicken bones until they were damn near nonexistent.

Amanda walked back over with a form and a pen and said, "Here, fill this out and give it back to me when you're done."

"What's this?" I asked, feeling very leery about signing anything. Signing shit without reading it is what got me in this predicament in the first place.

"One of our waitresses quit today and we're short staffed. If you're looking for a job, fill this out. I've got pull in here, and can get you working as early as tomorrow evening."

I couldn't believe the words coming out of her mouth. I've heard of being in the right place at the right time, and I know that God works in mysterious ways, but this was unbelievable. Finding a job had never even crossed my mind but it made perfect sense. I was incredibly appreciative of all Amanda's help, but I couldn't help but wonder why she was so caring and supportive to a perfect stranger. And most important, how does she know my situation so well?

"Not that I'm being ungrateful for what you've done for me,

because I'm truly thankful, but why are you helping me so much when you don't know me?"

Amanda quickly looked around, took a seat at my table, and began to explain. "I'm being so nice to you because I was in your place about two years ago when I moved here to pursue my modeling career. I see a lot of people come through these doors with hopes, dreams, and no money. Shit, girl, I was living out of my car for three month before I got this job. I know the state of mind I was in and wouldn't wish that on my worst enemy, so I try to offer people the help I never got. You look very young, and Atlanta could chew you into a million pieces and swallow you if you're not grounded. I don't know what your motivation is for being out here, but take my advice, always put reality before fantasy."

Amanda then got up and continued to do her rounds. I sat there thinking about the knowledge that she'd just dropped in my lap. I hurried to fill out that application as if my life depended on it; well, it actually did.

When I finished completing the application, I motioned for Amanda to come pick it up. She looked it over, gave it back, and pointed out that I had missed a very important question. "Umm, sweetie, you forgot something very important. You need to put an address down. You don't have to actually live there; just ask a friend or family member if you can use their address for employment purposes."

Again I sighed as I came to another wall in front of me. "I don't have an address, and I don't have any friends or family living out here. I literally just came off the highway from Pennsylvania a few hours ago. As a matter of fact, the only clothes I have are the ones on my back. I planned on living out of my car until I found somewhere to live just like you did."

"Oh, you think it's that easy?" she asked. It was as if she'd jumped out of the nice-waitress role into that of a protective mother. "I'm telling you, you're heading down a dangerous path, little girl." She stood and stared into space like she was contemplating something. She kept looking over at me and shaking her head just like my parents used to do. Then, after an extremely long deliberation, she threw a generous offer on the table. "Listen, I live not too far from here. I planned on looking for a roommate in the near future anyway, so if you want, you can stay with me rent free for a month. After that we have to split everything fifty-fifty. I'm talking about rent, utilities, cable, phone, groceries, and anything else to do with the apartment. It's a one bedroom, but the couch in the living room folds out into a bed. That's the best I can offer."

"That's more than okay with me," I replied. I felt overwhelmed with joy because my luck was finally taking a turn for the better. "Amanda, I truly think you're my guardian angel. You've shown me more love than I've ever known. Thank you, girl. I sincerely thank you from the bottom of my heart."

"Yeah, I may seem like a guardian angel now, but trust me, I can be a bitch too. You just hold down your end and keep your promise and you won't see that ugly side of me. I'm about to get off in thirty minutes or so. You can wait for me outside until then."

This girl could have been a bitch, a witch, and a snitch and it really wouldn't have mattered to me. She had a roof over her head and very soon so would I. Amanda proceeded to walk off but suddenly stopped to ask, "Hey, roomie, by the way, what's your name?" We had already sealed the deal regarding being roommates without even formally introducing ourselves to each other.

We both burst out laughing and I answered, "It's on the application. My name is Melissa . . . Melissa James. You'll be hearing that name on all the radio stations very soon."

"Is that right?" she asked while still laughing. "Just be sure to remember to show me some love when you're doing those radio interviews. Give a shout-out to the 'ever so sexy' Italian bomb-shell Amanda Scintilla."

Scintilla? I knew this girl was mixed with something. She was tall and light-skinned, with beautiful bold eyes, and had long dark curly hair that fell to her ass. And it was no wonder she was a model; she had a washboard stomach and a bodacious yet toned ass and curvy hips. She was an exceedingly gorgeous woman.

"You'll be the first one I give a shout-out," I assured her as I gathered my belongings and exited the restaurant. I waited outside in my car for her to get off work. I used that alone time to reflect on my past, present, and future. I even thought of my parents for the first time in a long time and wondered if they were thinking of me. I remembered that my father had said the door would always be open, but I wondered if the offer still stood. The way I saw it, if they had really wanted me, they would have found me and tried to take me home a long time ago.

I thought of Tiffany, Jasmine, and Mrs. Tarsha, although those thoughts were way different from the ones I had for my parents. Those bitches were on my payback list, and I would get them for what they did to me if it killed me. I looked down at Fatz's cell phone number sitting in my ashtray and thought about the show I had just put on in his truck. And, yes, I do feel utterly ashamed of having sex with him so quickly, but time is money, and I desperately needed his help. I compromised my body and self-respect but it was all in good faith.

Now, here I am about to live with yet another person who could kick me out whenever she pleased and I could possibly end up back on the streets again. No, I wasn't going to let that happen this time around. I'm not getting comfortable here, and will always be on my grind from here on out because it's about time for me to have my own. Amanda seemed like a very nice girl, but I always say if it's too good to be true, then it probably is.

I sat in my car for a while singing and writing a heartfelt song about life as I perceived it. After that, I drifted off to sleep. I had just dozed off when Amanda knocked on my window. "Wake up, sleepyhead," she joked. "You better watch how you fall asleep around here. This is Atlanta, girl; you might wake up with a dick in your mouth." I quickly jumped up out of my sleep, almost forgetting where the hell I was as she sat down in my car. "Real talk, Melissa, it's crazy out here, girl. I could have been a rapist and it would have been easy for me to get in your car, stick a gun in your side, and make you drive to a secluded area before raping and killing your ass."

"Oh, I just dozed off a minute or so ago. I won't make that mistake again."

"Okay, make a right at the light and then a quick left by the gas station." I followed her directions and in less than two minutes, we were parked outside her condo. She wasn't lying when she said she lived near the restaurant.

As soon as we entered, Amanda gave me a tour of her chic, neatly furnished condo. I could tell she had good taste. Her red-and-cream living room set and carpet complemented each other perfectly. Even her paintings and accessories were very bold and dazzling. She had pictures of herself from various magazines displayed in crystal picture frames throughout the apartment. I still couldn't believe I was actually living with a model. I had really hit the jackpot this time around.

Amanda showed me where everything was and told me to make myself at home. I felt extremely happy, to the point that my eyes felt like they were dancing to the cheerful beat of my heart.

As soon as I walked into Amanda's bedroom, it was apparent that she was a model. Fashion magazines were thrown everywhere, along with a million and one outfits, shoe boxes, and accessories. She showed me her portfolio, which was quite impressive. The girl was out here doing her thing, and I knew right then and there that I was right where I needed to be. We sat up and exchanged stories about our pasts, and both promised to help each other as much as possible. I didn't know this girl, but somehow she felt like the sister I never had. We had a lot in common, including our birthdays; how ironic is that? It totally freaked me out, but I knew God always worked things out and this was his plan for me.

I took the liberty of taking a long, well-deserved bubble bath, which felt like winning a million bucks. The heat felt soothing to my skin, and for the first time since I touched base in this city, I could sincerely say that I felt a sense of home. I wasn't stressing or worrying about where my next meal was going to come from. I wasn't thinking about where I was going to lay my head night after night. True, I was sleeping on someone's couch, but I was extremely grateful.

I sat in that damn bathtub until my fingers resembled those of an elderly woman. Just when I got the willpower to leave the bathroom, Amanda knocked on the door. "Come in," I said pleasantly while wrapping my towel tightly around my body.

"My boss just called and said you're on the schedule to work tomorrow. Girl, you got the job. He said he's going to start you off with something easy until you get fully trained. You're going to be a hostess."

"Hostess?" I asked, not knowing what the hell a hostess really does.

"Basically all you have to do is smile, politely greet the customers, and escort them to their seat. I'll train you on everything else."

"Are you kidding me? I got the job! Did I really get the job?" I began to jump around for joy. "Thank you, Jesus, thank you so much. Thank you too, Amanda. I owe you my life."

"Girl, I didn't do anything that you couldn't do for yourself," she modestly replied. "Just don't make me regret this shit. I've seen a lot of girls get caught up in a lot of bullshit; don't be one of them." We exited the bathroom, and she made her way to the refrigerator and took out a bottle of Deer Park Spring Water. "If you're serious about this music thing, you'll need photos, a bio, and a demo. What do you have?"

"Not a damn thing," I replied. "I don't have shit to my name. Those bitches took everything from me. Now, I can write my own bio, but I don't have any pictures or music. But I met a guy named Fatz earlier and he's going to manage me, so I'll have something very soon."

Amanda did a 180-degree turn, nearly breaking her neck. "Fatz? Fatz from NBE?"

"Yeah, he said his label is called . . ."

"Never Broke Entertainment," she finished. "Girl, he's nothing but trouble. He's a big fat-ass freak. Because he's got money, these bitches are out here throwing themselves at him left and right. He's all about him and no one else."

I almost vomited. I felt horrible because I was one of those girls she was talking about, and what makes it worse is that today was my first damn day in Atlanta and I already managed to do some smutty shit. "Well, all I want him to do for me is take me to the studio and introduce me to some producers so I can get this demo completed and then I'm bouncing."

"Melissa, please don't get caught up with that nigga. Get your songs recorded and bounce like you said. That fool is a nasty fat ho." Amanda then wrote down a number and handed it to me. "Anyway, call this guy Greg tomorrow morning and tell him I referred you to him. He studies photography at Georgia State University and is always looking for new faces. You can help him build his portfolio, and he can give you pictures. He was one of the first people I worked with out here, and trust me, he knows his shit."

"Girl, I don't have any clothes to do a photo shoot. After I get my first paycheck I'll call him and make an appointment."

"Chill out, Melissa. I have more than enough clothes in my closet, as you can see. All I ask is that you respect my shit. I told you we're going to help each other, and I mean that. Get your photos done, write your bio, and hurry up and get your songs recorded. After that, I expect you to be grinding by day and working at the restaurant by night."

"Trust me, I plan to do just that," I assured her.

The next morning I called Greg to schedule my photo shoot, wrote my musical bio, and gave Fatz a call to discuss our little business arrangement. He told me I could record in the mornings, but I had to be out of the studio by 6:00 p.m. because other artists had those time slots locked. That was perfect for me anyway because I'd be working in the evenings and could only record in the mornings.

Later that evening, I went to work and did the damn thing, even making a few of my own tips. I was doing an excellent job, if I did say so myself, considering that this was the first job I'd ever had. The following weeks, I worked six nights a week and spent my days in the studio with Fatz. Just as he'd promised, he introduced me to many producers, who were eager to work with me as soon as they heard my voice and saw my potential. Pretty soon I started making money on the side by writing for local artists and collaborating with a few, even jumping on a couple hip-hop mix CDs to get my name out there in the streets.

But of course everything came with a price. As long as I continued to make Fatz and his friends happy, they made me happy. I'd had threesomes before, but now you could add foursomes to my list. While other artists were paying top-notch dollars to record, all I had to do was suck and fuck a little and my debt was paid in full. It took me no time to record an entire CD greater than the songs I wrote and performed for Pretty in Pink.

So there I was living out my dreams in Atlanta just as I'd planned. To be perfectly honest, I no longer needed Fatz to manage me because I was doing a damn good job all by myself. I really didn't enjoy compromising my body and dignity day after day, and now that I'd established myself, I could finally break free from Fatz and his friends. Once again, the stars seemed reachable, and I knew I was only seconds away from getting my big break. This time around, I was much stronger and wiser, and I had destiny eating out of the palms of my hands. No one was going to stop my shine, and I meant *no one*!

FFB

I contentedly walked into the radio station holding my CD with pride because I knew it was phenomenal; every track was a banger. I worked with some of the best producers in town, and of course my writing and vocal skills were off the meter, so it came as no surprise that this CD would ultimately get me signed. I had all my ends covered so I figured this should be a walk in the park. My bio was well written, thanks to me. My photos were breathtaking, thanks to Amanda's friend Greg, and on top of it all, I had a remarkable CD, thanks to Fatz and his many, many friends. Furthermore, my single, "Shake That Water," was popping off in all the strip clubs, which threw my name out in the streets. I'd been in Atlanta for eight months and already I'd accomplished way more than I did with Pretty in Pink, or should I say Jazzy Girls.

My appointment was scheduled for 2:00 p.m., but at 3:15 I was still sitting in the waiting area in anticipation of the program director coming out and meeting with me. It wasn't like I just up and came in unannounced; I'd called and made this appointment a week ago, so I really didn't understand the holdup, but I guess situations like these came with the territory.

I was damn near dying of boredom when suddenly a very prissy lady walked out from the back laughing at a joke shared among her co-workers and called out, "Are you Melissa James?"

"Yes, that's me," I enthusiastically answered as I quickly jumped from my seat and walked over to formally introduce myself. "Good afternoon, how are you? Are you the program director?"

Miss Thing barely looked my way as she turned and snobbishly replied, "Follow me." Deep down inside I wanted to tell this bitch off, but I couldn't because my future lay in her hands. I wanted to ask her why she was acting so high and mighty. She was probably more approachable when she was interning at the radio station, but as soon as she got that promotion she thought it gave her the right to treat local artists like myself like crap because we needed her to play our music. This was the part of networking that I dreaded the most. The part where you have to kiss up to people who are undeserving.

"Take a seat," she ordered. "Jay Spinz will be in shortly to meet with you." Oh, my goodness. This smart-ass bitch wasn't the program director after all. I wish I knew that a minute ago. I wouldn't have been so obedient toward her bony ass.

So once again, I was sitting in a room waiting for the program director. This was a very humbling experience for me. I swore, as soon as I got this deal, I was going to put this radio station on blast, especially that prissy little bitch. You'd have thought I was in here asking for handouts. All I was asking for was some airtime.

I did everything I could think of to keep from losing my sanity, including reading all the banners and flyers hanging on the walls. When the door finally opened and a very tall man walked through, I hoped and prayed it was finally the program director and not another wannabe like Miss Priss.

"Hello, pretty lady. I'm the program director, Jay Spinz. How are you today?"

Thank God. Those were the words that I'd been waiting to hear all damn evening. "Oh, I'm fine," I answered with a warm smile. "I'm a little nervous, but happy to be here."

Jay was different from the others I'd seen so far. He was far more hospitable, with a very pleasant attitude. "Oh, don't be nervous, sweetheart. I've heard about some of your work, and you're hot, Melissa. To be honest, I wonder why it took you so long to come in here to holler at me." At that very moment, my confidence level rose to the roof. A huge smile crossed my face to the point that my cheeks were actually hurting. It was so fulfilling to know that the people at the radio station actually knew of me. "You really know your stuff, baby girl. From what I hear, you're the shit."

"Thank you so much. I've been working tremendously hard on this album, and I really wanted to showcase my talent. There's so many things I can do if I only have the opportunity and the right people in my corner." Of course your girl knows how to sell herself, so it should come as no surprise that I was working the room. Jay sat for almost ten minutes as I ranted and raved about my progression as a solo artist and how I ghostwrote for many local artists here. "Like I mentioned before, I just need the right people in my corner," I emphasized, hoping he was willing to jump on the bandwagon to help promote me. "So do you think my song will do well on the radio?" I asked.

For a second there was silence as Jay began to lustfully scrutinize me from head to toe like I was a piece of meat he was getting ready to sink his teeth into. Again, I repeated my question, because it was obvious that his mind was traveling to all the wrong places, like a typical man. "Do you think my music will do well in the eight p.m. mix?"

Jay immodestly smiled as he leaned closer toward me and turned the lock on the door. At that moment I was wondering what the hell was going on because the mood had suddenly shifted from professional to personal. "Yes, I agree with you one hundred percent, Melissa. You are certainly talented, and I for one want to be in your corner."

Feeling a bit awkward and out of place, I tried to steer the conversation back to my music, hoping he was still on that subject, although my better judgment was telling me he wasn't. "So here's my CD." I reached into my bag for it. "Tracks 1, 5, and 9 are my favorites because they really showcase my range and versatility."

Jay took the CD, set it on the table behind me, and took the liberty of putting his hands on my thighs. At that moment I knew exactly what was up, but there was no way I was sleeping with this man. Who does he think he is to leave me sitting in this fucking office for hours waiting for him, just to have him bluntly make sexual gestures toward me?

"Maybe you don't get what I'm trying to say to you. I heard about *you,* not your music. Fatz told me all about the good work you put in, and I really want to see if you're as good as they all say you are." *Oh, my God,* I thought. The moment he said Fatz's name, I knew my secret was blown. No one knew what was going on behind closed doors at the studio but me and the family, but it's apparent that Fatz couldn't be a real nigga and keep his mouth shut. Still, I wasn't going to let this fool put me down and, furthermore, he wasn't going to insult my character like that.

"Excuse me," I replied, as I pushed his grimy hands off me. "I came here for you to listen to my music and hopefully to get my songs played on the radio. I didn't come in here to get insulted."

Jay looked at me as if I was speaking Chinese. "Come on, FFB. You slept with the whole damn NBE label and you're in here talking all proper and saying you didn't come in here to get insulted? Did you feel insulted when you fucked Fatz in his truck five minutes after you met him?" FFB? What the hell does that mean? He started to laugh dead in my face as I sat stunned and quiet. "Now, that's what you call an insult, a nigga blowing your back out in his truck. I, on the other hand, am simply asking you to provide me with some of your wonderful services. Maybe you can show me a little something right now. I heard you're mad flexible."

I wanted to sink into the ground and never show my face to anyone ever again. The way he labeled me as a first-class whore was inexcusable. Yes, I did sleep with the whole NBE label, and yes, I did have sex with Fatz as soon as I met him but that didn't make me a freak. I was only doing what I had to do to survive at that moment. I was damn near homeless and starving when I first arrived in Atlanta. I needed some friends to have my back until I got on my feet. Every time I slept with someone, I always reminded myself that once I got my record deal, I would never degrade myself like that again. Jay Spinz didn't know me from a can of paint, and he'd never understand where I was at. Mrs. Tarsha told me a long time ago that there's nothing wrong with having sex to get a check. She said she did it and it landed her a rich lawyer husband, so I could only have faith that it would work out for me too.

Jay continued to proposition me, but I was in no mood to hear any more of his offensive proposals. "I thought you wanted to make it in this industry," he said. "I heard you were serious about getting signed and becoming big and famous."

"Yes, I want to make it, but I don't have to sleep with you or anyone else to accomplish my dreams because I've got talent, and my CD speaks for itself."

"Man, the only talent you got is sucking and riding a hell of a dick, from what I was told, so I thought you wanted to add me to the roster. But I see you're not serious about your music career." Jay then stood up, opened the door, and practically put me out of his office. "Now I feel insulted," he said in a joking manner as he rubbed his hand across his face and looked in the mirror. "I know I look waaaay sexier than Fatz's big ass, and you treated him like a king. I guess I'm not fat enough, is that it?" He lifted his Polo shirt to broadcast his washboard abs in hopes of me getting turned on,

I guess. "Look, baby girl, come back when you get your head right. Remember this, though: If you want me to play, then you have to lay! Have a nice day, FFB."

FFB? He said it again and I had no clue what those initials meant, but I was too ashamed to even stand there and argue with this jerk. I couldn't believe what I'd just heard. Worst of all, I couldn't believe that Fatz had sold me out like that. I got down with him and his crew because I didn't have any money to pay for production and studio time. Words couldn't explain how ashamed I felt walking out of that radio station as Jay and the other disk jockeys pointed, laughed at me, and called me an FFB. Usually I would have stood up for myself, but how could I? I was foolish to believe that everything I did in-house would actually stay in-house.

That one embarrassing day led to many others like a domino effect as every door I knocked on was slammed in my face. Everyone wanted to use me to write and sing background for their artists, but no one wanted to work with me as a solo artist. I didn't understand what the hell was going on. My CD was ten times better than a lot of garbage I heard playing on the radio, yet other female artists were getting the love and exposure I deserved.

Trying to switch things up a bit, I decided to change my stage name from Melissa James to "Mel-J." I even began to sport a superlong weave down my back and bought a pair of grayish contact lenses to add some spice to my look. I tried every damn thing to give myself that extra push as I continued to grind in the streets every single day but it seemed as though I was blackballed.

I was at work one afternoon when a huge party came into the restaurant. I'd moved up to waiting tables and I prayed and prayed that the hostess wouldn't seat those loud, obnoxious motherfuckers in my area, but as luck would have it, she did. I was in no mood to deal with this bullshit, especially with the messed-up week that I was experiencing. I was depressed, cranky, and irritable, which was a bad combination, especially when dealing with the public.

I walked over to Amanda and pleaded with her to cover that table for me. I knew that I was on the edge and one slipup could leave me unemployed or even worse, in jail. "Girl, if you do this big favor for me, I swear I'll owe you one. I'm just not in the mood to smile and be nice to those motherfuckers, and I don't want to say or do anything that might cost me my job."

Amanda looked at me as if I were insane. "Melissa, don't you know who that is over there? I thought you would be happy as fuck to wait on that table. Girl, that is Reggie, the CEO of Big Dream Records. That nigga right there can take your music to the next level. That's one of the hottest local labels. You need to take your ass over there and leave a CD in his lap, but be sure not to let anyone see you, because you know the rule: absolutely no solicitation of customers."

"I heard about Reggie, but I never actually met him in person. Everyone speaks highly of him and his label, and I always hear his name all over the radio. He just threw that big all-white party last week with Young Jeezy, right?"

"Yes, that's him. Go fix yourself up in the bathroom real quick and get over there."

I ran into the bathroom, reapplied my makeup, and hurriedly returned to wait on my table. But then my boss decided to move me from the area and put a more experienced waitress at the table since the party was so big, about fifteen people. Every time someone big comes into the restaurant they always send the same lame-ass people to wait on their table, knowing good and well that they would do anything to get big tips, including kissing ass. Damn, lately I can't get a fucking break to save my life.

For about an hour, I walked back and forth, watching everyone eating and enjoying their meals. I particularly kept a close eye on

Reggie and prayed that he made eye contact with me at least one time but he never did. Furthermore, I was still on the clock and had my own damn tables to wait on, which kept me pretty busy and out of commission.

I walked toward the kitchen area to put in an order and realized that Reggie and his entire entourage were getting up from the table and proceeding to leave. I looked over at Amanda, who in return looked back at me like, *girl, you better do something and fast.* For about a minute or two I contemplated whether I should just walk over in front of everyone and hand this dude my CD. With the luck I'd been experiencing lately, he'd probably yell at me for interrupting his social time and make me feel worse than I already did.

I thought over what I should do as Reggie and his crew began to head my way. My heart began to race and my thoughts became flustered. Before I knew it, he walked directly past me and toward the door. It was like I was watching a golden opportunity pass me by, and at that moment I didn't know what came over me, because out of the blue I screamed the nigga's name as if my life depended on it.

"Reggie . . . Reggie, wait!" I screamed. Everyone turned around, including my co-workers. "I . . . I . . . I wanted to give you a copy of my CD."

Reggie turned to his friends and began to smile. Instantly I felt a sinking sensation in my stomach. "You screamed my name like that just to hand me a CD. Girl, I thought you saw someone about to assassinate my ass." Everyone began to laugh and I felt sick to my stomach. "What kind of CD is this, anyway? You're a rapper?" I guess he figured I rap because of my edgy look on the CD cover.

"No, sir," I replied, looking down at the ground and wishing I had kept my damn mouth shut. "I'm an R&B singer and songwriter. This is my first album. I wrote every song on there, so if you . . ."

"Okay . . . Okay. I get what you're trying to say." Reggie cut me off in the middle of my thought and once again I was utterly embarrassed. "My CD player is broke so if you want me to hear your song you have to sing live right now."

"You want me to sing right here in front of everyone? Right now?" I nervously asked.

"Yeah. I wouldn't want you to sing to me after I leave because that wouldn't make much sense, now would it?" Some of his friends started to laugh. "Go ahead and sing the first song on this CD."

Perfect, I thought. I absolutely loved the first song on my CD because it was a slow ballad called "Self-Destruction." I began writing that song when I first arrived in Atlanta and was waiting in the car for Amanda to get off work. It practically tells my life story and my inner thoughts. I knew a million motherfuckers were looking at me and I could possibly make a fool out of myself. And even worse, I knew I was going to lose my job for creating such a scene, but this could be the break I needed, and I wasn't going to let it slip away. So without giving it a second thought, I opened my mouth and sang like I never had before.

"I've been down so many times that I've found comfort in the ground. Running from my own shadow is what led me out of town. Finally I realized that it's me and no one else. How can I defeat this enemy? Tell me, how do I protect me from myself? I need some protection from my own self-destruction."

My eyes were closed and for that moment everyone else in the room disappeared in my mind. I let my soul flow free and got lost in the emotions of the song. Every note was on point, the melody was soothing, and I didn't need anyone to tell me how great I sounded because I knew. It took me back to the days when I was singing in my father's church choir. I was belting out from my diaphragm as if I were an opera singer at the peak of her aria. I didn't know what it was, but this moment was real for me and I just couldn't let it slip out of my hands.

Then Reggie cut in. "Whoa . . . Whoa," he said, while shaking his head. Everyone in the room began clapping. "I haven't heard anyone sing like that in a long time. When I told you my CD player was broke, I was really just testing you. I didn't think you would actually sing in front of all these people, and on top of that, I didn't expect such a powerful voice to come from that little body."

"Thank you," I answered, feeling my spirit soar. "So are you willing to bring me onto your label?" If you knew anything about me, you knew that I didn't waste time because I was always racing the clock. I didn't need to hear that I could sing because I already knew that. I needed to hear him say that he was going to work with me.

"Girl, as good as you sound, you should be picking, choosing, and refusing labels. Here's my business card. Give me a call first thing in the morning and I just may have an amazing opportunity for you." Reggie then made his way out of the restaurant as he simultaneously flipped over my CD to view the cover. "Melissa, be prepared to put in some hard work because we grind hard at our label."

"Trust me, Reggie," I replied. "I will grind harder than anyone you already have signed to that label. For one, I know that I'm hungrier than any other artist you've worked with past or present. And two, I live for this, so bring it on." Instantly, I saw some of the people with him start to look me up and down like I had crossed the line with that remark. I knew I might have touched someone's sensitive spot and already made a few enemies, but my goal at the moment was to impress Reggie and no one else.

"I like what I hear," he stated as he turned and looked at a young lady who was standing not too far from him. As a matter of fact, she was one of the people who was giving me the evil eye. "Do you hear that, Shay? I hope you have that grind in you as well." Let's just say that the look Shay gave both of us answered his question loud and clear. She wanted to tell both of us to kiss her ass.

Once Reggie and his friends left the building, I was called to the manager's office, which was expected because I had broken the rules. Amanda had drilled into my head that I must never let anyone see me promoting my CD on the job, and I had flat-out auditioned for Reggie like I was on stage at a talent show. It was okay to slide someone your CD or phone number on the down low and pray that no one ratted you out. But I took it to the next level and held a concert in this motherfucking restaurant.

I walked into the office employed and in less than fifteen minutes I walked back out unemployed. To make a long story short, I was jobless once again but I was cool with that. I could always find another job on any given day or night, but running into someone as prominent as Reggie was very rare.

That night when Amanda came home from work she had some words for me and I had some for her as well. My parents put my ass out years ago; I wasn't confined to any rules and surely wasn't going to let this wannabe-diva talk to me like I was her child.

"Why did you pull that stunt today?" she asked with an attitude. "Why would you do something that I told you would get you fired? I told you to hand over a CD, not sing a fucking song to the entire restaurant. We've got bills to pay and they're not going to fucking disappear because you lost your job, and I'm certainly not going to cover your ass."

"I did it because I had to do something before Reggie walked out that door. It's been almost a year, and so far nothing has popped for me out here. Girl, I can get a job anywhere, so why are you tripping like it's a big deal?"

"Because I put my neck out for you to get that job and you just don't give a fuck about putting me in a bad position with the boss.

Now they're never going to take my word about anything because I highly recommended you and you basically shitted on me."

"Look, Amanda, I apologize, okay? But I have to follow my heart, and my heart beats for music and you know that. Maybe you can put your dreams on the back burner and serve motherfuckers fried chicken and collard greens all night long, but I can't do it."

"Oh, my dreams are on the back burner now? If I'm not mistaken, I get paying gigs month after month while you're out there begging motherfuckers to listen to your demo. If it wasn't for me, you wouldn't have gotten this far, and you want to sit in my house and talk like my life is pathetic."

"I didn't say that, but if the shoe fits, wear it," I replied as I looked directly into her eyes so she knew I meant business.

"Oh, honey, the shoe is definitely five sizes off from my petite feet, but I think I have a perfect fit for you. Try this on for size. Get the fuck out of my house and go mooch off someone else."

"With pleasure," I snarled. "I was planning on leaving anyway; better sooner than later."

"Get the fuck out of my house" were words that I'd gotten used to, so this time around I wasn't fazed one bit. My parents were the first ones to tell me, then Mrs. Tarsha, and now Amanda. That shit was getting pretty redundant at this point in my life.

I packed up all my belongings, put them in my trunk like I'd done before, and drove around until I found a cheap hotel to lay my head for the night. I had to get some rest because I had a long day ahead of me. I had to find another job fast, before my savings ran out. I also had to give Reggie a call to see what was on his agenda for me. To be perfectly honest, working with him would be the highlight of my day.

I tried to lie down to get some rest but the stench and filth of the cheap-ass room I was in kept me up all night long. On top of that, the junkies shooting up and fucking like dogs in the next room were making so much noise it was impossible to sleep for even a millisecond.

The next morning, I was already up, dressed, and out of that hellhole before sunrise. There was no way in hell I would ever live my life like that. This was my wake-up call to get my shit in order because I had never laid my delicate head in such places.

Before doing anything that morning I called Reggie to show him that I meant business. At first he didn't answer, but when I called him the third time he finally picked up.

"This is Reggie," he answered.

"Hi, Reggie. Nice hearing your voice. This is Melissa, the young lady you met yesterday at the restaurant."

"Oh, yeah, my little songstress. How are you this morning?"

"I'm doing fine," I lied, knowing good and well that I was doing bad as hell. The smell from the dirty hotel was haunting my every thought. "Are we meeting today?"

"Yes, but first I have to talk to you a bit to see what you need from me and how I can benefit from you. You know it's all about money, right?"

"Yes, I know that. I'm trying to make some money myself, so I can't knock you for managing yours wisely." Reggie and I then talked on the phone for almost half an hour. He asked me a lot of questions to see who I'd worked with in the past and to see if I was bound to any contracts.

Reggie said he'd listened to my CD over and over because it was really hot and put together well. He said what really impressed him was the fact that he didn't have to do much to make some money off my CD right away. All he had to do was mix and master the songs and get me to open for a few of his famous friends who were already signed. Overall, it was music to my ears. I couldn't stop smiling to save my life.

As we went deeper in conversation I decided to make him aware of the sacrifice that I'd made to work with him. "You know, it's a good thing you like my music and want to work with me, because after you left I got fired and my roommate, who helped me get the job, got mad at me and put me out, so I'm jobless and homeless."

"A talented and pretty lady like you shouldn't be working in a restaurant in the first place. I would have made you quit anyway because I need you to focus on your craft one hundred percent."

"Well, how am I supposed to support myself without income coming in? I need a job to keep a roof over my head and food on my table."

Reggie laughed. "Listen, baby girl. From now on you work for me on a paid weekly salary, but you have to do some grinding. I need you working hard in the studio, performing at shows, and doing some other side promotional ventures. As far as a roof is concerned, I'll find a nice little apartment for you, so don't worry about all that. You just have to play your part and I'll play mine as your manager."

Hearing those words was like hearing the man of my dreams saying, "Melissa, will you marry me?" This is the life that I was supposed to be living a long fucking time ago. You know, living in an apartment without worrying about the expenses, recording in a professional studio, and performing in front of an actual audience like a real star. In fact, I wanted to call Amanda and thank her for putting me out of her apartment because my life had just taken a turn for the better.

Later that evening I met Reggie at his studio and instantly began writing and working on some bangers. His production team loved me from the moment they met me, and for the very first time I was part of a family. Reggie put me up in a one-bedroom apartment and even took the liberty of helping me furnish it. He gave me his credit card and told me to buy new clothes, and sent me and the other girls on the label to get our hair and nails done on a weekly basis. After a while I parked my old beat-up ride and began to push various luxurious cars that Reggie had bought for his artists to share. Perception meant everything to him, so if you were associated with his label, you had to represent excellence in the streets. He was like a savior to me, and I showed my gratitude by being the best damn artist signed to his label.

Months passed and we were working on various projects when out of nowhere it happened—I began to receive recognition and started performing all over the city. Reggie promoted me everywhere he went by giving out samples of my demo, flooding the streets with flyers and posters, and arranging for me to host many events. The club owners and clubgoers liked what they heard, so in no time, I was being put on some of the hottest shows in Atlanta. They introduced me as Mel-J, the R&B princess of Big Dream Records, and I would melt. The other artists on the label, especially Shay, hated on me every chance they got but it never fazed me because I was on my way to the top.

One night after a big show in Decatur, Georgia, Reggie formally thanked me for all the hard work I'd been putting in. We were in the studio dropping off the microphones and other equipment when he began to pay me mad compliments.

"Melissa, you rocked that stage tonight, girl. You were born to be a star. I'm thinking about launching you full force."

My eyes lit up with glee. I was so happy that he was proud of me, because to be honest, Reggie was very hard to please. He didn't play around with money, so if you're not on your A game, he'll cut you from his team as if you were never there in the first place. So to hear him speak so highly of me made my heart swell.

"Well, I wouldn't have gotten this far if it wasn't for my wonderful manager," I assured him. "So when you say full force, what do you really mean?"

"I mean, leave all this local shit alone and start shopping you to some major labels like Def Jam, Sony, and Universal Records. With a voice like that, you need to let the world hear you."

"Are you serious, Reggie? You're going to try to get me signed with some major labels for real? That's what I moved here for. This is what I've worked for all my life."

"Well, baby girl, I'm going to make it happen for you. You deserve it because you work harder than a motherfucker. You're going to have to do some hard work that you may not like, but it will be beneficial to you, I promise."

"Oh, I'm willing to do anything, Reggie. Anything, just name it."

Reggie moved closer to me, to the point that I could see the lust pulsating deep in his eyes. The truth is, I never fucked him before because his girlfriend was my stylist and she was always around. There were always weird moments when sexual chemistry filled the air but we'd never acted on it.

"Melissa, you know I like you and I know you like me. I think both of us could take this industry by storm if we play hard with the cards we've been dealt." He moved my head slightly to the side and began passionately kissing my neck, which caused me to melt into his arms. "Do you want me to stop?" he whispered in my ear.

"No, I've wanted this for so long, Reggie. I want you to make love to me right here, right now in this booth." I then walked over to the power button and turned it on. "Let's go inside and create some feel-good kind of music." I unbuckled his belt and pulled him into the booth. Turned on with outrageous passion, he threw my body against the foam-filled wall in the booth and began licking me all over. I moaned in elation as he pulled my thong down and began to suck on my clit like it was a Blow Pop. "Oh, yes, baby. That feels so fucking good. Suck this tasty pussy," I chanted as he sucked my clit in and out of his wet mouth.

The next thing I felt was my body being lifted off the ground while still being planted on top of Reggie's face. The nigga damn near bench-pressed my pussy over his juicy lips as his long tongue explored me. My entire body felt like butter that was melting away in this man's mouth. I closed my eyes tightly as I screamed and called out his name. "Reggie . . . Reggie, I'm cumming, baby!" Just knowing that we were actually recording this made me cum even harder. I couldn't wait for us to listen to the music our bodies were producing.

As I mentioned before, my eyes were tightly shut, to the point that I didn't see a damn thing, especially his friends Mike and White Boy walking into the booth. When I finally opened my eyes, the sight of them made me jump off Reggie's face. "Oh, my goodness, Reggie. Your friends are watching us."

Reggie held me tightly as he lowered me to the ground and climbed on top of me. "Come on, baby. Don't worry about them. We're a family. We play hard with the cards we're dealt, remember."

I had to take a real good look at this nigga because I didn't understand what was going on. Now, I've had threesomes and "thensomes" like I told you before, but I thought Reggie sincerely liked me. I didn't understand why he would let his friends walk in on us like this.

"What's going on?" I asked. "I thought you wanted us to be partners. I thought you liked me, Reggie."

"I do like you, baby. But you have to keep the family happy if you want to be with me. Remember I told you that you're going to have to work hard and do things that you may not want to do. Just tell me no if you want to stop because I won't force you to be down if you really don't want to."

I laid on the ground and thought long and hard about the situation I was in. Reggie was paying my bills and taking care of my expenses, and at this point in my life, I couldn't afford to lose what I'd worked for. Plus he was about to blow me up in the industry, so I guessed I could just charge this one to the game like I did the others.

"Okay, baby, let's have fun," I whispered into his ear as I

opened my legs and looked back at his two friends. "Let's all have some fun!"

That night we all became extra well-acquainted with one another. I fucked Reggie, Mike, and White Boy like a professional porn star, which led to other sexual episodes. Then all of a sudden Reggie began offering my services outside the family to local DJs, club owners, and anyone who he needed to do business with. I didn't particularly like it, but he said I needed to do this to prove myself in the industry. To make matters worse, I ended up fucking Jay Spinz at Reggie's command, although he did play my single "Your Eyes" on the radio. Every other week it was a different man and a different reason I had to sleep with him *for the team.* I was beginning to become emotionally and physically drained from it all. Deep down inside, I knew that what I was doing was wrong, and the more I went against my better judgment the worse I would wake up feeling on a daily basis. It was getting to the point where I hated to walk past a mirror and see my reflection, because I didn't recognize myself anymore.

One night I was coming out of the studio when White Boy and his brother confronted me about having sex with them. Reggie hadn't left me any orders to, so I declined the offer and walked away. White Boy then grabbed my arm and began arguing with me. "Wait a minute, bitch. I'm not *asking you* for some pussy. I'm *telling you* to take off your fucking pants and open them legs."

I pulled away and smacked him across the face. "Don't grab me like that!" I yelled. "I am not fucking you or your brother, so get out of my fucking face." Again I tried to walk away but his brother grabbed both my arms and threw me down on the floor.

"Look, bitch, don't get righteous all of a sudden when it's my turn to get some. From what my brother tells me, you don't mind getting fucked, so open your legs or your mouth because I got a load to let off." Their speech was slurred and imprecise, and it was evident to me that they were both drunk and high. I began yelling and fighting as much as I could but they were too strong. While White Boy pinned my arms to the ground, his brother climbed on top of me and spread my legs. Right before entering me, he said something that sounded too familiar. "Yeah, now it's my turn to get some FFB."

FFB? The first person who called me that was Jay Spinz, and now this motherfucker is raping me and saying the same shit. What the hell does that mean? It didn't even matter at the moment, because I was being raped by two guys who chose to beat my ass too. For damn near thirty minutes I was forced to fuck both of them and perform oral sex. It was the worst feeling of my life, and I wouldn't wish that pain on my worst enemy.

As soon as the nightmare was over I called Reggie because I knew he was going to take care of the situation. I told him what went down after he left the studio and just as I expected, he told me he was on his way to come get me. I could actually hear the concern in his voice.

Twenty minutes later, when I saw Reggie's truck pull into my apartment complex, I ran out crying and jumped into his arms. "Baby, I told them no and they raped me."

"Calm down and tell me what happened," he said.

I told him every nasty detail. I couldn't help but cry because I felt so violated. "White Boy and his brother took turns holding me down and raping me."

Reggie became very tense and angry, as if he were the one who'd gotten raped. "Stop saying rape, Melissa. You can't throw that word around like that. I don't need that kind of attention for my label." Wait a minute. If he didn't want me to say "rape," then what the hell was I supposed to say when two guys forced themselves on me after I told them *no*?

"Well, what should I call it, Reggie?" I asked. "I said *no* and they said *yes,* and had sex with me against my will. I think that's called rape."

"Again, I'm warning you to watch your mouth. White Boy has made me a lot of money and I can't let you get him or his brother in trouble, so just forget about that shit. You're acting like you never fucked him before."

"Yeah, I did it for you, but I didn't want to then, and I damn sure didn't want to today."

"So are you going to say I raped you too?" he asked, while looking at me like I wasn't making any sense. "It's the same fuck-ing scenario, Mel. You didn't want to fuck him the first time but you did, so how was he to know you really meant it this time?"

"Because I said *no!*" I screamed. "Look, I'm going to the police and telling them everything, and I'll let them decide if I was raped or not."

Reggie then began smirking like this was a laughing matter. "Did you forget that we have a tape of you fucking me, White Boy, and Mike in the studio? Shit, it was your idea to make it! What judge in his right mind is going to believe you? I got about a mil-lion motherfuckers who will come to court and testify that they fucked you. Do you know what your name is? They call you 'FFB.' I heard about you before I met you at the restaurant. They say there's a bitch that's talented as shit and she Fucks For Beats. Every pro-ducer in Atlanta knows they can give you a track and lay you down on your back. Give it up while you're ahead, sweetheart."

"So you were using me all along?"

"No, you were using yourself. I was only playing hard with the cards that I was dealt. Look, I can see that you're going to be a problem for me now, so keep the clothes and everything else I bought you. You have two months to find yourself somewhere to live, and please just leave quietly with some dignity."

No, no, no, this was not happening to me again. Was my life moving in a circular pattern? Was I back in the same fucked-up position once more? Worse, was my name really on the streets as FFB?

I didn't wait for my two months to expire before packing my shit in my trunk and heading back to the dirty crack hotel that Reggie had taken me from. Because I didn't have any other skills except music and being a waitress, I managed to get hired at Slabs Rib Shack, yet another demeaning job, but it helped me rent an apartment and paid living expenses. Atlanta wasn't what I'd expected after all. To be honest, the music industry wasn't what I'd expected either. I remembered Amanda warning me to put reality before fantasy. I didn't understand what she meant then, but I sure as hell did now. I had to face the facts: I am not now and will probably never be a big star.

The whole situation of being raped and humiliated made me sick to my stomach, literally. I couldn't hold down any food, and I kept getting sick. It was like I had a flu that I just couldn't shake to save my life. It would go away one week and come back the next. Some mornings I woke up to what felt like the worst headache known to mankind. I guess going through the drama that I'd experienced had taken a toll on my body so deep that it was making me sick.

I was at work one morning vomiting everything I had eaten that day when Trina, a co-worker, came in to see if I was okay. I told her how sick and exhausted I'd been lately and she asked something that blew my mind. "Are you pregnant? It sure sounds like you are, girl."

Oh, Lord, I didn't remember the last time I saw my period, and the sad part was, if I was pregnant, I didn't know who the father was. My life was sinking further and further into the ground.

Trina gave me her doctor's number and told me to give her a call. "She's an excellent doctor, girl. Call her and tell her what's going on with you. She will help you with any decisions you make. Trust me, she's awesome."

So the very next morning I called Dr. Lawrence and made an afternoon appointment. I told her everything that had been going on with me lately. She took some notes and gave me a full physical. Afterward she sent me to a lab to get some blood drawn for a pregnancy test.

After taking those damn tests, she told me that she'd call me as soon as she got the results, in a day or so. I thanked her for seeing me on such short notice and went home to lie down because I was feeling tired as hell. Before I even made it home, I got a call on my cell from her office telling me she needed to see me back in her office the next morning. *Oh, my God,* I thought. *I'm about to get more bad news. I can barely take care of myself, much less bring a life into this world. What am I going to tell Dr. Lawrence when she asks me about my child's father? I can't say "Well, I slept with like a million niggas and got raped by two, so I have no clue who the fuck the father is."*

A Star Was Born

I was back in Dr. Lawrence's office bright and early the next morning. My appointment was for 10:45 a.m. but I was there at 8:00 a.m. The thought of being pregnant made me sicker than I had been all month. First of all, I wasn't ready to share my life and time with anyone, including a baby. Having a child means that your every moment and your every step is spent being a mother, and most important, that has to be your purpose for living; there's no break in that. Second, I damn sure wasn't ready to dismantle this well-defined body that God blessed me with. I wasn't prepared to see my waistline increase ten sizes, my nose stretched way across my face, and even worse, I wasn't mentally prepared to see one fucking stretch mark on my abs. Yet the greatest anxiety-producer of all: Who was the damn daddy, and where would I begin looking for him? I got so apprehensive I had to walk outside to catch a breath of fresh air.

"Girl, calm your nerves," I said to myself as I caught a glimpse of my worried face in the mirror. Sweat was running down my forehead, which was a sure sign of nervousness, since the central air had that building feeling like the North Pole. "You can get through any situation, so don't let this one break you down." I've been in worse predicaments than this, and it's not like I never had an abortion before. However, I felt so guilty the last time I had one that I had vowed that it would *be* the last time.

After taking a moment to get myself together and downing two cups of coffee, I made my way back into the office just in time to hear the nurse calling me.

"Yes, I'm right here," I quickly responded as I rushed through the door and ran over to greet her.

"You made it just in time," she joked. "Follow me, please." She gave me a warm, charming smile as she escorted me to an empty office. "Dr. Lawrence will be in to see you shortly."

"Thank you." I sat down, thinking over how my life was about to change, maybe for good, maybe for bad. One thing I knew for certain was that I wasn't having another abortion. Maybe this baby could be my blessing in disguise. Maybe this child could change my goal from becoming the world's greatest singer to becoming the world's greatest mother. There are plenty of single parents out there, and they're doing just fine. I'm not going to put myself through the embarrassing hassle of trying to find out who fathered this child. I'm going to do it all by myself. I'm going to give this child the love, attention, and support that my parents didn't give me. You know, the more I thought about the situation, the more comfortable I became with the idea of being someone's mom. Imagine someone calling me Mommy!

In the midst of my thoughts, the door opened and Dr. Lawrence and some white lady walked in. I didn't know if she was a nurse, another doctor, or an intern, but I did know that I didn't want a stranger all up in my business. Doctors' appointments are always private and confidential, so it was a safe bet that this extra ear in the room wasn't sitting right with me.

"Hello, Melissa. Nice seeing you again. I hope you feel a little bit better than you did yesterday."

"Well, I didn't get any rest last night, so I feel a bit tired. When your office called and told me to come back into the office today, I got extremely nervous."

"I understand your worries. The doctor's office is always the last place anyone wants to go." Dr. Lawrence then looked over at the white lady and gave a sort of sign for her to introduce herself, so she began talking.

"Hello, Melissa. My name is Dr. Linda Bloomsburg. I'm a licensed psychologist and on-staff counselor for the majority of Dr. Lawrence's patients. One thing I want to make clear before we explain why I'm present during your visit is that everything that's discussed in this office is strictly confidential and will never leave our office without your written consent."

Now, I'd been in plenty of doctors' offices to get pregnancy tests done, but that was the first time I'd had a counselor present. This must be some high-class fancy shit, but hey, I can live with it.

Dr. Lawrence opened a folder and began talking to me again. "Let me first tell you that we have the results of your pregnancy test. I ran two different tests on you, a urine test and a blood test, and they both came back."

Here comes the moment of truth. By this time I wasn't the least bit concerned about the situation anymore. All I wanted to do was find out the truth as quickly as possible so I could make preparations to deliver a healthy baby and get back in shape, if I was in fact pregnant.

"Both tests came back negative. You aren't pregnant, Melissa."

I was sort of disappointed, because I was just getting used to the idea of being a mother. On the other hand, I was utterly grateful that my body wasn't going to get stretched out like a pair of small tights on a three-hundred-pound woman.

"Oh, that's good to know," I replied. "At least now I get to plan my pregnancy for a more convenient time in my life."

I was smiling and feeling pleased with the good news, but then I noticed that the doctors were exchanging a look.

"Melissa," Dr. Lawrence continued. "Our lab noticed something when they collected your blood sample for the pregnancy test. Now, I don't want you to get alarmed, because they could be wrong, so we're going to need more blood to run some more tests."

"Well, what did they find in my blood, or think they found in my blood, should I say?"

"The results showed some HIV antibodies in your blood sample. However, we're going to conduct a rapid test today, which will confirm or dismiss our lab's assumption."

She was rambling, talking a bunch of medical terminology, but I was still stuck on, "The results showed some HIV antibodies in your blood sample." I felt light-headed. I knew I had heard her incorrectly.

"Did you say HIV? What the fuck do you mean by 'HIV antibodies in your blood sample'? I came here for a fucking pregnancy test, not to hear any bullshit like this."

Dr. Bloomsburg then pulled her chair closer to me. At that moment I understood why she was present. These motherfuckers knew I was going to go off, so they had a psychologist present to help calm me down. Well, they should have had the United States Army up in there, because I was about to explode like a ticking time bomb.

"I know you're feeling confused, upset, frustrated, and stressed-out right now, but I'm here to help you through this transition. Let's take the rapid test to see what measures we have to take next. There have been cases where the labs have been wrong, and we're praying that this is one of them. The best thing to do now is to remain calm and levelheaded."

"Bitch, you can remain calm. I'm the one who's being told that I *may* have a disease that *will* make me extremely sick and then kill my ass. I'm the one being told that I *may* have a disease there's no fucking cure for."

The rage in my voice made Dr. Bloomsburg back the hell up out of my face. I wanted to kill her for even suggesting that I remain calm and levelheaded. "Melissa, many people are living healthy and normal lives after finding out that they are HIV positive. Times have changed, and we're getting closer and closer to finding a cure. However, in the meantime, there are many medications and therapy treatments that have proven effective."

Then tears began to flow from my eyes like the Mississippi River. I fell out of my chair onto the floor. "Why me, Lord? Why me? Haven't I already suffered enough?"

"This is not the time to give up. We have to take more tests, and then if you are in fact infected, we have to do all we can to keep you alive. I won't sit and tell you that it's going to be an easy road, but I can say that if you fight this disease, you'll stand a greater chance of survival."

My body was numb to the point that I could barely speak clearly. There were so many questions and regrets piercing my mind. *Who gave me this disease? Who did I pass it on to? Why didn't I strap up every time I slept with someone? If I am in fact HIV positive, I'm going to kill myself before it kills me. There's no way I'm living my life like that.*

After a long, drawn-out discussion, I agreed to take the rapid HIV test to see if I was infected with the disease. So once again I was back at the lab having my blood drawn for what could be the most devastating news a person could ever hear. As the phlebotomist wrapped the tourniquet around my arm and looked for my vein, I burst into tears. I wanted to pull my arm away and go home to take my life on my own terms, but I couldn't do it without actually knowing if I had this atrocious disease.

After my blood sample was collected, I was told to go back upstairs. When I returned to the office, Dr. Bloomsburg was still in the room reviewing my chart. In an awkward kind of way, she tried to pacify me, but to tell the truth, I was angry and didn't want to hear a word she had to say. This was routine for her. She had probably sat in front of a million motherfuckers and dropped a bomb on their lives. I wasn't trying to hear all that medication, therapy, and prayer shit. The fact still remained that this disease was going to kill me one day; maybe not tomorrow, but one day.

I was *angry* with all the men I had fucked. I was *angry* with these doctors and the lab for telling me that I *may* have this disease. But most important, I was *angry* with myself. How could I do this to myself? I knew that HIV was alive and very much real, but I had never in a million years thought it would catch up with my ass.

For about thirty minutes, I sat and listened to Dr. Bloomsburg telling me how healthy I could be should the test results come back against me. The bitch even popped in some bullshit DVD titled *Making Ways Out of No Way*. From the look of things, she was pretty convinced that I had the disease. She kept telling me to have hope, but on the other hand she was preparing me for the worst.

After waiting for what felt like a billion hours, Dr. Lawrence returned to the office with a folder in her hand. She didn't have to say a word; the look on her face said it all. Instantly I began to cry hysterically. My life as I knew it was over. I'd made poor decisions and now I would have to pay the price for them.

Dr. Lawrence sat down and said, "Melissa, you have to be

strong at this stage. If you want to *live,* you have to *give.* You have to give your all, and fight like you've never fought before. Don't let this disease beat you."

Despite the doctor's positive words, all I heard was, "You're going to die. You're going to suffer in the worst way before you die alone."

After taking more tests and listening to more bullshit, I finally went home. I had never felt so empty. For a while I just sat in the house and cried. I'm pretty sure I lost my job, since I didn't make the effort to call in, which meant that I would be living on the streets very soon; what else was new? I didn't bother to take a bath, change my clothes, or even pick up the phone when my co-workers and a couple of guy friends tried to call me. They were all going to cut me off once they found out I was HIV positive anyway, so I might as well beat them to the punch.

I was sitting in misery one afternoon when I heard a knock on the door. As usual, I ignored it and kept watching TV. Suddenly I heard the door opening, which caused me to jump out of my seat. "Who is coming into my fucking house?" I yelled.

"*Your* house," the woman repeated. "I sent your ass countless letters and you've ignored them all. You see, when you don't pay your rent and you don't show up for court and then turn around and ignore the notices on your door that say you have to be out of here by a certain day, which was yesterday, this is what happens." It was my nagging-ass landlord. She was coming in to put me out on my ass in the middle of *The Young and the Restless.*

"Look, Sheila, I'm sick, which caused me to lose my job. I'm going through something right now, but I promise I'll get you your money. I have no money right now and nowhere to go."

"That sounds like a problem for you to deal with just like I have to deal with the problem of you not paying your rent. I should have put you out a long time ago, but I gave you chance after chance. Now I have someone ready to move in here as soon as tomorrow, and I need your shit out of here. So these strong men are going to take your stuff out piece by piece until this motherfucker is empty. You can help them speed up the process."

She was being a total bitch, which was understandable, considering that I'd been ignoring her notices. I tried to plead with her to give me one more chance, but it was a losing battle; she wasn't hearing that shit.

I stood outside as three guys carried my furniture out to the street. Everyone was out on their front stoops looking at me and laughing. *So now I'm dying, homeless, and humiliated. What reason do I have to live at this point?* I looked horrible, smelled foul, and felt like shit. I didn't have the money to buy a soda, much less rent a U-Haul truck, and then have to turn around and pay a storage fee. So I said fuck it and told my junkie neighbors to have a ball with my belongings.

As if things could get any worse, in the midst of the turmoil, Reggie and White Boy drove past laughing. Typically I would have felt ashamed, but to my surprise I began to laugh too, which caused them to stop the car and roll the windows down. "Damn girl, you look fucked-up," White Boy joked. "This is what happens to people who are disloyal to the family."

"Yeah, I may look fucked-up on the outside, but bitch, both of you are fucked-up on the inside." I began laughing harder than before. "Seems like we all got something in common."

Reggie looked over at White Boy like I was insane before turning to me and asking, "What could we possibly have in common with each other? From what I see, we have somewhere to lay our heads tonight and you don't."

"Don't worry about where I'm going to sleep tonight. Worry about how you're going to sleep from here on out. That's all I have to say. It was nice knowing both of you gentlemen, but as you can see, I have my own problems to attend to."

"Ah, shut the fuck up, bitch," White Boy interjected. "Take

your raggedy ass somewhere and take a fucking shower. You look dirty as shit. I'm almost ashamed to have fucked your slutty ass."

Hearing those words were the therapy that I needed. It's funny how God can use something negative to make you do positive things.

"Thank you for the suggestion. I'll go and do that right now. But most important, thanks for making me see the bright side of my current situation."

I waved to them as they pulled off, thinking they had gotten the best of me. It wasn't until then that I realized that the same motherfuckers who had nicknamed me FFB might have HIV. Looks like we all have three initials tagged to our name now.

I got into my car. The only thing I had with me was a change of clothes, my phone book, a pen and pad, and my medical records.

I was experiencing a life-changing epiphany. I began to reassess my life and the decisions that I'd made and really wished there was a way for me to save others from making the same mistakes. Maybe my misfortune could shed light on the evils of the industry to a young woman who wants to become famous and thinks she can do it by pleasing others at all cost.

With the last drop of money that I had saved under my mattress, I bought some stamps and envelopes, filled up my tank, and prepared to jump back on the highway. It's strange but when I was driving to Atlanta I didn't know where I was heading. But now, driving away from there, I knew exactly where I needed to be. Before taking the long drive I had a couple of phone calls to make. I couldn't just walk away from this city without calling a few people.

The first person I called was Amanda. I didn't give her a chance to curse me out and hang up on me. "Hello. I know you may not want to talk to me, but I just called to tell you that I'm moving back to Pennsylvania and wanted to thank you for all you did for me. I know we both said things to each other that we didn't mean, but I do love and appreciate you."

To my surprise, she didn't hang up. It was as if she was actually happy that I called. "So you're giving up on your dreams and moving back home? You never seemed like the quitting type to me."

"No, I'm not giving up on my dreams. I finally realized that my priorities were backward. Look, there's no point in me hiding this from you, so let me just come out and say it." I took a deep breath. "I found out that I am HIV positive."

There was an extended period of silence on the other end of the receiver. "Are you sure?"

"Girl, I'm positive that I'm positive," I joked, trying to make the best of my misfortune. "Look, I already cried and put blame on everyone else, but at the end of the day, I am totally at fault. I'm going back home to find myself, because somewhere in the process of me joining Pretty in Pink and moving out here, I got lost."

Amanda began apologizing for all the evil things she had said and I did the same. It felt good to finally tell someone that I was infected and have them still accept me as their friend. She tried to convince me to stay and even asked me to move back in with her, but my mind was made up and I knew I had to get the hell out of Atlanta.

"Even if I wanted to stay I'd still have to leave. A lot of mother-fuckers are going to be looking for me when they find out I gave them that shit. Some of them I'm kind of happy about. But I feel sorry for their girlfriends that they cheated on and may have infected. I especially know Reggie and Fatz are coming after me."

"Wait a minute!" Amanda yelled. "Did you fuck Fatz after I told you not to?"

"Girl, I had already fucked him before I met you. It was some wild shit that went on in his truck but I did continue to sleep with him after you told me not to."

"Melissa . . . Melissa, girl, he's the one who gave you that shit.

That's why I told you not to fuck with him. A close friend of mine told me that he had that shit and gave it to her cousin. I didn't know if it was true or not, but I always warned people when they said they'd met him. He's the one who gave you that shit. I swear, I just know it."

I couldn't believe what I was hearing. Fatz. Fatz has HIV. Why the hell is he going around fucking women without wearing a condom? Shit, why is he even fucking anyone at all? I couldn't talk long with Amanda because I had a long day ahead of me, so I promised to keep in touch with her and prepared to make my second call, which would be the hardest of all.

"Hello," the soft voice answered. It's funny but in all the years of my knowing this woman, her voice had never sounded so warm and comforting.

"Hi, Mommy," I hesitantly replied. "How are you?"

She paused before stumbling on her words. "Melissa. Melissa, baby, is that you?"

"Yes, Mommy it's me," I answered as I began crying uncontrollably.

"Thank you, Lord. I knew you would answer my prayers." My mother began to cry and praise God all at once. "Baby, where are you?"

"I'm in Atlanta right now, but I'm on my way home. Is Daddy nearby?"

"Your father is sitting right here with tears in his eyes. We've missed you so much and even hired detectives to find you. I can't wait to wrap my arms around you, baby. What time is your flight coming in?"

"Well, actually I'm driving, so it will take me about a day, but I should be there by tomorrow afternoon at the latest." I then took a deep breath. "Mommy, I have some bad news to tell you before I get there. I want you to know exactly what you're facing when I arrive."

"What's wrong, baby? Are you okay?"

"Mentally I'm hanging in there, but physically I'm not quite as fortunate. Mommy, I'm HIV positive. I know you told me something like this was going to happen to me but . . ."

She cut me off. "Baby, I'm going to buy you a plane ticket. Go to the nearest airport and give me a call. You can leave that car or have it shipped; just get on the next flight out and come home."

"Don't you want to talk it over with Daddy to see if he wants me to come home like this?"

Unexpectedly I heard my father's voice. "Melissa James, you are my child and I love you. I loved you when you were healthy, and I will love you when you're sick. Do what your mother told you to do and hurry up and come home. Come on *home,* my child!"

Without hesitation I drove to the Atlanta International Airport and parked my car in the parking lot. As much as me and this ride had been through together, I had no intention of ever stepping foot back inside it. I planned to leave every single thing I owned in Atlanta, because I was making a new start.

Before calling my parents, I made a couple of copies of my test results and mailed them along with a letter to some of my little "friends" who had turned on me, like Fatz and his labelmates, Jay Spinz from the radio station, a couple of club owners and promoters, and most important, Reggie and his "family."

Dear Friend,

By the time you read this letter I will be long gone from Atlanta. I moved to this city with a dream and an open heart, and I feel that you took advantage of me. Enclosed is a copy of a recent HIV test that I took, and by the way, it came back positive; yes, you read it right: positive! *I've come to grips with the reality of it all and have taken responsibility for my actions and I hope you do the same. A good friend once told me to play hard with the cards that you're dealt, so I hope you play your heart out, because this is not a game. Well, I have doctors to see, medications to fill, and a lot of enemies to dodge after these letters are mailed, so I have to go now. Just remember that you can live a long and healthy life should your test results come back identical to the one enclosed. In order to live, you have to give; give your all!*

Sincerely,
FFB

An hour after talking to my parents, I was in the air looking down on the city of opportunities. I couldn't help thinking how eager I was to come here, and it was ironic, but I was even more eager to leave.

Still Shining!

Two years later. Los Angeles, California

I was standing behind the curtain waiting to go onstage as the announcer began to introduce me. To be honest, I wasn't nervous at all; I just wanted to hit the stage and do my thing.

"Okay, you guys are in for a treat. The next lady who's about to bless the stage is a singer, songwriter, and published author. She's been traveling and touring for the past year and gracing many of us with that beautiful voice of hers, and now I'm glad to welcome her. She's the founder and CEO of STAR: Stop, Think, And Reconsider. She's been bending over backward educating and serving as a mentor to young women everywhere who want to break into the music industry. Backed by her father, the Honorable Reverend Earl T. Booker James, and his lovely wife, Sister Patricia James, we bring you a true star. Ladies and gentlemen, please stand for Ms. Melissa James."

I made my way to the stage to face an audience of ten thousand fans. I opened the ceremony with my new single, "The Cards I Was Dealt," which was an open door to my life's story. So far, my single had sold over a million copies worldwide and gone platinum. My biography had also been flying off the shelves. Just as the announcer said, my parents and I had been traveling all over the world teaching parents and kids how to be successful without compromising their lives. It was too late for me to go back and make corrections, but it wasn't too late for me to help someone else.

STAR is a nonprofit organization providing vocal, spiritual, and intellectual training for young women aged 12 to 18. We offer them resources and outlets and a strong, positive role model in their lives. Maybe if there had been a program like that when I was younger, I wouldn't have gotten caught in the web of immorality that I crawled into and got tangled in. I teach these young ladies to think before they act. In a nutshell, *stop, think, and reconsider* your decisions. If it's something that can potentially come back to haunt you later, don't do it.

So there you have it. I actually became a star, just not like I thought I wanted to be at first. I finally got to perform in front of a big audience, make money, and had my voice heard by thousands, and all it cost me was my life. I guess when you think about it, I was literally dying to be a star!

TYSHA

Money, Stilettos, and Disrespect

Goodbye, Mama

Beverly "Mama Bev" Woods lay at the bottom of the staircase constricted with electrical tape. Her hands and feet were swollen and bound too tight. She had taken a massive blow to the head, and she faded in and out of consciousness while strangers riffled through her worldly possessions.

"Get that flat screen out to the van. Grab the surround sound, iPod dock, and anything else worth some dough," said the leader of the intruders.

The steady stream of tears and blood pouring from Mama Bev's eyes added moisture to the tape around her mouth causing it to slip off. Her eyes followed three masked robbers as they destroyed the home she'd worked a lifetime to buy. She had no strength to fight back.

One tall young man kept glancing over at Mama Bev. His actions offered false hope that he might become her savior. Unlike his partners in crime, his demeanor suggested that he would pay to be anywhere else. Tramond "Rocky" Clinkscale was always impressionable. He was weak and lacked any self-assurance. His insecurity made it easy for him to lie, rob, and steal when others wanted him to. Rocky felt bad for their victim but he wouldn't be the one to run to her aide. He wasn't built to be a hero. Rocky diverted his eyes from Mama Bev. She continued to suffer alone.

"Bitch, where's the money? Answer me! Where's the money and dope?" demanded Slick. He violently shook his victim. Even if Mama Bev could have replied, the aggressive boy wouldn't get the answers he wanted. There were no drugs or money to be found. The intruders had stormed the wrong house.

Things moved in slow motion for Mama Bev. Mama Bev faded away again with dreams of being by her daughter Aisha's side when she gave birth to her first child. In her dream, life was as it should be: peaceful, happy, and blessed. She worried about her two adopted daughters, Kayla and Terry. They had been best friends with Aisha since they were kids. Kayla and Terry had become family and Mama Bev loved them as if they were her own. The three girls' personalities complemented each other perfectly.

Aisha was strong-willed and, at times, stubborn. She often forgot how much inner strength she possessed but her mother never did. Terry was college educated, business-minded, and focused. Terry was sheltered as a child. She learned about the streets through her relationships with Kayla and Aisha. Mama Bev encouraged Terry to strive for success in every facet of life. Kayla grew up on the streets, hustling to survive. Her mother was addicted to drugs and her older brother was serving hard time. Kayla hustled her way to the top of the drug chain before the age of twenty. The streets knew her as Bossy, a hood legend. When she retired from the game, Kayla left her alter ego behind and preferred to be addressed by her given name. It took her loved ones some getting used to but they respected her wishes. Mama Bev knew how hard it was for Kayla to leave the streets. They often talked for hours about the pull the game had on her. Mama Bev would remind her daughter that she was the boss no matter where her lot in life took her.

She could feel herself slipping away. Her head began to spin, causing the visions to fade away as her vital organs began to shut down. Mama Bev took one last breath, causing her body to tremble. *Lord, forgive me of my sins. Please watch over the girls. Keep them safe and protected. I'm on my way home, Jesus,* she cried. Her prayer is what she left this earth with.

"I know you got a stash up in here. Now, where is it?" yelled Slick. His anger was over the top. His victim was limp, only moving because he was shaking her.

"Hold up, dude," said Rail. "You gon kill da bitch before we get her to talk."

"Fuck that, man! This bitch gotta come up off that shit," panted Slick. He kneeled over his victim, sweating like a pig.

"It's too late. Your dumb ass already killed the bitch! Look at her man, look at her!" Rail said angrily.

The inexperienced intruders had crossed the line. Killing the home owner took them from thieves to aggravated murderers.

"Fuck! Now what do we do?" asked Rocky. He stood off to the side, trying not to look at the battered body.

"Now we do what the fuck we came here for. We tear this joint up 'til we find the dope and money. It's here somewhere! Think, where could he have stashed it?" Slick didn't show it, but he was as scared as his friends were.

They stayed in the house so long the sun began to rise. Slick, Rail, and Rocky collected all the jewelry they found, even prying the rings off Mama Bev's fingers. Besides the electronics and the gold and diamond jewels, the robbery didn't give them anything close to what they'd expected. The jewels would net them a small fortune if disposed of properly, but becoming "hood rich" remained a dream.

"Let's go. We gotta get the fuck up out of here. Let's go!" demanded Rail, leading the way out.

The light shining through the window landed on a framed picture hanging on the kitchen wall. Slick, Rail, and Rocky all gasped in recognition of the woman in the picture. It had been dark when they entered her house. None of them had paid any attention to the pictures placed throughout it. They'd have realized from the beginning that they'd made a terrible mistake breaking into the house. Fear and regret took immediate hold of their minds, bodies, and souls. Invading the wrong address was only their first mistake. The second mistake was killing the mother of a hood legend.

Holding On

Three weeks crawled by at a snail's pace for Aisha, Kayla, and Terry. The sudden, cruel way Mama Bev had left this earth was proving too much for Aisha. Her weight had dropped eleven pounds. Her hair was becoming brittle, and dark circles had formed under her eyes. Crying had become her only proof of existence. She hadn't left her mother's home since the day of the funeral. It seemed impossible not to think about the torture her mother had endured. Aisha blamed herself for not being there when her mother had needed her the most. She had fallen so deep into a depression that her friends worried she might be suicidal, or even worse, homicidal.

Aisha sat in the middle of her bed staring at the program from Mama Bev's service. She smiled at the thought of all the people that turned out to say their final goodbyes. The caravan behind the family limo had seemed to go on for miles. It really touched Aisha's heart to see how many lives her mother had touched. Mama Bev's neighbors had loved and respected her dearly. She was a positive role model who had mentored and assisted every single mother, each wayward child, and any stranger she met in need. She praised the children constantly but was quick to chastise them when warranted. When she got word of poor behavior or low grades in school, she would step right in and turn the situation around. Even the local gangs and natural-born knuckleheads respected her. No one ever bothered her. That's what made her murder so hard to understand. No one could make any sense of it.

Tears streamed down Aisha's face. She had never experienced so much pain in her life. Losing her mother had never crossed her mind until it became a reality. Mama Bev was her hero. Aisha didn't know what to do without her and thinking about the agony she'd suffered before her death intensified her pain tenfold. Aisha thought her heart would never heal. Without Mama Bev around to guide and counsel her, Aisha was lost. She felt like a little girl as she curled into the fetal position and cried out for her mother. "Oh Mommy!" she sobbed. "Why'd you leave me like that? I should've been here for you. Please forgive me. I'm so sorry."

She had cried herself to sleep and didn't hear Kayla come into the house. "Aisha! It's me," announced Kayla. "I'll be up in a minute."

Aisha was dreaming that her mother was sitting beside her and they were talking. Mama Bev made Aisha promise not to let her death break her. She tried to remind Aisha that her strength was far greater than her grief and sorrow. Kayla woke Aisha at the wrong time. Her conversation with her mother wasn't over. Aisha hadn't had a chance to say goodbye.

Aisha dried her eyes and checked the time. It was much later in the day than she'd thought. Kayla and Terry brought her something to eat around the same time every day. She caught a glimpse of herself in the mirror and gasped. It wasn't like her to let herself go. *Mommy, I know you're disappointed in me right now. I promise you I'll pull it together and do better,* thought Aisha.

"Kayla!" yelled Aisha.

"What's wrong?" asked Kayla. She was startled by Aisha's yelling.

"I'm getting in the shower. I'll eat a little later," said Aisha.

Kayla was happy with the response. Getting Aisha to do anything these days was a battle. Kayla and Terry shared Aisha's pain. They felt like biological daughters of Mama Bev, especially Kayla. After her brother went to prison and her mother dedicated her life to being a crackhead, Mama Bev took on the responsibility of caring for Kayla. Mama Bev had embraced Kayla and Terry with open arms and never let them go.

Thirty minutes passed before Aisha emerged from the bathroom wrapped in an oversized towel. She found Kayla sitting on the bed thumbing through an old photo album.

"I haven't thought about life in the jets in years," said Kayla, smiling.

"Look at our hair! What were we thinking?" Aisha laughed and Kayla joined in.

Life during those days was rough. But looking back, they were also good times.

"Mama Bev beat us all that day," recalled Kayla as she pointed out a picture of herself, Aisha, and Terry sitting on C-Lok's '79 Impala.

C-Lok was Kayla's first love and business partner. They had formed an unbreakable bond over the years. Mama Bev, Aisha, and Terry loved C-Lok and he felt the same about them.

"How could I forget? She went off on us after she threatened those poor boys with the .22 she carried in her purse, remember?" asked Aisha.

"They ran out of the apartment with the quickness. None of them ever spoke to us again." Kayla laughed.

The sisters went through the entire album, laughing at all the memories it held.

"Aisha, you know it's time for you to fight this depression. I don't want to sound like I don't care. You know Mama Bev was the only real mother I ever had. She would hold me responsible for taking care of you. You've had time to feel every emotion known to man, and Mama would not want you in this state of mind for so long," said Kayla.

"You're right, Kayla, it's that time. Mommy told me the same thing in a dream I was having when you woke me up. It's time for me to show that I'm the strong woman she raised me to be." Aisha walked over to her dresser and grabbed a bottle of lotion. Kayla could see that she was carrying the weight of the world on her shoulders.

"I'm angry. Why would anyone pick this house to break into? Everybody knew Mommy, knows us, hell, and is afraid of you. Anybody beating the streets knew not to do this," Aisha said.

"Word's out and the streets will be talking very soon. C-Lok has his people on it," Kayla said.

"Good. I should have known he'd be on it," sniffed Aisha.

"He'll handle things. There's nothing to worry about. We have to decide what's going to happen with this house," Kayla replied, trying to steer the conversation in a different direction.

"What happens when C-Lok finds out who killed Mommy?" Aisha asked.

"Never ask the when, where, how, and especially the who. I taught you that lesson years ago."

"This is different, Kayla. They tortured my mother, our mother, in her own home. She was beaten and brutally raped. She didn't deserve to die the way she did. I have to know what will happen when they're caught," Aisha explained through her tears.

"Why? What do you want to happen?"

"They should suffer a worse death than the one Mommy went through. Shooting them is a kinder death than they deserve."

"I have to agree with that," Kayla replied.

"Will you see if C-Lok will arrange for it to go that way?" asked Aisha with pain and hatred in her heart.

"Yes, I will."

"I just need one more thing from C-Lok, I'm going to need your help to get it," began Aisha.

"What is it?"

"I want to be there when it happens. I have to be witness to the slow, painful deaths of the bastards who ripped my heart from my chest. I want revenge," Aisha cried angrily.

$ $ $

On the streets, C-Lok was a ghost, an unseen legend. People knew Cliffton "C-Lok" Boyd's legacy on the streets. He was head of the drug game and of a family he'd created from nothing. No one made a move without his permission. That included everyone from street soldiers to his queen, Kayla. His workers never saw him. He kept his hands on a buffet of drugs and guns. Many speculated that he'd move away from the impoverished city of Youngstown, Ohio. He was a man of honor, pride, and loyalty. In his mind, he could never abandon the city that had raised him, fed him, and kept him in business.

But now he was stuck. He'd never expected such a request, especially from Aisha.

"Aisha, you can't think for one minute that I'd permit this. I expected you to ask that whoever did this be tortured or some shit like that. What you're talking about is that bullshit right there," said C-Lok.

"Man, she don't mean that shit. She tripping and grief is a bitch. Kayla, man, you can't talk to ya girl?" asked Big Black. He was C-Lok's right-hand man.

"I know exactly what I want to do. Whoever did this shattered my life and left me in pain. My mother was all I had and they stole her from me," explained Aisha.

While everyone understood where Aisha was coming from, no one thought she really understood what the consequences would be. This wasn't the first time such a request had been made of C-Lok. In the other situation, he'd had no qualms or hesitations, but it was a decision that he'd come to regret.

"I gotta make a call, ya'll. Hold up," he said. Five minutes later, he returned to the living room and immediately made eye contact with Kayla. Not a word was spoken but much was said. He could see that she wasn't totally convinced one way or the other, but no matter what Aisha decided, Kayla would have her sister's back.

An hour later C-Lok was still on the fence. The more time that went by without an answer from him, the more anxious Aisha felt. Just when she was about to ask him the status on finding out who'd killed her mother, the doorbell rang. C-Lok passed the blunt he was toking on to Big Black and went to let his visitors in. The phone call he'd made was to his sister. He knew that if anyone could identify with Aisha, it would be Shy. Years before she'd been in a similar position.

"Hey, baby, how you doing?" C-Lok greeted.

"I'm good," Shy replied as she kissed her brother's cheek and gave him a quick hug. "Where is she?"

Everyone greeted Shy when she entered the room. Shy sat next to Aisha.

"C, do you mind if I talk to Aisha alone." Shy said it as more of a statement than a question. Besides Kayla, Shy was the only other woman on earth for whom C-Lok would lay down his life. Kayla stood up, with the men following suit. After everyone was gone, Shy turned her full attention to Aisha.

"You haven't returned any of my calls. I've been so worried about you. I knew Kayla and Terry were looking out for you, though," Shy began.

"I didn't want to bother you. It's bad enough that Kayla and Terry are going through this with me. You have enough to worry about," Aisha said.

"My brother told me you need me. He said you want to personally punish the bitches who did this."

"They don't understand what I'm feeling. I know they loved my mother, but it's different for me. She was my world. All my life, she sacrificed her own so I'd have anything and everything. She didn't have her own life while I was coming up. That's why I spoiled her when I started making money." Aisha cried.

"Do you get that if you do this, you'll be sacrificing life as you know it?" Shy asked with compassion.

"How do you deal day in and day out?" Aisha asked.

"Melvin was my life and I was his. Sacrificing my life for him was a no-brainer for me. My kids don't have their father and I don't have my husband. To be honest with you, I don't feel an ounce of remorse." Shy meant what she said. She'd never lost one night of sleep for taking the life of the man who'd shot her husband down in front of their ten-year-old son. "You have to ask yourself if you're willing to sacrifice your life for that of a memory."

"Absolutely," Aisha replied.

Shy called out for C-Lok, Kayla, and Big Black. They all returned to their seats with fresh drinks in their hands. Kayla handed a glass to Aisha, and C-Lok gave one to Shy. Once everyone was comfortable, it was back to business.

"Tell me what it is, Aisha? Do you still want to do this?" C-Lok asked.

"Without any reservations, yes," Aisha answered.

"She'll be fine," promised Shy. "Aisha knows exactly what she's doing."

"Rule number one: no government names when conducting business. There's no waking up from this. From now on, we'll address you as 'Dream,' " said C-Lok.

"Aisha, you're a hood girl without a doubt, but there's a lot for you to learn on this side of the fence. I respect your decision and

I got your back. I'm going to tell you the same thing I told Shy: Life after getting revenge can be a sweet dream or a beautiful nightmare."

Bad Boys, Come Out to Plaaayyyy . . .

Slick, Rail, and Rocky found it near impossible to sell the goods they'd stolen from Mama Bev. The entire city was ablaze, and the flames were out of control. Everybody in the hood was gunning for them. Word was that there was a $50,000 bounty on their heads. Everyone with a foot on the streets was searching for Mama Bev's killers. As a result, they remained just as broke as they'd been before the heist.

"Man, this is some bullshit! What da fuck?" Rail fumed.

"We all in the same boat, playa. Just calm down so we can put our heads together to figure a way out of this corner," Rocky reasoned.

"Ya little soft ass would say some shit like that. If you haven't noticed, we been trying to come up with a plan for months now. We can't even slang enough rocks to get out of town. This is da bullshit fo' sho," said an irritated Slick.

Rocky stared at Slick. He'd gotten tired of Slick putting him down.

"This is stupid. We don't even know if our names have dropped. If they not lookin' for us, we making it obvious that we did this shit by disappearing," Rocky said.

"Oh, we numbers one, two, and three on the most-wanted list. The police ain't figured it out, but the streets know our names. My boy told me that everybody at the club was talking about us. He said he even heard whispers at the barbershop. We need some cash fast. I ain't tryna dic bchind this shit," Rail said as fear settled into his heart.

"You think I don't know that shit? What da fuck can we do?" Slick demanded.

"I have a plan to get us some money," Rocky interrupted.

Slick and Rail both looked at Rocky like he'd grown a second head right before their eyes. "What's up?" asked Slick. He usually shot down anything Rocky said but desperate times called for desperate measures.

"My boy from the jets is looking for a couple of runners. We came up together since third grade. His supplier relocated to New York and he needs some dudes to make the trip for him every other month. His plan is to switch up on drivers to fool the troopers. I think we should hook up with him. We can at least make one run and get that money," Rocky explained. Rocky misled Slick and Rail on purpose. He and Prince lived in the same housing projects and attended the same schools but they were not close friends. Nor were they enemies. Their relationship could be described as mere acquaintances. Rocky was anxious to get as far away from Youngstown as possible. He believed Prince was his one-way ticket out and he needed Slick and Rail to see things his way.

"That ain't a bad idea," Rail said.

"Yeah, instead of delivering that cash, we can get the fuck up out of here real quick. We just rob da nigga instead of making a damn delivery. Fuck Youngstown and every bitch in it!" Slick said.

"Hold up a minute. How do we know this job is legit? There's a big-ass price tag on our asses. Dude could be setting us up just to get paid. Shit, I know I would," Rail said.

"Naw, Prince ain't like that. His dad was Melvin Shaw," Rocky said before Slick interrupted him.

"Da cat who got shot in his own crib by the po-po? They

gunned him down in front of his own seed, right?" Slick asked excitedly.

"Yeah, that's him. It was Prince who witnessed that shit. Ever since then, Prince been a young-minded hustler out here getting it done. He just waiting on the okay to come here and rap to us about the job," Rocky said with a grim look in his eyes. He was fully expecting Slick to go off on him for suggesting that someone know their whereabouts.

"Shit, get dat nigga over here. The po-po kill ya pops right in front of you, hustling and killing is in your blood. I've been hearing stories about his dad Melvin since I was a little kid. I heard the streets used to call that nigga Legend." Slick remembered wanting to be just like the man called Legend when he was growing up. It was going to be an honor for him to meet the seed of his hero.

"That's what's up, my nigga. Let's get this poppin'," Rail said.

Rocky walked over to the kitchen/dining area of the old house. Its original four legs were barely holding up the wooden table. The two vinyl-covered chairs were torn and ripped so bad all their insides had long been pulled out. Rocky moved the strewn newspapers in search of his prepaid cell phone. He had been anticipating making the call for a week. It had taken him that long to work up the nerve to discuss his plan with his partners in crime. He began pushing buttons as fast as his fingers would move.

"Yo, come on through," Rocky invited when his friend answered his call.

"One," Prince replied and ended the call.

$ $ $

"Nephew."

"Meeting now, it's on, Unc," Prince said into his phone.

"Get back at me," instructed his uncle.

Prince and his uncle ended their conversation with a mutual understanding. The meeting with Mama Bev's killers was about to take place and Prince would report the details soon. With that information, his uncle would start getting his end of the matter in order and wait on the go-ahead from his nephew to get things going.

Prince drove down Hillman Street five miles under the posted speed limit. The police had never stopped him, and it was in everyone's best interest that they never did. He hated anyone wearing the blue and he knew that if he ever interacted with them, someone would end up dead—and it wouldn't be him.

The area at the bottom of the city's south side was nicknamed Smurf Village back in the eighties. All the houses were small, crammed together, and the same color, just like the village the little blue cartoon characters called home. It was now home to three young men who'd signed their own death warrants the second they broke into Mama Bev's house. Rocky's bad luck continued to follow him the day he bumped into his childhood friend at the corner store.

Prince had showed major self-restraint by not putting a bullet through Rocky's neck the very second their eyes met. Mama Bev had been like a second grandmother to Prince and his twin brother Jayden. Her death had devastated the McGee family, especially their mother. Unaware of Prince's relationship with the woman whose blood stained his hands, Rocky walked right into a well-laid trap. Rocky was clueless that the time for reckoning was near.

When Prince had mentioned his need for trustworthy runners, Rocky had jumped at the opportunity. With their history, he was certain his friend trusted him enough to hire him. He decided that he'd venture out on his own if Slick and Rail refused to play along. Rocky was determined to get as far out of harm's way as he possibly could.

"What up, my man?" Rocky greeted Prince.

"I can't call it. You tell me," Prince said with a smile. He gave

Slick and Rail firm handshakes and nods as Rocky made the introductions.

"I just want to tell you that your pops was a hero of mine. Legend is a true legend out on these streets," Slick gushed. Prince looked at the man as if he were an ugly woman at a bar trying to go home with him.

"My old man lived up to his name. I aspire to be just like him," Prince admitted. "Let's get down to business." He could do without all of the small talk. "I need some runners outside my camp to take care of business for me. This business needs to be handled at least once a month. I want the drivers to rotate to avoid any unwanted attention. It's a five-hour drive one way, so turnaround will be two days. Drive up, make the delivery, get the pickup, stay the night, and drive back in the morning. This schedule is etched in stone. Each person should rotate the hotel as well. One throwaway phone will be supplied for the ride up and another for the return drive. Never take anyone on the trip except for your assigned backup."

Slick, Rail, and Rocky hung on every word. It was impressive how detail-oriented Prince was at age sixteen. Slick wondered how he'd climbed so high up the totem pole at such a young age. Considering that he'd witnessed the police killing his father, Slick reasoned that the streets had raised Prince. He was a young man with an old mind and soul.

"I don't mean to be rude, but can I ask you a question?" Slick asked.

"What up?" Prince responded.

"Most cats at the top like that don't let many into their house. How does your supplier feel about working with different runners each month?"

"That's not for you to worry about. If I'm sending you to do a job, the details have been worked out far ahead of time. I got that," Prince snarled. He hated stupid questions. It should be obvious that what he put down was going to be picked up by the other players.

"As I was saying," Prince continued, "should a shipment be lost, it falls on your shoulders to replace it. If it can't be replaced, your life will be lost. It's as simple as that."

"What do we get hit off with for each run?" Rail asked.

"My bad, fella. The cash is the most important part, right?" Prince laughed. "Each run brings in fifteen thousand dollars per person. Since that type of paper ain't a monthly guarantee, you gotta be able to handle ya business. Put some of that shit to work for you and put some up, if you're smart, that is," he finished.

"What's up, dudes? Y'all down with it or not?" Rocky asked.

"Why you asking them? If you take this gig, it's your life and freedom at risk. What do you want to do, Rock?" an annoyed Prince asked.

"Put me on," Rocky replied with complete certainty.

"What's up wit you, Slick?" Prince directed the same question.

"I'm wit it fo' sho."

"Rail, what about you?"

"You had me at fifteen grand, my man. I wanna be down." Rail smiled.

"Done," Prince replied. "We leave tomorrow at nine to take the first ride into New York. I'm going to show you the route, introduce you to your contact and make sure each one of you is comfortable with the job," Prince said before turning to walk out the door. "One."

Inside his car, Prince made the call that many had waited months to receive.

"Nephew."

"Nine, Unc," Prince announced.

"Done," C-Lok replied before ending the call. He needed to notify all involved that revenge was in motion and that Youngstown's three most wanted would be leaving the city at nine o'clock the next morning. It was time to rumble.

Trust No Man

Prince drove to his destination with the sounds from Above the Law's classic song, "Uncle Sam's Curse," coming through his car speakers. The urge to pull out his .380 and kill his passengers was overwhelming. It was not in his character to show such restraint. He was proud of himself. His destination slowly came into view. Prince slowed the car down.

"Man, what's up? I thought we were going to ya dude's crib. Ain't nothing out here but an old empty warehouse," Slick said suspiciously.

"Where'd you get that bullshit from? Don't nobody operate where they lay their heads, not if they got any true hustle in their bloodline. We're here to meet up with my man. Be cool," directed Prince.

"So this where all the drop-offs and pickups gon be?" Rail asked.

"Unless my man says differently." Prince smiled and turned the volume up on the car stereo. He knew the three victims were getting suspicious, but they were in no position to act upon any instincts. Before leaving Youngstown, Prince had convinced them to hand over their guns in order to hide them in a special compartment. He explained that, if they got stopped for any reason, they didn't want the police to find four young armed black men. Prince, on the other hand, remained strapped. Because of what had happened to his father, he'd rather the police catch him with a gun than for an enemy to catch him without one.

All the men bobbed their heads to rapper Kokane explaining why his neighborhood considered him a Black Superman as Prince pulled up to an old abandoned building. The steele mill had closed before any of the car's occupants were born. It was the perfect place to exact street justice.

"This the place?" Rocky asked. He looked around, taking in his surroundings. Nothing could be seen but old abandoned buildings covered in soot. Rocky trusted his boy Prince. The idea that he might betray him never entered his mind.

"Yeah, my mans and 'is already here. Their cars are over there. It was a long ride, so we're about to blaze this blunt before we go conduct this business," Prince said while lighting the end of the cigar paper.

"Shit, I'm wit that fo' sho." Rail smiled. He had slept the entire five-hour drive and was just waking up.

As the car filled with smoke from the blunt, Prince pulled a throwaway cell phone from underneath his seat and speed-dialed his uncle's number. If his passengers took notice, it would just seem like he was checking for any missed calls. He pushed the SEND button, waited five seconds, and finished the signal by pushing the END button. The blunt found its way around the car a couple more times until it burned down to a mere memory. Prince popped the car locks and opened his door. It was time to get things popping.

Payback Is a Bitch

"**G**ood work, nephew. We'll square up when I get back to the spot. Now get the fuck up out of here. Your mission is over."

Prince gave his uncle a nod and a quick handshake with a

bump of the right shoulder before turning to leave. C-Lok was the only male role model Prince had had in his life after his father was murdered. His uncle always looked out for him and his family. Prince admired him for that. He would go to hell with flammable drawers on if C-Lok asked him to.

Aisha could feel her blood boil as she stared at the three men in the dog cages. The hate Aisha felt as she thought about her mother's terror and fear was so powerful her head hurt. She could hear her mother's cries for help when her eyes fixed on Slick. Somehow she knew Slick was the rapist and she wanted him to suffer the most. The desire to inflict pain on him was so intense, Aisha almost had an orgasm.

Kayla watched Aisha. She knew exactly what she was feeling. Years before, one of Kayla's best friends had been killed in a drive-by. She had put her ear to the streets, found the shooter, and executed him. At the time, pulling the trigger had felt exhilarating, but living with the reality of taking a life was a different battle altogether. Almost twenty years later, the face of her victim occasionally found its way into her dreams. Kayla had never imagined that she'd find herself in a similar situation with her sister Aisha. And at that moment, standing next to Aisha was the only place Kayla would be.

"Are you okay?" Kayla asked, placing her hand on Aisha's back for support.

"I will be as soon as these muthafuckas start screaming like bitches," Aisha replied. She kept her eyes locked on the dog cages while she spoke. "Where are the guys?"

"C said we don't need the dogs until later, so they went to tie them up out back."

Within arm's reach lay an assortment of tools: a power drill, sharp and dull knives of various sizes, a staple gun, a hammer, a mallet, acid, table salt, rubbing alcohol, a plumber's snake, dog food, and a plunger. There were also Tasers, a cattle prod, and small boxes containing live rats and poisonous spiders nearby. Meth and PCP were on hand to keep the victims awake. The last thing Aisha wanted was for them to pass out from the pain. Right now the three were napping, thanks to hits on the backs of their heads.

Aisha looked around and yanked the water hose off the floor. She turned the nozzle on full blast. "Wake the fuck up, you bas- tards!" she demanded. One by one, her victims coughed and struggled to figure out what was restricting their movements. The dog cages were big enough to stuff the men into with ease but small enough to prevent them from finding any comfortable po- sition. Aisha turned the water off after five minutes of getting the men soaking wet and wide-awake. She took a moment to step back and smile at her prisoners.

"What the fuck is going on?" Slick spoke between coughing fits.

"Where in the hell are we?" Rail asked as he looked around.

"What's going on?" a frightened Rocky questioned.

"It's time to get this party on and poppin', playboy," announced C-Lok. He, Devin, and Big Black had returned from the back of the abandoned building while Aisha was showering the caged men. "You niggas knew the streets would cough you up sooner or later, didn't you? I mean, ain't no love in the game," teased C-Lok. "Am I right, Black?"

"Right as rain, my man. If you do the crime, you have to be willing to do the time," Big Black responded. "What do you think, Dee?"

"I think this right here's a little different. These little niggas fucked up in the worst way, but we 'bout to see to it that the pun- ishment fits the crime, fo' sho," said Devin devilishly.

Devin was Kayla's older brother and a dedicated member of C-Lok's team. Kayla may have retired from the game, but Devin had only semiretired. Doing wrong flowed through his veins. He enjoyed the rush that stealing and killing gave him, and just like his addiction to nicotine and weed, he couldn't give them up. Memories of his twenty-five-year stint in prison kept Devin's menacing to a limit. Devin was enjoying his freedom and not willing to give it up again.

"Who the fuck is ya'll niggas, and what you want with us? I thought we were hooking up with Prince and his peoples," Rocky said. His entire body shook with fear.

"We're your worst nightmare, muthafuckas! How's that for an answer?" Devin said.

"Let me tell you pieces of shit who I am," Aisha said. "I'm the daughter of the saint of a woman you tortured and killed in her own home." She spoke through clenched teeth to keep from crying. She ran her hand along the top of each cage as she circled them. "It pleases me to have you here. This is where each of you will take your last slow, painful breath before death comes to claim you. I'm personally going to see to it that you suffer the same pain and agony inflicted upon my mother." She wanted to cry, but she wouldn't give them the satisfaction of witnessing any weakness on her part. It took great willpower to keep her composure. "You beat her, we'll beat you. Her bones were broken and yours will be too. You raped a defenseless woman, and I will take great pleasure in stripping you of any measure of manhood you have right now. My mother called me Baby Girl, but you may refer to me as Dream. Just know that this is far from a bad dream—it's your new reality."

"Now that the introductions have been made, Dream, tell us where you want to start." Kayla said. The two women, along with C-Lok, Big Black, and Devin, were dressed in hospital scrubs covered by white hazmat jumpers. To protect their footwear, their feet were covered with booties like the ones hospital workers and crime-scene investigators used. Multiple boxes of surgical gloves along with masonry and utility gloves were on hand.

Aisha walked over and picked up the cattle prod as an evil smile washed over her face. "They're wet, so let's play with this right here," she said, holding the prod in front of her.

"Make your dreams come true, girl. The world is yours," C-Lok said.

"So y'all got us caged up like fuckin' animals over that bullshit? It was a mistake! We went to the wrong damn address. We didn't mean to do that old lady. Shit just got fucked up," Slick began, begging for his life.

"Shut da fuck up, bitch! You don't get to have a say in this. Did my mother have a say? Did she tell you you had the wrong spot? Fuck you!" Aisha screamed. She stormed over to the cage that held Slick and jabbed him with the cattle prod. The more he screamed in pain, the harder her nipples got.

Rail and Rocky were scared to death. They both prayed to God for mercy, asking for a quick death. Tears streamed down Rail's face as Slick lay in a fetal position next to him, yelling in agony.

"This ain't right. Just shoot me. Ain't that what you want in the end? Our lives?" Rail demanded a say in how he left this earth.

Aisha yanked the cattle prod out of Slick's cage and focused her attention on Rail. "When you broke into my mother's home, did you ask her how she wanted to die for *your* mistake? It took hours for my mother's suffering to end. She lay slowly dying while your bitch asses ransacked her home. So you already picked your fate, bitch." Aisha picked up a metal bucket filled with some sort of liquid and began slowly pouring it through the top of the dog cage. She took her time, careful not to splash any on herself. Rail's head was her target, and she was hitting her mark. His skin made a sizzling sound as the acid met his face, neck, back, and arms. The smell of his flesh melting away was overwhelming. Being witness to the pain gave Aisha a feeling of euphoria she'd never experienced.

Rail squirmed inside the cage. His attempt to flee his jail was wasted energy. He screamed, yelled, and hollered at the top of his lungs until he couldn't anymore. "Please kill me! Oh, my God, please kill me," Rail pleaded for an escape from the torment and agony. His skin was boiling from the acid. Rail's burning skin sizzled. Breathing was more difficult by the second. All he wanted to do was die. "I'm sorry, I'm sorry. Just kill me." Rail's cries went unanswered.

She turned with the bucket in hand and was met by her sister's worrying eyes. She nodded to indicate that she was all right.

"Dream, you have one left before you take a break. We'll get them ready for the next round," C-Lok said while passing a blunt to Big Black.

Rocky was so fearful he shit his pants. Growing up in Youngstown had offered very little to him and those around him. All his life, he'd tried to avoid the drug scene and the gangs. He went to school, played sports, and got the high school diploma his mother had urged him to strive for. At the end of the day, his efforts got him nowhere and nothing. School didn't prepare him for life. He had a diploma but no skills. Living a life of poverty after watching his mother work two and three jobs at a time was discouraging. He was frustrated with their situation and wanted to help his mother financially. She was getting older and deserved to relax a little while she could still enjoy it. The only option he had was to sell rocks. He was tired of being hungry and needing basic things like shoes. He felt horrible for what he'd allowed to happen to that lady. They'd hit the wrong house, thanks to Slick's illiteracy, and the outcome haunted him on a daily basis. It was his turn to be punished and he would take it like a man.

"What? You too big to beg and cry like your friends?" Aisha asked.

"I'm sorry," he replied. "It was my fault your mother suffered because I wasn't strong enough to stand up for what was right. I can't bring her back to you. All I can say is I'm sorry."

"What's your name? Rocky?"

"Yes."

"You're the one who grew up in the Victories with Prince?" Aisha's voice was void of anger.

"Yes, I am, " Rocky said.

"I respect what you've said. I respect you for manning up," Aisha said as she walked over to the table and picked up the chrome .380. She turned back around to face Rocky. "Because I respect that, I won't make you suffer." She raised the gun, aimed it toward Rocky's head, and fired.

Then C-Lok forced Aisha to take a break to give her time to get her thoughts together. It would be her decision whether to continue with the torture herself or allow Big Black and Devin to finish the job.

Kayla grabbed her duffel bag from the corner. She followed Aisha to the opposite end of the abandoned steel mill. Aisha was calm, quiet, and wet with perspiration. It devastated Kayla to watch her sister dive headfirst into the world of money, drugs, and murder. She knew Aisha's life would be in ruins due to her thirst for revenge. "Sit down right here," Kayla said, pointing to a chair on their right. Aisha did as she was told without hesitation. Despite her demeanor, she was fighting against herself on the inside. Her mind knew that what she was doing was wrong, but her heart felt like it was oh so right.

"Here, drink this," Kayla instructed as she passed Aisha a cup of Ciroc and a pre-rolled blunt. Kayla twisted off the top of a water bottle and took a big swallow. It had always been her policy to keep a clear head when putting in work. Though she didn't intend to get her hands dirty, she'd step in for her sister if it became necessary.

"These niggas are trying to pass out. Get that meth into them and wake them up," C-Lok said.

Devin and Big Black grabbed the water bottles, which were

filled with drug cocktails. Multiple pills to make one's system race were crushed and dissolved in the water. After being shocked by the cattle prod, Slick was jonesing for a drink of water. It drained what little strength he had left just to sip the weird-tasting liquid through a straw, but he continued to swallow as long as Devin held it to his mouth.

With acid having been poured over his upper body, there was no way Rail could drink or swallow. Big Black drew the meth into a syringe and shot Rail up between his toes. The drugs prevented Slick's and Rail's systems from shutting down.

Big Black opened the door to Rail's cage and dragged him out. Devin followed suit with Slick. The two broken men lay on the cold oily concrete floor fighting to bear the pain. After Big Black and Devin were finished, Rail and Slick would beg to feel their current level of pain again. They were beaten with fists and base ball bats before being stomped on with steel-toed boots. The pain was unbearable. They both prayed for death to end their suffering. The beating continued until Big Black and Devin were exhausted. Slick's right leg, left elbow, and left hand were all broken. He would spit in his mother's eye if it meant eliminating the pain he was in.

Rail lay six feet from his friend in worse shape. His skin was still sizzling from the acid. He was bleeding from his nose and mouth. The blood flowing into his open wounds was pure torture. He prayed to God repeatedly to take his soul. The idea of his own death had never entered his mind until he woke up inside a dog cage. At that moment, he wanted a gun put to his heart and the trigger pulled. He wanted to die and escape the pain.

Both of Rail's eyes were mere slits. He could barely focus on the activity going on around him. Then he heard footsteps drawing closer to him.

"I'm sure your stupid ass is ready to leave this world right about now. Well, what you're about to feel will not change your mind, playa. You have no one to blame but yourself for what you're going through," C-Lok preached as he walked circles around Rail's burned body.

C-Lok reached inside a medium-sized Baggie and grabbed a handful of its contents. Rail's body began to convulse as the table and sea salt rained down on him. The pain was too much for him to handle. He went into a seizure. Aisha and Kayla made their way back over to the men as he thrashed on the floor. Kayla had had enough. Aisha should be satisfied with the pain inflicted on the men. As far as Kayla was concerned, it was time for the group to leave and for the second team to come in and clean things up.

"C found out that it was Slick who violated Mama Bev, so Black and Dee, roll this one," Kayla pointed at Rail, "over to that furnace. He'll be dead soon. Infection has probably set in as we speak. After he gets what he deserves, it's done." Kayla spoke with great authority, and no one dared disagree. C-Lok was in a position to override her but even he knew not to go against her.

"Can one of you strip his ass naked?" Aisha said more as a demand than a question. She knew it was time to finish exacting her revenge and release her pain. Big Black used his foot to roll Slick onto his back. Slick screamed in agony as his broken leg was moved when his pants were stripped off. His high-pitched screams pierced everyone's ears. The crying began when Big Black kicked Slick back onto his stomach. He was now ready for Aisha to finish him off.

Aisha rammed the plunger inside of Slick's anus with all the force she could muster. "You bitch!" Slick yelled. "You can't break me." Next, she violated him with a wooden broomstick until blood started leaking from his anus. Slick continued to scream and cry from the torture. He was helpless to defend himself. Blood gushed from his anus forming a pool beneath him. Aisha was unfazed. She imagined the shame and disrespect her mother must have felt while he raped her. The thought infuriated Aisha to the point of no return. She hoped Slick's insides were being ravaged with each thrust of the foreign object.

Tears streamed down Aisha's face. She dropped the broomstick and walked over to where the two-inch Marcel curling iron was heating inside its oven. The curling iron was as hot as molten steel. "Fuck you, Slick! How about that? Fuck your mama and her mama. You're going to hell because I'm sending you there. When you get there, tell your boys I said fuck them too!" Aisha cried right before jamming the hot curling iron into Slick's rectum. Slick was semiconscious and near death. After giving the handle a good twist, she left it there and turned her back on him.

A smile covered Aisha's face as she walked away from Slick, feeling satisfied and lighter. Slick passed out from the pain and blood loss. The grim reaper was holding Slick's hand. Aisha had gotten her revenge, allowing her mother to rest in peace and her to finally sleep at night. She was happier than she had been in months.

I don't know what everybody was tripping about. I feel strong, guilt free, and hungry for more. I may have walked in here as Aisha, but I'm leaving as Dream. I can get used to this feeling. Just the thought of more victims is making me wet, thought Aisha.

Said and Done

Aisha and Shy were enjoying a late lunch at A Piece of Soul Café & Catering, which was owned by Shy's best friend, Cherise Peters. The ambiance was calm and relaxing in the quaint café as jazz played in the background. All her customers seemed to enjoy the setup, and Shy encouraged Cherise to keep everything the way it was. Aisha, Kayla, and Terry always used Cherise when their company, KAT69, needed catering services.

"I'm glad you called. We haven't talked since that day at your brother's house. What's been going on with you and the kids? How are the twins and that little beauty queen of yours?" Aisha asked between sips of coffee.

"Princess is spoiled as ever. How many five-year-olds do you know who have everything? Christmas and her birthdays always have me stumped. All I can do is give her an updated version of what she already has," Shy said half jokingly. "As far as the twins are concerned, Jayden and Prince are doing well." She picked at her apple fritter and savored the taste of her strawberry-banana smoothie while she and Aisha made small talk. After the two settled into their visit, Shy decided it was time to get to the point. "Aisha, I wanted to talk to you about what happened and how you're dealing with it. Are you okay?"

"I'd be lying if I said sleeping some nights was easy, but I'm doing well," Aisha said with complete honesty.

"I'm happy to hear that. Sleepless nights are part of the package when we choose to do what was done. The million-dollar question is, would you do it all over again?"

"I've asked myself that many times. When I think of my mother, all that comes to me are the good times we shared together. I miss Mommy every minute of every day," Aisha said as she reached for a napkin to dab the tears rolling down her face. Shy reached across the table to hold her hand.

"I'm okay, girl. I have bad days and I have good days. The good are beginning to outweigh the bad."

"I understand, girl. Your heart will slowly heal and the weight of your pain will get lighter," Shy promised.

"The only time I think about what went down is when I can't sleep. I feel no compassion for them, and I hope they're burning in hell. So to answer your question, yes. If I had to make the decision all over again today, I'd still want to be the one to punish the punk-ass niggas who ruined my life. They robbed my mother of the joy of being a grandmother. They stole our shopping for my wedding dress together. Those three boys deserved what they got, and I have no problem living with myself." Aisha had expected to feel guilty and experience nightmares about the torture she'd inflicted on her mother's killers but she hadn't. She was at peace with her actions and made no apologies for them.

"To be honest with you, I went through some bad dreams after my situation," Shy said. "The only thing is, the bad dreams weren't about the crooked-ass cop who gunned down my husband in the presence of our son. My dreams were about my husband. My conscience was telling me that Melvin was somewhere watching me." She agonized at reliving that difficult and emotional time in her life. Aisha listened intently and felt Shy's pain as she spoke.

"Why would Melvin watching over you make you feel bad?" Aisha asked.

"Because I thought that he might be disappointed with me. That he might have been angry with me for what I did. I mean, it was so out of character for me," Shy explained.

"Girl, that man loved you. It was obvious to everyone. He always took care of you, even when we were in high school. I wish I had a man who loved me with the level of passion and commitment Melvin had for you."

"Melvin was my world, my life. He became my life the day we met. We had time to enjoy each other before we had kids, and I cherish that time. When that cop pulled the trigger that day, he not only killed my husband, he killed the father of my children, my best friend, my protector. Aisha, he shattered my family's life and we're still trying to recover from it. I remember that day as if it had just happened.

"I was rushing home from a doctor's appointment. I was hurrying to tell Melvin I was pregnant. He died not knowing we had a baby on the way," Shy cried. Recalling the events of that tragic day still drained her. Now it was her turn to grab a napkin to dry her tears. It was not like her to get so emotional in public. She had buried her husband six years ago, and the pain was still overwhelming for her and her children. The twins were ten years old when their father was gunned down in their own home. Prince bore the weight of seeing his dad murdered while trying to protect him. He was a daddy's boy to his core. Prince and Jayden were identical twins but only physically. Their psychological, emotional, and mental makeups were as different as if they were strangers. Five-year-old Princess Lilac never knew her father. She saw pictures and heard stories from her brothers, but she was robbed of having a relationship with her father. She would never get to experience being a daddy's girl. Shy knew her husband would have adored his daughter. He would have spoiled her, overprotected her, and loved her as only a father could. Shy dried her tears and pulled herself together. She continued her conversation with Aisha.

"The city officials didn't care about my family. They covered shit up and made it seem like Melvin had attacked them. The trigger-happy cop got a three-month paid suspension, a vacation really, while the police chief and mayor worked out the details of all the lies they'd tell. I couldn't live with that. So I did what I had to do," Shy said with contempt in her voice.

"I don't think Melvin would be angry or disappointed with you. Had it been you who took a bullet and died, Melvin would have made the shooter pay."

"You're right, he would have. When he was here, my husband tried so hard to keep the twins and me from *his* world. Out of nowhere, strangers with badges kick in our door and all hell breaks out and I'm pulled into a foreign land. When it's all said and done, my heart knows that Melvin would understand why I did what I did," Shy said, as if trying to convince herself along with Aisha.

"Do the dreams ever come back?" Aisha asked.

"They only resurface around the anniversary of Melvin's death. Instead of chastising me, my husband praises me. Those are the sweet dreams Kayla referred to the other day. The beautiful nightmares are when Melvin's unhappy with what I did and I wake up with my heart racing and short of breath." Shy smiled. "I hated to have that man mad at me. It wasn't often but I still didn't like it." Both Shy and Aisha laughed.

Aisha was pleased with what she'd just heard. As far as she was concerned, the subject was closed, locked, and buried under cement. It was time for her to focus on running KAT69 and rebuilding her personal life. She was aware that her relationship with Kayla had become strained while all that ugliness was taking place. Kayla was her sister, and their relationship was important to Aisha. She was determined to start repairing things between them. Aisha was thankful that Terry had been away the last few months. Her daughter, Anissa Renée, was dealing with some difficult times, so Terry had temporarily relocated to North Carolina to be near her. The last thing Terry, or Anissa's two godmothers, Aisha and Kayla, wanted was for Anissa to withdraw from college when she was only one semester away from earning a double master's degree in business management and public relations. Terry was in the dark about what had gone down, and Aisha's and Kayla's involvement. Aisha wanted to keep it that way.

Aisha's thoughts were interrupted by the sound of Kayla's voice. She'd been invited to join Aisha and Shy for lunch. Aisha had given her a later time to allow herself time to talk with Shy alone.

"Good afternoon, ladies, I hope your day is going well so far," Kayla said.

"Hi, Kayla," Aisha and Shy said simultaneously.

"The day is much better now," Aisha added.

"Are you ladies ready for your soup and sandwiches now that Miss Kayla is here?" interjected Brianna. She was a part-time server and cashier. The sixteen-year-old was also the girlfriend of Shy's son Jayden.

"Yes, baby." Shy smiled. "Bring our soup out first and we'll let you know when to start making our sandwiches.

"Okay, I'll be right back," Brianna stated with a smile.

"How's business going with the spa and barbershop?" Shy wanted to start a lighthearted conversation.

"Business is holding strong. We might be in a recession, but women still need their hair and nails done. Nothing can keep us from it." Kayla laughed as Aisha and Shy backed her statement with positive comments.

The lunch hour went by much too fast. Before they knew it, all their soup was gone and every bit of their sandwiches was devoured.

"Wow, time just flew by," Aisha said.

"I know. Good conversation with great friends never lasts long enough," Shy joked.

"Yeah, I need to be getting back to the spa. Our paperwork has been backed up for way too long. Lunch was fun but I have to be going. Duty calls," Kayla said while gathering her things. "Are you coming, Aisha?"

"I'm right behind you. We better get caught up before the drill sergeant comes back to the office," Aisha said jokingly. "Terry does not play, okay?"

"Right, and you know she's been looking into our record keeping. Her laptop was the first thing she packed for her extended trip," Kayla stated.

Just when Shy was about to joke about Terry's overbearing business dedication, her phone rang with the ringtone set to alert her that one of her children was calling. "MomMomMomMa-MommyMommy . . ." It was Stewie Griffin's voice, the baby from the *Family Guy* cartoon. "Hello."

"Ma!"

"What's wrong, Prince?" Shy inhaled deeply as she waited for the answer.

"Man, something ain't right out in these streets. In the last month three of unc's soldiers have fallen." Prince spoke as if he was in a panicked rush.

"I remember you telling me about Ace, B.J., and Skip. I feel terrible for their mothers, but what does that have to do with what's got you so hyped and upset?" Shy asked, worried that her son was in some sort of trouble.

Aisha and Kayla giggled at the ringtone and watched Shy as she spoke with one of her kids. The look on her face went from relaxed and happy to stressed and concerned in just under two seconds. It was obvious that something was wrong. Aisha and Kayla sat back down to see what was going on. They waited to see if she needed them. When she gasped and put her hand over her mouth, they held their breaths. Shy looked at Kayla and told her son, "I'll take care of that right now. You meet me at the house. We'll call your uncle when I get there. Are you okay to drive?"

"Yes, ma'am, I'm cool," Prince answered.

"Okay, I love you and be safe," Shy said before hitting the END button. Her heart was pounding; she took deep breaths to try to slow it down.

"Tell us what's wrong, sweetie," Aisha said with her hand on one of Shy's shoulders. "You're turning pale."

"It's about Devin," Shy began.

"What about my brother? He's working at the barbershop today," Kayla said.

"Kayla, I'm so sorry to tell you this. There was a drive-by shooting in front of the barbershop. Devin was hit by multiple bullets. I'm so sorry, sweetie, your brother died on the scene." Shy began to cry.

Kayla's hands went over her mouth and she began shaking her head. Aisha jumped up and immediately embraced her sister. Shy ran her hand up and down Kayla's back. She felt horrible having to deliver the bad news to her close friend. Devin was the last blood relative Kayla had left. He'd been doing well rebuilding his life after serving twenty-five years in prison. Dealing with his death was going to be very difficult for Kayla. It went without saying that Aisha and Shy would remain by her side as long as she needed them. Aisha was certain Terry would come back home after receiving the horrible news.

Kayla began rocking back and forth, holding onto herself for dear life. She screamed in pain with a steady stream of tears pouring from her eyes. Aisha held onto her and rocked with her. She knew the pain Kayla was feeling. Grief was a difficult emotion to jump into a boxing ring with. Aisha held on tight as Kayla released some of the pain she felt down in her soul.

"Let's go, baby. Shy and I are going to take care of you," Aisha said as she and Shy helped Kayla to her feet. Shy drove and Aisha sat in the backseat with Kayla, holding her while she cried. Aisha leaned her head back and asked herself, *What's going on? It seems like C-Lok's team is under fire. What could possibly happen next?*

Only time would tell, but when the answer came, no one on C-Lok's team would be prepared.

Love and Business Do Not Mix

Kayla dedicated great time and detail to putting her brother away beautifully. She didn't dress him up in a button-down shirt, suit, and tie. That wasn't Devin's style when he was alive, and she refused to change it now that he was dead. She went out and bought her brother the latest Rocawear attire. Devin was draped in Rocawear from head to toe, even to his underwear. The day Kayla went to view the body, she sprayed the newest Rocawear cologne on her brother. She demanded that the funeral home not shave her brother or cut his hair. She had one of his employees at his barbershop take care of grooming Devin. He was buried wearing the white-gold ring, watch, and matching bracelets he never left home without. Kayla slid in a wallet-size photo of herself with her brother, taken when they were much younger. A four-year-old Kayla sat on the shoulders of her fourteen-year-old big brother. She had the biggest smile on her face. Devin was larger than life in her young eyes. She loved her big brother more than anything.

It was Devin's love for his baby sister that got him an extended bid behind bars for attempted robbery. He'd been trying to get money to take care of her after their mother turned to drugs. After Kayla began hustling and making money, she took care of Devin while he was in prison. When he came home, she set him up with a place to live, a business to run, a full wardrobe to flaunt, and every essential he'd need to live. Like any other set of siblings, they had their differences, but they always had each other's backs. Nothing but death could keep them apart.

$ $ $

A few weeks had passed since the deaths of C-Lok's three street soldiers and Devin. Prince had a bad feeling about the entire situation. It was no coincidence that people affiliated with C-Lok were falling down. Prince's gut was telling him that whatever was going on was directly related to Mama Bev's death. He watched his every step, thinking hard before making any moves. He knew his uncle could take care of himself. But he was worried about himself, his brother, his sister, and his mother.

When C-Lok ordered everyone to his house, Prince was certain it was to discuss the deaths of their workers. Killing street soldiers was bad enough, but reaching out and touching a general like Devin was clear disrespect.

C-Lok was sitting with Big Black and Prince when Aisha and Kayla arrived.

"Something ain't right out dere in dem streets," Prince said, shaking his head.

"It's almost as if there's a hit out on our team. It wasn't a big deal when the little homies started getting knocked off, but three in just as many weeks?" Big Black said.

"Killing Devin is a high jump on the food chain," C-Lok responded.

"The problem with that is that Devin was out of the game," Kayla said. "He retired a couple of years ago and was legit with the barbershop. I'm sure this bullshit didn't have anything to do with my brother. He was back in the game for only one reason—the same reason I came out of retirement: Aisha revenging Mama Bev's death. Y'all need to get this shit right before we all get laid down," Kayla demanded, a frown on her face and anger in her heart.

"You sound like all this is because of me." Aisha was offended by the insinuation.

"Those boys had families too. They had people who loved them the way we loved Mama Bev. Let me make this clear to everybody involved so there are no misunderstandings on where the fuck I stand." Kayla stood up and spoke with an authoritative tone. "No one is untouchable. I survived over twenty damn years on these streets trying to make a living and eat. I made it, and I made sure that not one of my family went hungry. We getting older, and we all know this shit don't have a retirement plan. I went legit and got used to living the life of a business owner. I stepped back in to complete one task, and my brother did the same because I asked him to. My sacrifice is too great for a battle that wasn't part of my war. I'm telling each one of you, the aftermath of this shit better get handled."

"So this is my fault? Is the boss wagging her finger in my face?" Aisha asked, offended.

"If that's the way you want to take it, Aisha, that shit is on you."

"I don't remember putting a gun to your head and dragging you along for the ride. Kayla never does anything if she ain't benefiting from it," Aisha spat.

"How did I benefit from getting my hands dirty behind your ass? Was having to bury my brother my big payoff?" Kayla yelled with one hand on a hip.

"So was I supposed to let those niggas ride after what they did to Mommy?" Aisha asked in confusion.

"No, they weren't supposed to get a free ride on that foul shit, and they were going to get handled. You wanted to be in the game. You wanted to make a name for yourself on these streets, right, Dream? You ran up into a world that you have no business being in. We all backed you. Everybody in this room did what was done for and because of *you*! And do us a favor, Aisha. Stop pretending like it was all to avenge your mother's death. This shit was all about your selfish ass." Kayla pointed her index finger in Aisha's face. "So what are you going to do to fix this shit? Tell me, Dream, what the fuck are you going to do?"

Aisha couldn't believe the things her sister was saying to her. In the life span of their friendship, Kayla, Aisha, and Terry had never fought like enemies. There were always disagreements between them but they were always able to talk out their issues. Aisha felt like Kayla had jammed a hand deep inside her chest and jabbed at her heart with each nasty word. "You're throwing one of your famous tantrums just because you not in control? Fuck you, Kayla!" That was all Aisha could come back with. Kayla's delivery may have been harsh, but her words were true and Aisha knew it.

"Bitch, *you* ain't in control," Kayla spat out. "C-Lok handles everything that goes on in his team. No players can move without his permission. He put a bounty on those boys' heads. He already had a plan in place to stop them from breathing weeks before you begged to take part. That nigga is always in control. Dream, you should know who the true boss is. Mama Bev is gone from your life forever. My brother is gone from my life forever. There are six mothers out there grieving and hurting for the loss of their sons, three on our team and three on the other team. And for what? So the bitch who killed Devin can be caught and face street justice? The cycle will never end. That's why I walked away from it all. Those are the things I tried to protect you and Terry from all those years I put in work," Kayla cried. "So fuck me? Fuck me, Aisha? Bitch, fuck you back, how about that?"

Kayla was blind with rage as she lunged forward, grabbing Aisha around the neck with her right hand and punching her with the left. Aisha was caught totally off guard. She grabbed the arm around her neck, trying in vain to free herself from the death grip her sister had her in. Before the men could react, Kayla had slammed Aisha to the floor and repeatedly punched her in the face.

It took C-Lok, Big Black, and Prince to pull Kayla off Aisha, who lay in a coughing and choking fit. Kayla's fingerprints were visible on her skin, and the beginnings of a black eye had formed. And even worse than the physical pain was the emotional hurt. Aisha was dumbfounded. She couldn't wrap her head around what had just taken place. She and Kayla had never physically fought each other. Her feelings were hurt and her ego was bruised. More important, their friendship was in disrepair. There was no going back from what had happened.

Aisha was stuck. Everything Kayla had said was right. No argument can be had when one person had all the facts right. Aisha began to cry once her breathing found a steady pace. The pain of losing her mother had eased with each new day. The pain of losing her sister had now taken its place. She thought to herself, *I hurt today. Not as much as I did yesterday and less than I will tomorrow. Kayla's pain is fresh. She attacked me like I was some bitch on the streets. She needs me to be there for her the way she was for me.*

"Both of y'all calm the fuck down," C-Lok growled. "Fighting each other ain't right! What da fuck, man? This blaming each other ain't solving a damn thing. You know the shit coming out of y'all's mouths is foul as hell." Like every other man, C-Lok and Big Black knew not to get between two women in a heated argument, but they had to intervene when the sisters started calling each other bitches and things turned physical.

"This is not what I wanted or expected!" Aisha cried.

"I'm sorry to disrespect your house like that, C. Please forgive me," Kayla said. "As for right now, between me and her, keep her away from me. After all I've done for her, she got the nerve to say 'fuck you' to my face? She got me fucked up. I don't know what's going to happen between Kayla and Aisha but Bossy and Dream are enemies."

"What the hell is happening to our family? This shit ain't right," Big Black fumed.

"Kayla is right," Prince said. "I don't know what to do with this shit here. I never thought about the aftermath. I mean, those boys are dead and missing. Who would avenge their deaths? Nobody but us knows what happened to them."

"Aisha, let me clear something up for you," C-Lok said. "Once Dream stepped on the scene and got not one but three bodies under her belt in a day, she will forever be in the game. Whether she's active or not is up to Dream. What we do know at this point is that our team's being disrespected. Our people are being hunted down on the streets. Somebody's calling us out. We have to figure out how to answer the call." He remained standing beside the armchair where he had made Kayla sit.

Prince was running through a list of his enemies and his so-called friends when an overlooked detail came to his mind. "Unc, dem niggas you sent to clean that shit up," Prince said with urgency.

"What about them?" C-Lok asked.

"Besides the people here right now, they the only ones with dirty hands," Prince replied.

"He right, man!" Big Black said through clenched teeth. "Those niggas are the only common denominator. We need to have an intimate discussion with them. We need to have it *now*!"

After the family had left the old steel mill that day, C-Lok had paid three of his most trusted workers to clean the scene. They'd received orders to remove everything used as torture tools. As far as the bodies were concerned, they could've rotted right where they lay, but Big Black had suggested differently. The hired help had received specific instructions to dispose of the bodies without a trace.

"I'm going to set that shit up as soon as possible," C-Lok said. "Until then, Kayla, I want you and Aisha staying together. It don't matter whose house the two of you chill at, but Big Black is going with you. He'll keep you safe until we can get this matter resolved. I'd lay down my own life before I'd let something happen to one of y'all."

Aisha and Kayla gave C-Lok a look of total disbelief. They both knew it was an argument they might not win, but Kayla was sure to veto his decision.

"C, baby, I just told you to keep her away from me and not five minutes later you're trying to force us to live together? Have you lost your mind?"

"Baby, your safety is—" C-Lok was interrupted midsentence by Kayla's raised hand.

"That did not require an answer. You just told me what to do. Now let me tell you what I'm *going* to do. I will stay here, in this house, with you. It's a man's job to protect his woman anyway. I'm going upstairs to take a shower. Have the house cleared by the time the water stops running. I've had just about enough of family to last me a fuckin' lifetime."

C-Lok watched Kayla disappear.

"Look, Unc, I'm up and out. We'll take care of this tomorrow, first thing," Prince promised. "Look for my call. One love." Prince went out the back door on a mission to find the cleanup crew.

"You call me if you need me, girl," C-Lok said to Aisha.

"I will, but Big Black always takes good care of me. Promise me you'll take care of yourself and Kayla. It'll take some time and effort but we'll come back from this. I love her and I know she loves me. Kayla is just, well, Kayla." Aisha spoke low so only C-Lok heard her.

"Promise," C-Lok replied.

C-Lok set the alarm and went in search of Kayla. He walked up behind her and whispered something in her ear to make her smile.

"I don't care who knows anymore. We're too old to be hiding our relationship anyway. It's about time the world knew that I have a man who loves me from my toenails to my hair follicles."

She turned to face her man and put her arms around his neck. He met her lips with a wet and passionate kiss. Then he unwrapped the towel covering her wet body and said, "Let your man take care of you now."

Rah, Rah

The following day, C-Lok was determined to squeeze the identity of the killer from the belly of the street. Another of his soldiers had been knocked out and died after three days on a life-support machine. His death made headlines. The city's murder rate was steadily climbing, and the mayor wanted control of his streets back. As a result, the police were harassing all black males.

Monk, Cuddy, and Red sat across from C-Lok as nervous as a teenage boy caught with his pants down by the drill-sergeant father of his first girlfriend. The boss had a multitude of questions, and he expected the right answers.

"How did you get rid of the drills, hammers, and shit?" C-Lok barked.

"We buried that shit in an old mining shaft somewhere in Pennsylvania," Monk said with complete honesty.

"The guns too? Please tell me y'all niggas weren't dumb enough to dump all that shit in the same spot," C-Lok demanded.

"My mans and me gots more experience at dis. Naw, we ain't do no dumb shit. We dropped shit everywhere between New York, Pennsylvania, West Virginia, and Ohio. In various spots and in different ways," Cuddy explained.

C-Lok looked at the kid like he was a piece of gum stuck to the bottom of his shoe. *Listen at this nigga here. I know my English ain't the best but damn,* he thought.

"I have more years of experience at this shit than you've been on this earth," C-Lok said. "Something tells me I'm not getting the complete truth from you niggas. Just so I give you fair warning, this shit is about to get real nasty for the three of you if somebody don't tell me something," he threatened.

"Okay, why don't we try this?" he continued. "I'm going to ask questions, and each one of you will give me an answer. A detailed answer. How about that?"

The men all nodded. They had sweaty palms and racing hearts. C-Lok studied each man closely. Decades in the game had taught him how to read people, and what he was seeing now made him nervous. *I don't know how, but these niggas here done fucked up roy-*

ally, he thought. C-Lok was getting a bad vibe from his soldiers. He made decisions and formed opinions off instinct. Sensors were blaring in his head but C-Lok couldn't put his finger on whatever was demanding his attention. He knew that whatever it was, it was going to be bad.

"Who disposed of Rocky's body?" C-Lok asked.

"That was me, boss," Red replied.

"What did you do with him?"

"I laid that bitch nigga out in the old furnace that was in the warehouse. It was big enough for the cage and everything." Red spoke with confidence. "I poured the kerosene in and lit that muthafucka up. Believe me, that dude is dust." Red was being cocky. He was certain he had nothing to be worried about. He'd followed directions to the letter and Rocky was reduced to ashes for sure.

C-Lok watched Red as he spoke. He sat up straight and looked C-Lok directly in the eyes when he spoke. There was nothing alarming about Red in C-Lok's opinion. Rodney "Red" Samples had impressed his boss and saved his own life.

"Aight, my man, you can go," C-Lok said, nodding at the door.

Red stood and left without looking back. Friends don't exist in the game, so his boys were on their own. He was just happy to walk away with his own life and control of his limbs.

"What about that nigga Slick? Who took care of putting that mu'fucka in a grave?" C-Lok looked back and forth between Cuddy and Monk. By the way he was fidgeting with his hands, it was obvious that Monk had handled Slick's remains.

"Talk, Monk. What went down?"

Before Monk could find his voice, the meeting was interrupted by Prince. Prince made eye contact with C-Lok, telling him that he needed a minute with him in privacy. C-Lok beckoned Prince over. He whispered something in his uncle's ear. C-Lok frowned and pressed his lips together. He shook his head and Prince left the room the same way he had come in: with a mission.

"Do you have an answer for me, Curtis Jackson, Jr.?" C-Lok called Monk by his government name.

"Slick is in a swamp somewhere up in Michigan. Abandoned land with nothing on it but muddy-ass water. I was happy to get out of there with my own life. You can't tell where quicksand or sinkholes are, feel me?" Monk said.

"Get out of here, nigga," C-Lok instructed.

"One," said Monk over his shoulder as he ran for the door before C-Lok could change his mind.

As Monk walked out, Big Black walked in to join the meeting. Prince had notified Big Black that C-Lok needed his help. Big Black left Prince to sit with Aisha while he was gone. He knew Prince was capable of holding his own. Big Black reasoned that Prince had been taught by the best. C-Lok stood and glanced toward the door. "Why don't we move this meeting somewhere more comfortable," C-Lok snarled at Cuddy.

"What's up, boss? You don't have any questions for me about Rail?" Cuddy asked nervously.

"Fuck you think? Getya bitch ass up, nigga, and follow C. Playtime is over, mu'fucka," Big Black barked.

Cuddy had no choice but to do as he was told. He was sandwiched between two killers and knew he was taking his last breaths. All Mark "Cuddy" Williams could do was pray he didn't have to suffer a painful death. If he was going out, he wanted a quick bullet to the heart so his mother could have an open casket.

In the basement of C-Lok's house, Cuddy sat in a small room, much like an interrogation room at a police station. Sweat poured down his face like an open faucet. His stomach was doing flip-flops, and he fought the urge to vomit and piss his pants.

"I hear you have something to tell me," C-Lok said calmly.

"We obviously already know what it is, so don't insult us by lying to our faces," Big Black warned.

"I didn't know who or what our assignment was until we hit the spot, I swear," Cuddy whined. "When I saw my man on the floor, it made me sick. He scared the shit out of me when I grabbed him by his wrist and a grunt came out of his mouth. But I still ain't trip. I was going to put him in the furnace too and just finish him off."

"Then why didn't you?" Big Black yelled. He was so angry it made his dick hard. He wanted nothing more than to wrap his hands around Cuddy's neck and choke him to death, but they needed more information before killing him.

"I recognized him. There was no way I could do that shit to my family. We got the same blood running through our veins. Me and Rail are first cousins. I'm sure that's what Prince rolled in and told you, boss. I love that nigga. We came up together, lived together, struggled together. What else was I supposed to do? Tell me, man, what else could I do?" Cuddy cried. He and Rail had been as close as brothers. When Rail went missing, it damn near drove him crazy. Seeing his favorite aunt cry over her missing child broke Cuddy's heart.

"Did you know that nigga was in on killing Mama Bev?" C-Lok demanded.

"No, no, no, I swear," Cuddy promised.

"I went back out to the spot, and there's no sign of a body. What did you do with Rail's body?" Big Black asked.

"There was no body," Cuddy replied.

"Fuck you mean, wasn't no body? Dat nigga was as close to dead as anyone could be," said a confused C-Lok.

"He wasn't dead, so there was no body to get rid of. We all drove different cars so we could complete our assignment. Instead of burying my fam, I got him some help by leaving him at a little hospital in New York. He was fucked up, man. His own mother didn't recognize him."

"His mother? *Fuck!* You saying that nigga alive?" yelled an enraged C-Lok.

"As far as I know, they had a 'copter fly him to a hospital in D.C.

or Maryland somewhere. Some burn specialist worked on him at one of the top hospitals in the country. My Aunt Tracey says he'll never be the same, and it might have been better to just let him die," Cuddy said in shame.

"You listening to this mu'fucka, man?" C-Lok said in amazement. "He took that murdering bastard to a hospital and collected money from us to compensate him for the work he put in. Let me guess what you did with those fifty Gs. You gave them to old Aunt Tracey for the care of her baby boy Terrell. Am I right?"

"Ain't that some shit! This dumb-ass nigga couldn't have fucked us better if we gave up our asses willingly. I ain't even with this bullshit. Off dis mu'fucka, Black," C-Lok instructed before storming out the door. He had to find out what hospital Rail was in and if he was still receiving treatment. If he'd been released from the hospital and was back on the streets of Youngstown, everyone involved was at risk. Cuddy's loyalty to his family had probably cost Devin his life and Aisha and Kayla their lifelong friendship.

C-Lok heard three consecutive shots as he walked up the stairs. Big Black put three holes through Cuddy's face. Anger got the best of Big Black, and he couldn't help but make a closed-casket funeral a necessity.

Who's the Bitch Now?

Aisha was on her hands and knees scrubbing the kitchen floor. Her mother had never allowed her to use a mop. Mama Bev had been adamant that elbow grease was far stronger than anything made by man. Aisha still cleaned the way her mother had, with a bucket, rag, bleach, Pine-Sol, and gloves. Two hours went by and Aisha was still cleaning things that were already clean. The sounds of Calvin Richardson, Lyfe Jennings, and Donell Jones helped her sort things out. Her fight with Kayla was weighing heavily on her mind and heart. No matter what had happened between them, it didn't outweigh all the good years the sisters had shared.

Aisha missed her mother and really needed to talk to her. Kayla had jumped on her like she was a born enemy. Aisha could forgive the physical assault but not the verbal. But she reminded herself that Kayla was hurting the same way she was. *Her brother was her protector, even when he was in prison. They made huge sacrifices for each other. I know Kayla was proud of the changes Devin made in his life. How could I ever compare her grieving to my own? Pain is pain, and it takes over your soul.* "What do I do, Mommy?" Aisha cried out.

Aisha threw the cleaning rag across the room and sat on the floor crying. She pulled her legs up to her chest, wrapped her arms around them, and rested her head on top of her knees. Then she asked God for just one more conversation with her mother. That was the one thing she needed more than she needed air to breathe.

She sat on the cold tile kitchen floor for over an hour waiting for God to answer her prayer. Her legs cramped and her behind was sore from sitting in the same position so long. She decided to go upstairs and take a long, hot shower. Her swollen eyes were red, and her nose was running. She needed someone to talk to. Terry was in North Carolina with Anissa, Shy was at work, and Kayla wasn't speaking to her. She stepped into the shower and let the hot water beat on her back, closing her eyes as she felt the tension leave her body. She stepped under the water to wash her hair. *It's not me you need to talk to, baby girl. You must go talk to Kayla. She's the one who needs you now,* Aisha heard a voice say.

Her eyes shot open and she looked around the bathroom. "Kayla! Is that you?" she yelled. The voice was too clear to be her imagination. Someone else had to be in the house with her. No one but Kayla and Terry had keys to her home. *I'm tripping. I must have left the TV on or something*, Aisha thought, trying to convince herself that she didn't hear anyone talking to her. She applied conditioner to her hair and picked up a cloth to wash her body and let the conditioner sit on her hair for a few minutes. *Kayla needs you, Aisha. Go to her, go help her now. Mommy is gone, but your sister is still there with you. Go to her now.* Aisha jumped and dropped the cloth. She quickly rinsed her hair and body. Something deep inside her said she needed to listen to the voice. It might just be in her head, but Aisha couldn't stay away if her sister needed her help. If something happened to Kayla and she did nothing to help her, Aisha wouldn't be able to live with herself.

She quickly dressed, grabbed her keys and purse, and ran out of the house. She used the keyless entry to unlock her BMW but then rushed back inside. With everything that had been happening, she felt that she needed protection. After retrieving her new .9 mm from its safe, she headed to her destination.

$ $ $

Kayla locked up the day spa. She couldn't wait to get home. It was Sunday and the shop was closed, but she'd wanted to do inventory and finish payroll before Terry called with questions. She was exhausted from all the stress, fighting, and uneasiness surrounding her. Her brother was shot down on the streets like a dog, and Aisha didn't seem to understand how his death was connected to her need for revenge. It all seemed so senseless to Kayla. As she got into her Lexus, she got a weird feeling in the pit of her stomach. "What the hell is this about?" she said aloud.

"Revenge of my own," said a voice so piercing and raspy it made Kayla's skin crawl. She nearly jumped out of her skin when she looked in the rearview mirror and found that she wasn't alone.

"Who the hell are you and what do you want?" she demanded.

"You don't remember me or is it that you just can't recognize me?" the stranger asked.

Kayla stared. The disfigured face was sickening. Three-fourths of his face was horribly burned. He had only one eye and a fraction of a nose; both lips and ears were missing. The strange man wore a ball cap pulled low but it did very little to hide the ugliness that was his fate.

"What do you want?" Kayla asked.

"Stop looking at me and drive to your house," he said.

"You asked me if I recognized you. How can I recall if I can't look at you?" Kayla asked. She wanted to make the monster as uncomfortable with his presence as she was. He had unknowingly just given her a way into his head.

"Don't try anything, Miss Boss Lady. This gun in the back of your seat is cocked and ready to blast," the strange man warned.

"What did you come for?" Kayla asked.

"My own brand of justice. Unlike you and your crew, I've been much more considerate of how I send my enemies to their deaths."

"No amount of justice or revenge is going to take away your pain or make you look human again. So what's the point?" Kayla asked.

"What was the point of torturing me? What type of satisfaction did ya girl get out of it?" Rail asked through clenched teeth. "Look what she did to me!"

"You'd have to ask her what it feels like. I don't know, but I'm sure it felt better than the pain her mother suffered at your hands. Aisha had the right to demand that you experience the same fear and terror you inflicted on her mother," Kayla said snidely.

"That was a mistake. This shit done to me was on purpose. Fuck all of y'all!" Rail said as loudly as he could. His vocal cords were severely damaged, and his voice was little more than a whisper. The doctors considered him the luckiest man alive, but he laughed at the thought of his current situation being luck. He loved his cousin Cuddy for doing what he did, but Rail wished he'd died on that cold oily cement floor.

"Going to the wrong house was a mistake," Kayla said. "Beating, raping, and killing Mama Bev was on purpose. It was done with malice, so don't sit in my car and try to justify what you did. The hell on earth you're living is kinder than the price Mama Bev paid for your fuckup." She refused to show any fear. She had done too much wrong over the years to too many people to think that karma would not one day come back on her. She'd always looked for it and told herself that she'd take her punishment in spades because there was no doubt that she'd earned it.

"Fuck you, bitch! Just drive and quit fuckin' lookin' at me. Don't make me tell you again," Rail warned.

"And if I do? Who's gonna check me, Boo? Not you. You're weak, Rail. Weakness oozes from your veins like rain falls from the sky. I'm driving, so shooting me in the back only kills us both. By my calculations, you have a few more people to lay down. I mean, Aisha, C-Lok, Big Black, even your cousin Cuddy. We all still breathing. You can't leave things like that. Am I right?"

Rail was incensed by Kayla's arrogance and disrespect. Though every word she said was true, he didn't want to hear anything but cries and pleading from his victims. The only reason she was even still breathing was because she hadn't had a hand in torturing him. And he needed her to lure the others into his trap. He knew that before the night was over, she'd be just like every other person in fear of losing their life. She'd suffer by watching everyone she loved drop dead before her feet.

§ § §

"Where that coming from?" Big Black asked. A weird beeping was sounding.

"Ah, fuck! That's my girl's distress call. She's in trouble. Let's raise," C-Lok said. The ringing was coming from his home alarm. He and Kayla had programmed a code years before, but this was the first time it had ever been used. He had no idea where she was, but thanks to modern-day technology, it wouldn't take him long to learn. The GPS on her car would help him find her. He only prayed he reached her in time.

$ $ $

Kayla's heart dropped when she saw Aisha's car in front of her house. C-Lok would be coming to her rescue soon, but she didn't know how Rail would react to seeing Aisha. Kayla feared the sight of her would set him off, sending her and Aisha out in a blaze of bullets.

As soon as Kayla had realized that Rail was in her car, she'd pressed the button on her steering wheel. She knew that wherever C-Lok was, he'd get the signal that she needed him. She doubted that Rail would be able to touch C-Lok and Big Black. Killing them would prove much more difficult than getting to the street soldiers had been. They were constantly surrounded by armed security. All Kayla could do now was to play along with Rail and keep navigating her way through his mind. She knew the cavalry was on its way.

"We're here. Now what?" Kayla asked.

"Now we walk into the house the same as you do every other day. Don't worry about what's next until then. Now quit stalling and get out," Rail ordered. He held the gun at his side as he followed Kayla up her front porch steps.

She was surprised that Rail hadn't noticed Aisha's car. His slip confirmed Kayla's suspicion—Rail had no idea what he was doing. She knew she'd be able to distract him until her backup arrived. She knew Aisha was inside and wanted to keep her sister out of harm's way. Despite whatever was going on between them, she still loved Aisha and felt responsible for protecting her.

Aisha was pacing back and forth in the family room when she saw the headlights shining down the driveway. She went to open the garage door for Kayla but then noticed that the car was stopped at the front of the house. Aisha stood away from the window so as not to be seen. Kayla never used her front door. There was no need for Aisha to wonder if something was wrong—Kayla's actions screamed that there was. Her suspicions were confirmed when Kayla turned off the ignition and slammed her car door. When Aisha heard another door slam, she grabbed her purse and rushed up the back stairs. She knew Kayla would stay in the front of the house. This scenario had been a fear of Kayla's for years. She and C-Lok tried to protect Aisha and Terry at all costs. At times, Aisha had thought they were going overboard with all the planning, escape routes, and distress signals they created. But as she pressed nine on her cell phone, she was grateful for their overprotectiveness.

"We're less than two blocks away. What is it?" C-Lok asked. He needed as much information as he could get to assess the situation.

"I heard two car doors slam. They're in the front room, as far as I can tell. I ran up the back stairs," a frightened Aisha whispered.

"Stay there but don't hang up. Open the cabinet and flick on the red button that turns on the cameras. Tell me what you see," C-Lok instructed.

Aisha tried to steady her hands. Her sister's life was in her hands, and she couldn't let her down. Aisha knew everything was riding on her. *Power is a dangerous thing. This is what you asked for. Now do the right thing with it,* Aisha thought. She got the cabinet doors open on the fourth try. Then she cried a river when she saw a gun pointed at her sister's head.

"Aisha, come on, girl. You strong, and we need you to talk to us." Big Black's voice startled Aisha. He was right. She took a deep breath and quickly wiped the tears from her eyes.

"Someone is pointing a gun at her. I can't make out who it is," Aisha said.

"Are you sure they're alone?" Big Black asked. He took over trying to occupy Aisha while their team got into place. C-Lok and Big Black were watching the same screen Aisha was. The built-in TV screen had multiple uses. Big Black needed to be sure Aisha kept her head and stayed out of sight. He screwed the scope onto his assault rifle while C-Lok gave his security team instructions.

"Yes, but I can't see who it is," Aisha said in frustration.

"We know who it is, Aisha. It's Rail," Big Black replied.

Aisha gasped in disbelief. It couldn't be Rail. He was dead. She'd sent him to his grave herself.

"We don't have time to explain now, but it's true," Big Black whispered. "Rail has been killing our team one by one. He wants you, so don't make a sound. We're right outside. I'm not going to say anything else, but don't hang up." He ran to get in place to wait for the signal to pull the trigger. He lifted his rifle and adjusted the scope in search of his target.

Aisha's head was spinning. She knew that her sister was standing where she should be. Rail wanted revenge on her the way she'd wanted it on him. Guilt overwhelmed her. She'd let grief and anger take over her life. For months all she'd thought of was getting revenge. Her irrational decision had led her to a point of no return. Multiple families were now mourning the loss of loved ones because of her. Her sister had buried her only brother as a result of Aisha's vengeance. She wondered how Kayla had stayed sane living in a world of drugs, money, and death.

$ $ $

"You do exactly what I say and you just might save your life," Rail stated.

"What do you want? Or do you even know the answer to that question?" Kayla asked. Rail's hands shook, and his balance seemed off. She was relieved that Aisha had paid attention and remembered the distress signal. C-Lok and Big Black had to be outside. Too much time had passed for them not to be in place. All she had to do now was get Rail to stand in front of the huge picture window.

"I told you what I want. Get your phone out and call up ya boys. Invite them to our party, and don't try anything slick. Put that shit on speaker so I can hear," Rail coached.

"Yeah, what up, Mama? I've been waiting on you," C-Lok answered. His words let Kayla know that he was in position.

"It took longer at the shop than I'd anticipated. I just came home. I'm tired. Would you mind coming south? I just don't have the energy to drive all the way out there," Kayla said in a steady voice to make Rail think she was following his instructions.

"Don't I always do what you ask me to? Look, Mama, let me finish up with Black and I'll be on my way. Do you need anything?"

"I picked up enough food for Black to eat with us. I figured he'd be with you. I'm going to call Aisha to come by. Maybe we can play some cards," Kayla said with very little emotion. Her words were clear and full of important information. They told C-Lok that Aisha was inside, and that Big Black should be ready to take the target out by aiming south.

"One, Mama," C-Lok said and ended the call.

Kayla hit the MUTE button instead of ending the call. She set her phone down next to her before driving her way into Rail's psyche.

"Rail, all of this won't solve your problems. Your life will forever be a living hell."

"Don't worry about my life. If I were you, I'd focus on your own life." Rail was physically tired and in enormous pain. He tried to push his physical discomfort to the back of his mind. It would all be over as soon as his plan played out. "Go on and call ya girl. Get her over here."

"That won't be necessary."

Rail jumped at the sound of Aisha's voice. Kayla rose to her feet, wondering what Aisha was trying to do. She had to let C-Lok know what was going on. The last thing any of them needed was for Big Black to shoot Aisha by mistake.

"Aisha!" Kayla screamed.

"It's okay, Kayla. I know what I'm doing," Aisha said while looking at Rail.

"Yeah, you knew what the fuck you were doing when you did this to me. Look at me!" Rail yelled. The gun was now trained on Aisha, who was standing directly in front of the window.

"This is between me and you. My sister did nothing to you. Let her go," Aisha pleaded.

"Naw, we have more joining the party."

"It was me, Rail. I made the decision to track you down and make you pay for what you did. If anyone disrespected you, it was me," Aisha explained.

"Aisha, what are you even doing here?" Kayla was confused.

"I came by tonight to apologize to you. I've never forgotten what you did for me that day you came to my rescue. You risked your life for me back then and you've taken care of me ever since. If it weren't for you, I wouldn't be anything in this life. No matter what happens, I love you," Aisha said through tears.

"You didn't have to do this. Everything is going to be all right," Kayla said. She had no idea if Aisha had remembered to call C-Lok. Kayla was trying to let her know that help was within arm's reach.

"Both y'all bitches shut the hell up," Rail demanded.

"Rail, revenge tasted so good. Seeing you trapped in that cage like the animal you are made my panties wet. Hearing you scream like a bitch gave me the most intense orgasm I've ever had. You have no one but yourself to blame for what happened. You made the choice to become a murderer, so you had to suffer the consequences," Aisha taunted.

"Who gave you the right to decide our punishment?" Rail retorted through pain and regret.

"I gave it to myself. That was my mother you killed. The disrespect you showed her can never be justified."

Rail took a step forward, aiming his gun at Aisha's head. Within the blink of an eye, Aisha pulled her arm from behind her back and trained her .9 mm on Rail's heart.

"Aisha, no!" Kayla screamed.

Three shots rang out simultaneously, sending broken glass, blood, and brain matter splattering everywhere.

"Aisha, what did you do? What did you do?" Kayla cried as she kneeled down and cradled Aisha in her arms. "What did you do, baby girl?" Aisha's body swung limply as Kayla cried and screamed.

C-Lok, Big Black, and the others rushed through the front door and stopped in their tracks at the sight before them. Rail lay dead from a shot through the back from Big Black's assault rifle and the shot in the heart from Aisha's gun. Rail's bullet had pierced Aisha's skull.

C-Lok raced over to Kayla and tried to console her, but she wouldn't let go of Aisha's body. Big Black walked slowly toward them and bent down to pick Aisha up. It was only then that Kayla released her sister. C-Lok carried the only woman he'd ever loved away from the bloodbath. He held her tightly in his arms, wanting to take all her pain away.

"I told her C, I told her," Kayla cried.

"I know, Mama. Shhh, baby."

"I tried to tell her that this life ain't for everybody. She wasn't meant for this side of the game. She said something about owing me. Why didn't she know that her life was hers? She sacrificed herself for me!" Kayla cried.

"You did everything you could to save her, Mama. I'm here. It's going to be okay," C-Lok promised.

"It'll never be okay again. Everybody wants to hustle and juggle power, money, and respect, but don't nobody want to accept the disrespect. Revenge and greed have taken my brother and sister from me," Kayla said. She wrapped her arms around C-Lok's neck and held on for dear life.

"I got you, Ma," C-Lok whispered.

"I don't want to be the boss anymore," Kayla said, weeping. Her heart was broken. "I don't want this anymore. What could possibly happen next?"

LAKESA COX

Southern Girls' Escort Service

Prologue

Oblivious to the airplanes flying above, Abie sat in her car at the park 'n' ride, hand on her gun, daydreaming about how she'd be thousands of miles away from everyone who'd ever used her in a few hours. Every emotion swept through her body as she waited—anxiety, nervousness, even fear. But the hissing sound from her back tire proved to be her death trap, because she was shaken from her daydream into reality. She stepped from the car to investigate what turned out to be a flat tire, only to be approached by an assailant from behind. The unidentified man wrapped one hand around her throat before knocking her out cold. The sad thing was, Abie had left her gun on the passenger seat in the car when she got out. After he slapped her back to consciousness, she couldn't figure out if she'd made it to Mexico, whether she was on the airplane, or where she was. Her vision was still a bit hazy but as her eyes focused, she realized she was still in Richmond, Virginia, stuck in a town that had used her up. Her attacker said things to her, but she was still in a daze, the back of her head throbbing from the butt of the gun, and her dreams were slowly drifting away. She sat helplessly as her attacker held his .22 with a silencer to her side. Surveillance cameras caught the abduction, but the tape was too blurry to clearly see her attacker. He led her to room 308 at the Red Roof Inn. How strange that there were no people in sight anywhere—no guests, house-keeping, nobody. Abie thought he was taking her to the hotel to rape her, since that's all men wanted from her anyway. But as she was pushed to the floor inside the hotel room, she realized that she was about to come to the end of her life. Forced to strip naked and kneel on the floor, she didn't try to fight. In fact, she couldn't have, because she was still shaken from the blow to her head. Instead, she just closed her eyes and dreamed of Mexico. And as the assailant put the gun to the back of her head, she let go of the life she'd been trying to run away from.

Abie's Dead

"**M**a'am, can you tell me your name?" repeated the short, pudgy Henrico County police officer. Rachida stared straight ahead in a daze. The officer snapped his chubby fingers in her face, but all she could think about was her friend's body on the other side of the hotel room door lying in a pool of blood with a gunshot wound to her head.

"Ma'am, what's your name? How do you know the victim?" The police officer's voice echoed in Rachida's ear, but her mouth couldn't form a response. The only person in the world who she'd considered family was now dead. Three years ago, Rachida was an eighteen-year-old runaway from Greensboro, North Carolina, homeless and alone on the streets of Richmond, Virginia, until she met Abie, her now-deceased best friend.

They'd met while Rachida sat on the curb outside the Greyhound bus station on The Boulevard. Abie was there to pick up her boyfriend, Scoot, who used the Greyhound bus as his method of transport for his heroin re-up in New York. Rachida noticed Abie right away with her long legs, double Ds, and extremely tight skirt that left nothing to the imagination. Abie's coal-black wavy hair was waist length, and her skin reminded Rachida of a brand-new copper penny. Rachida couldn't tell what nationality Abie was, but she knew that girl was mixed. Abie spotted Rachida when she pulled up in the Greyhound parking lot driving a souped-up Cadillac Escalade. She parked the car illegally in a handicap parking space. It was ninety degrees outside, but that didn't stop her from rocking a pair of thigh-high stiletto boots. She moved her oversized sunglasses from her eyes to the top of her head before beckoning to Rachida. Rachida turned her head, looking toward the street, thinking that Abie couldn't possibly be talking to her, with her disheveled hair and dirty T-shirt and jeans.

"You! C'mere a sec!" Abie yelled. Rachida pointed to herself, mouthing "Me?"

"Yeah, you, c'mere." Rachida stood up, ran her hands over her messy ponytail, and walked toward Abie.

"Can you do me a favor? Twenty dollars if you watch this truck for me for one minute. I just have to run in real quick. And don't try nothing slick." Abie smiled and rushed into the bus station, not giving Rachida a chance to accept or decline. The bass from the music inside the Cadillac vibrated under her worn Reeboks as she glanced in the tinted windows at her own reflection. She was actually a pretty girl underneath the dirt, with huge light brown eyes and long eyelashes. Her lips were full and exotic, and were complemented by high cheekbones and small freckles. *How did she know I wasn't a thief?* she thought to herself. She was just sitting in front of the station trying to figure out her next move when Abie blew her way. She hoped Abie would keep her word about the twenty dollars because she hadn't eaten in almost two days. As promised, Abie quickly returned with a tall, light-skinned brother sporting shoulder-length cornrows, baggy jean shorts, and a white T.

"See, this is the shit I'm talkin' 'bout. How you gon go all the way to New York and lose your goddamn cell phone? That's just stupid, Scoot."

"Stop talking to me like I'm a fucking kid, yo. I told you I was in the middle of a situation I had to get out of real quick. The phone was prepaid anyway, so why you trippin'?"

"Why am I trippin'? I'm trippin' because this bus was two hours late and I had clients. I've been calling you for two hours to see where you were when I could've been making money."

"Abie, man, just get in the truck, damn! You be on some bullshit sometimes. How much you lose today? I'll double that shit. It ain't that fuckin' serious. You bringing too much attention to me and shit." Abie stopped in her tracks and turned to face Scoot.

"Bringing too much attention to you? Oh, now I'm a fucking distraction?"

Scoot sighed heavily before opening the cargo door and placing a duffel bag inside. He reached the driver's-side door, where Rachida was standing, unsure if she should ask for the twenty dollars or not.

"Get the fuck from my truck, you crackhead bitch," Scoot said.

"Don't talk to her like that. I told her to watch the truck so I could go inside to find your ass."

"How you gon get a crackhead to watch my shit? Is you crazy?" Scoot asked, pushing Rachida out of the way so he could get in.

"Shut the fuck up, Scoot, and just get in the car." Rachida headed back to her spot on the curb to take a seat beside her garbage bag. *So much for the twenty dollars,* she thought to herself.

"Hey, wait! I got your twenty!" Abie yelled. Rachida breathed a sigh of relief as Abie dug her neatly manicured fingers into her tight pocket, fishing out a twenty-dollar bill.

"Here you go. What you doing on the curb anyway?" Abie said.

"Thanks. Got nowhere else to go. Trying to come up with a plan, I guess."

Abie stood back and studied Rachida for a moment. Abie knew that with a bath, the right clothes, and makeup, Rachida would be perfect for the business.

"You need a job?" Abie asked, putting her fingers in Rachida's hair. "This yo' real hair?"

"Yes, I need a job, but why you all up in my hair?" Rachida asked, jerking her head away.

"Look, how long you gon be out here?" Abie asked.

"Until whenever."

"You not on drugs, are you?" Abie asked, pulling at Rachida's arms, inspecting them for track marks.

"Hell, no, I ain't on drugs."

"You sure? You don't snort or no shit like that?"

"No, I ain't on no drugs."

"Okay, I think you'll work out. My Uncle Brick will be over here in about twenty minutes. He'll be driving a black Mercedes S550. I have to go with this nigga right now to get straight but Uncle Brick will take you to my house. We'll talk then, okay?"

"Okay, I guess, but what kind of job?"

"Don't worry about all that. I'll fill you in later. Just go to the house, get a bath and some food, make yourself at home, and I'll be there in an hour. Oh, I'm Abie, by the way. What's your name?"

"Rachida."

"Aight, Rachida. Trust me. I got you." Abie hopped in the Escalade and Scoot sped away, leaving Rachida in the dust. She held the twenty up in the air, looking through it, making sure it was real. She was going to buy herself a hot dog and Big Gulp from the

7-Eleven about half a mile away. She squinted, almost angry that the sun had to be so hot. She eased inside the lobby of the station with her garbage bag of belongings in tow. She'd been warned earlier by the clerk that loitering was not allowed, so she did her best to blend in with a family heading inside. The musty, moldy smell reminded her of the homeless shelter she'd slept in countless nights before leaving North Carolina. The ladies' restroom smelled even worse. She turned on the water and washed her face, using a damp paper towel to clean her breasts, under her arms, and around her neck to cool off. The image in the mirror looked unfamiliar to her. Once a star cheerleader in high school, Rachida was now a runaway who had escaped rape and brutal beatings by her mother's alcoholic boyfriend. Since her mother didn't believe her, she'd taken matters into her own hands and stolen her mother's gold earrings, pawning them and buying a one-way ticket to Virginia. Why Virginia? She really didn't know. It just happened to be the next state away, plus the earring money wouldn't take her very far. Once in Virginia, she was hoping to find a job and a place of her own and eventually go back to school.

Leaving the restroom and hurrying through the lobby, Rachida stopped dead in her tracks at the sight of the shiny Mercedes Benz that was parked in front. A man who looked like an NFL linebacker exited the car and walked toward Rachida.

"You Rachida?" he asked.

"Yeah."

"I'm Uncle Brick. Abie sent me for you. You ready?" Rachida looked up at this six-foot-four-inch giant with gentle eyes, a bald head, and a full beard. He looked to be in his late thirties or early forties, and was dressed in a Polo shirt and plaid shorts.

"Wait. She didn't tell me anything about the job. Do you know what it is?" Rachida asked. Uncle Brick smiled.

"Abie does this all the time. Always trying to rescue stray puppies."

"You calling me a dog?" Rachida yelled.

"No, no, I didn't mean it like that. Look, Abie can explain everything to you when she gets home. In the meantime, you can come back to the house, get something to eat, a hot shower, and clean clothes. You can get off the street. If the job isn't for you, you're free to go on your way. Abie has a soft spot for homeless girls, and she invites them to the house all the time. I didn't mean to offend you." Rachida crossed her arms, upset at being referred to as homeless and a stray puppy, although in actuality, that's what she was.

"That all sounds good, but I don't know you and I don't know Abie."

Uncle Brick studied Rachida for a moment before turning to walk away.

"Wait!" Rachida yelled, just as Uncle Brick had thought she would. "You sure you're not some crazy killer or something?" she asked.

"Rachida, I understand your hesitation. But I have no reason to hurt you. My job is to protect Abie and the other girls."

He saw the look of concern on Rachida's face. He took out his cell phone and handed it to her.

"Here. You take this and keep it until we get to the house. If anything happens, you can dial 911. How's that?" Rachida grabbed the phone from Uncle Brick's huge hand and smiled at him. The sun was getting hotter by the second, and she could definitely use a shower, fresh clothes, and food. She held the phone tightly and followed her instinct to go with Uncle Brick. Abie had been nice to Rachida, so Rachida didn't think Abie would go through the trouble of sending someone to hurt her. After staring at the phone and making a mental note of where the talk button was, she agreed to go with Uncle Brick. He took the garbage bag from her other hand and put it in the trunk of his car.

Ne-Yo's melodic voice filled the car on the long drive to Abie's house. Rachida took in the sights of the unfamiliar city and watched as the scenery began to change from the city to small dirt roads, farmhouses, and an abundance of maple trees. Her eyes grew wide as they pulled up in front of the estate. Seeing the other women on the lawn and front porch put her nerves at ease.

Abie and Rachida hit it off immediately. The pain from the abuse they'd both suffered in their former lives seemed to seal their bond. It was easy for them to talk to each other, and the fact that they shared a room brought them closer. When Abie felt that Rachida was comfortable taking on work, Abie helped her with the transition into the business. That's how Abie was—she took all the new girls under her wing and taught them the ropes, especially since the madam relied on Abie to bring new women into the business. But the relationship between Abie and Rachida was different. They became best friends. That was three years ago. Now Abie was dead and Rachida was left to pick up the pieces.

Almost three years to the day that Abie had come into Rachida's life, she left it. Even at two-thirty in the morning, the summer heat stifled the Richmond air.

"Ma'am, we really need you to help us out here. If you don't tell us what happened, we can't get justice for your friend in there." Rachida wiped the tears from her face. She was standing on the balcony of the Red Roof Inn, and the flashing blue lights from the police cars were making her nauseous. *What the hell was Abie doing at the Red Roof Inn anyway?* Rachida thought.

"Her name is Abie Thornton. She's my sister," Rachida lied. She knew the officer would want to know her relation to Abie, and she couldn't tell him they were prostitutes. Just like Rachida, Abie was a runaway with no known family members, at least none that Rachida knew of. The officer flipped through a small notepad and scribbled some notes. Rachida watched as several other cops tried to control the crowd that was forming. They placed yellow tape around the perimeter of the crime scene to keep it from getting contaminated.

"What was Abie doing here?" the pudgy officer asked Rachida.

"I don't know. She wasn't supposed to be here."

The crime-scene investigators arrived and pushed their way past Rachida and the cop. The door opened and Rachida caught another glimpse of Abie's naked lifeless body lying near the door. Before she knew it, Rachida had purged herself of the waffle and eggs she'd just eaten an hour earlier. Her body trembled as her tears flowed.

"Why would somebody do this? Why?" Rachida cried. The officer put one arm around her shoulder to keep her weak legs from giving out beneath her. After making her way down the steps, she tugged at her skintight minidress to keep it from rising. The officer led her to a cluster of police cars. The scene was chaotic, with hotel guests standing outside their rooms trying to figure out what had happened. The people behind the police tape pointed and stared at Rachida, whispering about her, wondering who was dead and whether she'd had anything to do with it.

"Come on, have a seat in here for a minute," the officer said, opening the rear door of his car. Rachida sat in the back, looking around. She'd never been in a cop car before and it felt strange to her. She tried her best not to look at any of the people in the crowd. Instead, she focused on what was happening upstairs in front of room 308. The door was propped open while CSIs snapped pictures of Abie's body.

The pudgy policeman talked with another cop, giving Rachida time to make a phone call. She dialed several numbers on her cell phone before finally reaching someone.

"Uncle Brick. It's 'Chida. I need you to come get me. Abie's dead! She's dead, Uncle Brick! Somebody killed her!"

"What! What do you mean? Abie? No! No! No! Where are you?" Uncle Brick asked.

"The Red Roof Inn on Laburnum, right across from the Waffle House."

"What happened? Have you called the madam yet?"

"I tried but she didn't answer. I tried Scoot too but it went straight to voice mail."

"What about the police?"

"The police are here. I'm sitting in a cop car now."

"Stay there, 'Chida. Don't let them take you to the station. I'm on my way."

Rachida tried dialing Scoot's number over and over, but each call went straight to voice mail, which seemed strange to her because these were normally Scoot's working hours. Rachida shook her leg nervously, hoping what she was thinking wasn't true. As much as Abie and Scoot had fought, they loved each other and had had plans to get married one day.

Rachida watched the coroner's van pull up and be slowly ushered through the crowd by a cop. Two people exited the vehicle, pulled a gurney and body bag from the back, and headed up the stairs to collect Abie's body. Just the thought of them hovering all over Abie, handling her like a piece of garbage by putting her in a plastic bag, set Rachida off. By the time the pudgy policeman saw Rachida, she was up the stairs and past the pair of grim reapers.

"No! Leave her alone! Don't touch her! Stop it!" Rachida yelled. A female cop guarding the door tried to keep her from entering, but the strength of a grieving friend outweighed that of a woman trained at the police academy.

"Ma'am, you can't go in there. Stop, please, ma'am!" The tussle between the two resembled something from the show *Cops*, and before Rachida knew it, a male officer had stepped in and lifted her hundred-and-twenty-pound frame.

"No! No! Please, don't put her in the bag! Please!" Then the heel on one of her stilettos snapped. The other shoe was still lying in the doorway, not far from where Abie's body was being placed in the bag. Rachida's squeal was deafening, almost like a siren. The officer managed to get her down the stairs, but by the time they reached the bottom step, Rachida had collapsed. Her lungs tightened and she felt dizzy. There were about three cops surrounding her, all trying to keep her under control. She couldn't find the strength to stand; every inch of her body felt numb. She lay there on the sidewalk, not caring that her thong was exposed or that her dress was partially unzipped in the back.

"Come on, miss, let us help you." Rachida shook her head. She was on the verge of passing out when she saw Uncle Brick's two-hundred-fifty, six-foot-four-inch frame pushing through the massive mob that had now formed.

"Let me through! I'm family!" Uncle Brick yelled. His physique intimidated the officers, especially when he reached down and scooped Rachida into his arms like a rag doll.

"I'll take her home," Uncle Brick stated, letting the cops know that anything they needed to discuss with Rachida would have to take place another time.

Councilman Big Daddy

(One Month Earlier)

"**C**ouncilman Big Daddy, you want me to suck your dick?" Abie whispered coyly to her client as she rode him like a wild horse. Councilman Sullivan couldn't speak because she was putting it on him so good. She sat straight up on him and placed his hands on her breasts before leaning over to suck on one of her own nipples. Sullivan moaned in ecstasy as he watched Abie's show while she simultaneously massaged his balls.

"Shit! Shit! Wait, Abie! I'm not ready to come yet!"

"I got something to make you come. Give it to me in my ass, just the way I like it." She stood up on the bed and turned her back on Sullivan. In stripper fashion, she bent her body forward, grabbed her ankles, and slid her chocolate tunnel down around his erection.

"*Ooooohhh,* Abie, *Ooohhhh,* shit!" he moaned in elation.

"You like fucking me in my ass, don't you?" Abie asked, going up and down. She was a pro, taking every inch of him without flinching, and it was only a matter of minutes before he exploded. When his body stiffened, she knew her job was done. She slid off him, pulling the loaded condom off at the same time.

"Where you going?" he asked.

"Councilman Big Daddy, I need to go to the bathroom."

"Wait, sit down with me for a minute." Sullivan was fifty-something and represented the East End Sixth district in Richmond. Married to his college sweetheart for over thirty years, he'd been one of Abie's regular clients since she began working for Madam Celecia's Southern Girls' Escort Service.

Abie sat naked on the bed beside Sullivan. She smoothed her hair out of her face and gave him her attention.

"I don't want you to work with any more clients."

Abie looked at him matter-of-factly.

"Councilman Big Daddy, this is my job. If I don't work, I don't get paid."

"I can take care of you."

"Until when? Until your little wife gets wind of it? No, thank you. I told you before and I'll tell you again, there's nothing but work between us. That's it for me. Put the money on the nightstand before you go."

Abie stood up, her coal-black hair cascading down her back, ending right above her firm butt. The only thing she cared about was getting paid her $500 for the hour of sex she'd had with the councilman and for him to leave so that she could take care of her next-highest-paying customer.

Sullivan grabbed her by the arm. The room was dark with the exception of the light coming from the bathroom. Even in the dark she could sense his sincerity although she could hardly see his face.

"I love you, Abie. I'll give up everything to be with you." She smirked at him in the darkness. Quite frankly, she didn't have time to listen to the bull he was dishing. She really didn't care. The man who had her heart was Scoot.

"Okay, listen. You're a customer. This pussy, this is my product. Now, I'm trying to run a business, and right now I have another paying customer on his way. All those feelings and shit, they don't mean a thing to me. I told you that before. If you keep this up, I'll have to tell Madam C. to get you somebody else."

"No, don't do that, Abie, please."

"Then cut out all this love shit. You know how this works. We fuck, you pay, and then you go. That's it." Abie's tone was frank and crass. She walked into the bathroom and locked the door behind her, making sure she had her cell phone in hand. The linoleum tile was cold under her feet and she wished she'd thought to bring something to walk around the hotel suite in. She wrapped an oversized towel around her, compliments of the Candlewood Suites and Hotel, where she'd been servicing her clients since about six p.m. Her reflection in the wall-sized mirror indicated that she needed to freshen her makeup and comb her hair. The councilman was her second client of the evening, and she still had two more to go before finishing for the evening. Two thousand dollars for four hours of work wasn't bad, and after she paid Madam Celecia her portion, she'd take home $1,000. She couldn't make that type of money working a regular nine to five. And she definitely couldn't do it working two days a week.

Abie had been the first to join Southern Girls' Escort Service, a brothel of about twenty girls who worked around Richmond and the surrounding area, and she brought in the most money. The majority of the clients requested her, and sometimes there was a waiting list. The business was a discreet one, since prostitution was illegal in Richmond. What made the business more distinct was the fact that the woman in charge kept her identity a secret from the women who worked for her. They talked to her on the phone and she handled their business affairs, but none of them had actually met her. They didn't even know if Celecia was her real name. Uncle Brick was her assistant and the liaison between her and the girls. With that amount of secrecy, it was also much easier to protect the clients' identities. All the women lived together in a fully renovated, three-level eight-bedroom Victorian farmhouse in Charles City, a small town right outside Richmond. The sprawling home featured a wraparound porch, double chimney, and oversized windows, and it sat on five acres amid sprawling farmland. In the town it was known as a halfway house and shelter for young female runaways. Charles City residents had no idea that the women they saw coming and going there were prostitutes. During the day, the women were attending classes, doing housework, or relaxing on the grounds. Their courses were training them to be independent. All the women were between the ages of seventeen and twenty-three, with the exception of Abie, who was twenty-five. Madam Celecia viewed Abie as her prize possession, the one who'd helped build an empire in which she grossed close to $30,000 a week. Her program trained the women in a trade, and they saved enough money so that when they left her business, they could live on their own. The situation was different from the normal brothels, where the women waited on lounge chairs in lingerie for their "gentlemen friends." Madam Celecia had a different vision for her women—to use what they had temporarily until they were able to go out on their own. Most of the women who'd been at the "shelter" for a while already had enough money saved to live on their own. However, since they were all mostly runaways, women who were hiding from someone or something, they found solace at the house, where they were surrounded by women they considered family.

None of the women serviced their customers at the house. They all took care of their clients at hotels in the city or one of the surrounding counties. That was one of the rules: Never bring a customer to the house. Never bring a male friend to the house. The house was strictly for the tenants and Uncle Brick, who stayed in an in-law suite that was detached from the house but only a stone's throw from the front door.

Abie pulled back the shower curtain. She grabbed the white bath mat and placed it in front of the tub beneath her feet. Unzipping her cosmetics bag, she pulled out her shower gel and deodorant. She sat on the toilet, waiting for the steam to fill all the empty space in the bathroom. The knock at the door took her away from her thoughts, and she was a bit perturbed that the councilman was still there.

"Abie?"

"Councilman Big Daddy, what are you still doing here?" She watched as the locked chrome doorknob twisted back and forth.

"Abie, can I just see you for one minute, please?"

She sucked her teeth and leaned over to open the door. She didn't bother getting up. Sullivan, now fully dressed in a black suit and crisp white dress shirt, stared at her naked body. The butterfly tattoo on her inner thigh was in full view since her legs were wide open.

"I thought about it and I'm going to talk to Madam Celecia. I'll pay triple, just so she can save you for me. I don't want you with any other men." The wrinkles on his forehead and his graying hair told the story of a man who'd fought his way from community activist to councilman over a twenty-year period. But tonight, he was willing to throw it all away over a piece of pussy. Abie stood up and pulled him into the steam-filled bathroom. She stood on her toes so she could kiss him on his cocoa-colored cheek.

"Go home, Councilman Big Daddy. Your wife is probably looking for you."

"Didn't you hear what I said? I'll give it all up to be with you."

"If you give it all up, how will you be able to afford me, huh? This is just business. That's it. I've told you that over and over again. Go home."

"Why won't you let me be your man? I can take good care of you."

"What if I told you I already had a man? Huh?"

Sullivan's eyes transformed. He didn't like the sound of that.

"What do you mean?"

"I mean, the same way you go home to your wife, I go home to my man. Do you still want me all to yourself?"

"You think this is a joke? A game? I'm standing here telling you that I'd give up my whole world just to have you in my life and all you can do is mock me?" Sullivan grabbed Abie's upper arm and twisted it. She noticed a vein popping out of the side of his neck. She'd never seen him this angry before.

"No, I don't think this is a joke, but you need to get your fucking hands off me. Then you need to stop taking this whole thing so personally. Look, I'll have to call Uncle Brick if you don't leave now."

Sullivan pushed Abie with just enough force for her to hit the door—face first. She grabbed her cell phone from the bathroom counter and held it up in his face, taunting him. He was becoming more and more aggressive with her, and she needed to let Uncle Brick and the madam know.

Sullivan nodded in defeat and left the hotel room quietly.

What Happens in the Dark

The sound of Abie stirring in the darkness woke Rachida. From the side view of Abie's silhouette, Rachida could see her shoulders going up and down quickly, indicating that she was crying.

"Abie?" Rachida asked.

She heard a loud sniffle and then Abie said, "Go back to sleep."

Rachida squinted at the clock on the nightstand. It was after four a.m.

"Abie, are you crying?"

"No, 'Chida, now go back to sleep."

Rachida reached in the darkness until she felt the antique lamp on her beechwood nightstand. She closed her eyes briefly so they could adjust to the light. Focusing on Abie, she noticed bruises on her arm, and the side of her face was red and swollen.

"Abie, what happened to you?" Rachida quickly pushed the down-filled comforter from her body and jumped to her feet. The hardwood floors creaked from the impact.

"'Chida, go back to sleep!" Abie said again. Rachida ignored her, turning Abie's face toward her.

"Who did this to you? Huh? Who? Did the councilman hit you again?"

Abie, always the strong-willed, boisterous one, sat on the edge of her bed and sulked. She had defeat in her eyes.

"Abie, tell me what happened. Do you want me to go get Uncle Brick?"

Abie jumped to her feet so fast she startled Rachida.

"No! You can't say anything to Uncle Brick or Madam. I'll deal with this myself," Abie snapped.

"But, Abie, if someone hurt you, you know you have to tell Madam."

"What did I say?" Abie yelled. Rachida raised both hands in defense, looking like she was under arrest. Based on Abie's tone, Rachida knew she had to leave the situation alone, even though she was concerned.

She went back to her side of the bedroom. Before turning off the lamp, she stared at Abie for a moment, hoping her friend would open up to her. But Abie quickly turned away, not letting Rachida's eye contact affect her. Rachida turned off the light and though she could see very little in the darkness, from the sound of it, Abie was putting on her pajamas and getting in bed.

"Abie, I'm worried about you. If the councilman is beating you, you need to say something."

"Maybe I have already. It doesn't matter. All Madam cares about is her goddamn money," Abie said. Rachida reached to turn on the lamp again.

"'Chida, just let it go, please. I'm so tired of this. This whole life. I'm just tired. Nobody cares about me. Everybody just uses and abuses me. All for the money. Turn off the light and go to sleep." Abie rolled over so her back was to Rachida.

"Abie . . ."

"'Chida, let it go. I'll be fine. Go to sleep." Rachida did what she was told. She hated to see her friend upset, but what could she do if Abie wouldn't let her in?

Risky Business

The grandfather clock in the foyer chimed, indicating that it was four p.m. Today was Wednesday, the day all the women at the brothel huddled around the speakerphone in the large parlor as Madam Celecia gave them their assignments, made special announcements, and filled them in on highlights of the past week's events.

The parlor, with its oversized columns, hardwood floors, and antique furniture, had an eighteenth-century flair with twenty-first-century amenities. The madam's taste was far from contemporary, and the entire house boasted pricey antique furniture, expensive wallpaper, and original Persian rugs. The parlor was one of the biggest rooms in the house; it had been designed that way when the home was renovated. The wall between the living room and dining room had been removed to expand the parlor, which had enough room to seat about twenty comfortably on various sofas and chairs that circled an oval table in the middle of the room.

The women filed into the parlor slowly, all of them chatting with each other, except for Abie. She wore dark sunglasses to cover her swollen eye, and she'd done a good job covering her bruise with makeup. Rachida walked in behind her, still unnerved by the sight of the bruise, which Abie refused to discuss. That wasn't normal, because they were tight, tighter than sisters, and they shared everything. Rachida was concerned.

The sound of the speakerphone ringing was the women's cue to be quiet and start the meeting. They all shuffled to their seats, and before Uncle Brick pressed the TALK button on the phone, he held a finger to his lips.

"Hello, Madam," he answered.

"Good afternoon, Brick. Good afternoon, ladies." All the women responded with hellos of their own.

"Is everybody doing okay?" Madam Celecia's southern drawl was thick and syrupy, like one of those southern belles from Mississippi during the Civil War era. Rachida noticed that Uncle Brick's eyes went immediately to Abie before he answered.

"Everybody is doing fine, Madam. Old business first?"

"Good. Well, I first wanted to commend you all for doing an amazing job last week," the madam said. "All your clients had nothing but good things to say about you. One thing to note: Since the seasons are changing, you need to be sure you're all taking your vitamins and drinking plenty of water to keep your skin hydrated. Brick told me a couple of you had a few minor breakouts, so the dermatologist is scheduled to come in tomorrow at ten."

"Old business—we have two ladies who are eligible for the transition program," Uncle Brick said. "Both of them have done outstanding work while in the program, and are ready to transition into independence, and I've approved their release. Zakia and Jasmine, congratulations!" He motioned for them to stand as the remaining women—except for Abie—applauded. Uncle Brick gave Abie a look, and if looks could kill, she would've been dead on the spot. Rachida was beginning to think that Uncle Brick and Abie were at war over something. Their scowls weren't evident to anyone but Rachida, and she made a mental note to get to the bottom of it. As Uncle Brick put his finger to his mouth again, Rachida noticed several scratches on his arm. Could he have been behind Abie's injuries? But why?

Then Abie, who'd been unusually quiet, spoke out of nowhere.

"Madam, I need to talk to you privately." Abie's abruptness startled everyone in the room, and the celebration was swept under the rug like dirt.

"Is that you, Abie?" The southern voice spoke through the speaker.

"Yes, it's me."

"Well, there are no secrets here. Whatever you need to say to me, feel free to discuss right here. We're all family, you know."

Abie looked around at the other women, all of whom had puzzled looks on their faces. Abie was always the vibrant leader of the pack, keeping the women in order, teaching them the business, leading them as they progressed. They all put her on a pedestal and considered her, along with Uncle Brick, Madam's right hand. Today she was different—cold and aloof—and they didn't know what was wrong with her.

"I submitted my transition paperwork two weeks before Zakia and Jasmine, and I haven't been approved yet," Abie said. "I was wondering when I'd be getting my transition package. I mean, I have more seniority than anyone here."

The transition package was the official release from the "shelter," which provided the women with a bonus check of ten thousand dollars to get them started on their own, a key to an apartment in the city, and documents regarding a real nine-to-five job.

"Abie, dear, I didn't receive a transition request for you. Brick, did you send me a package for Abie?"

Uncle Brick stared coldly at Abie.

"I thought I sent it to you, Madam. You didn't get it?"

"No, I most certainly did not." The sarcasm seeped through the speakerphone. It was obvious to Abie and everyone else in the room that Brick and Madam were playing Abie. But no one could understand why. Why wasn't Abie given a chance to leave like everyone else?

Abie sighed heavily. She knew what was happening. They were trying to keep her there because she was Madam's cash cow. Sure, Abie had saved enough money to leave on her own. But she wanted what Madam had promised her, had promised every girl there: an apartment and the cash, particularly the cash. She'd worked hard, damn hard for Madam, and she deserved everything that was due her.

"I'll send it again," Abie said. "This time I'd rather mail it to you overnight. Can I send it myself?" No one could see Abie's expression behind the shades, but she squinted as she stared at Uncle Brick.

"Brick, make sure I receive Abie's paperwork this time, okay?" the madam said.

"No problem. Not sure what happened to it."

The women listened attentively while Madam listed their assignments for the week. One of the women would be servicing a senator from Washington, D.C., who was scheduled to be at a town hall meeting with Virginia's governor. Another was assigned to one of Richmond's delegates, who used the services at least once a month. Abie, who was often requested by some of the elite clientele, would be servicing the co-pastor of one of Atlanta's largest megachurches, who'd be in town that weekend for a Christian leadership conference.

As some of the women scribbled notes and others whispered comments to one another, Rachida kept her eye on Abie and Uncle Brick.

Letting Go

"**Y**ou have to let me go, Brick." Abie moved slowly through his in-law suite, a place that had become all too familiar to her. The one-bedroom apartment was stuffy compared to the main house, and sometimes Abie felt like Uncle Brick's physique was too big for such a small place. Standing with her back to the door, she closed it softly, staring at his massive collection of Washington Redskins memorabilia. It was obvious that Madam had allowed him to decorate his space himself, because it was a bachelor pad to the fullest extent: oversized matching La-Z-Boy chairs, a coffee table adorned with *Sports Illustrated*s and various car magazines, and atop a mahogany stand a flat-screen TV and several DVDs and CDs.

Uncle Brick walked to Abie, towering over her like a skyscraper. He gently touched her cheek before bending to kiss her on the forehead.

"If that's my baby, I need to know. Furthermore, I'll kill that motherfucker for putting his hands on you."

"Brick, this is all my fault. I provoked Scoot. I should've just, I don't know." Abie found a safe place to snuggle in Uncle Brick's arms. He stroked her hair gently and held her tightly while she cried.

"Listen, Abie, the best thing for us to do is just cut our losses here and leave this place—together."

Abie pulled away.

"How? We broke the rules. If Madam finds out about us, I could be put out on the street and forfeit my transition package. Then there's this baby. I just don't know what to do. I think I need to have an abortion."

"Abortion? But that's my baby, Abie. How could you kill our child?"

"You don't know that."

"You told me you always use protection with Scoot because he's out there in the streets. I know you use protection with your clients. I'm the only one you go raw with. I know that's my baby. You know I love you and you know we belong together. I can handle Madam."

"Brick, listen. What you did to Scoot today was wrong. You almost killed him."

"He hit you."

"Brick, listen to me, please. I have to work. For me to work, I can't be someone's mother. I can't have this baby. You have to give Madam my paperwork and let me go."

"So just like that, you're going to kill my baby and leave?"

"You don't understand. I have a lot invested with Scoot. You and I, we have something very special, but the more I think about it, the more I realize our relationship can't go any further. Everything we do is done in secrecy. What do you want to do? Run off into the sunset together, have a baby, and live happily ever after?"

"Hell, yes, that's exactly what I want to do. Be with you and my child. I can take care of you, Abie. Fuck this job. We can move to Atlanta, where I have a few connections, and set up there."

"Set up and do what? Me be a fucking prostitute? You want to take me somewhere else to pimp me out?"

"No, I didn't mean it like that. I can get a job, you can stay home with the baby. I have enough money saved to get us started. I know you have money saved too. You can get away from Scoot, I can get away from Madam, and we can start a life together."

"So you'd give up your life here and loyalty to Madam, all for me?"

"Yes, Abie."

Abie pulled away from Brick and sat on the tweed oversized sofa. She rubbed her temples, not sure how she'd get out of her predicament. First, she and Brick had a forbidden relationship that had backfired on her with the discovery of her pregnancy. Second, Sullivan was stalking her and abusing her every chance he got, but when Abie mentioned it to Madam, she told Abie to deal with it for the sake of the business. On top of that, she'd given Brick the impression that Scoot had roughed her up, when in actuality it was Sullivan's doing. As a result, Brick had given Scoot a beat down that had almost cost him his life.

Why did all these men want Abie, a runaway, a street girl who used her body for money to survive just so she could get away from her mother, who'd allowed her boyfriend to use her for free? All she wanted was to make enough money and go into seclusion somewhere, far away from the life of a prostitute, which she'd grown tired of.

Abie knew Brick cared about her. Hell, so did Sullivan, at least that's what he said. But her heart belonged to Scoot. Despite his aggressive personality and quick temper, she still loved him and wasn't sure if she was ready to give him up. Besides, Abie and Scoot had a plan that was about to be put in motion. It would put an extra $250,000 in their pockets—that is, if everything went the way it was supposed to.

Brick sank into the sofa beside Abie, wrapping his heavy arms around her.

"Let me handle everything. I'll talk to Madam. I'll tell her about us, tell her I love you and we're going to be together."

"But, Brick, what'll happen if she refuses my package? She owes me, and I'll be damned if I don't get everything I've earned since I started working for her."

"Abie, I promise you, you'll get everything you deserve and then some. I'll handle everything. But you have to promise me one thing you have to break it off with Scoot."

"And you'll make sure I get my package?" Abie asked.

"I told you, you'll get your package and then some. Let's just say that I have a way with Madam." Brick put his tongue in Abie's mouth and kissed her hard. His size made it hard to be delicate, but Abie was used to him. After having a relationship with him for over a year, she'd become accustomed to the gentle giant. He stood up, carrying Abie through the cramped living room to his bedroom, laying her down on his king-sized bed. He pulled her halter top over her head. He kissed her stomach, trying hard to connect with the unborn fetus growing inside her flat belly. She was about four weeks along, so she still had a ways to go before her stomach would swell. She decided that she'd just tell Brick what he wanted to hear for the sake of getting her package, because she had no plans to keep the baby.

"I just love you so much, Abie. You and this baby." Brick rubbed her stomach before cupping her breasts. He sucked them hard, causing her pussy to throb. Even though her body was excited, her brain was checking the clock on the nightstand, calculating when the whole event would be over. Abie hated having sex with Brick. His body was too big and heavy, and his dick was too small. Plus he always breathed heavily when he thought he was putting in a lot of work, when in fact all his dick did was tease. He barely reached her G-spot, let alone the full depth of her pussy, a major reason Abie didn't want to ride off into the sunset with him. She'd had her share of men, all flavors, and one thing she couldn't live without was sexual gratification.

She turned her head sideways to avoid being suffocated by Brick's body, fixing her eyes on the various Washington Redskins knickknacks that lined the marble-topped dresser. The bed squeaked when Brick got up on his knees, unzipped his pants, and pulled out the short, stubby dick that disappointed Abie so. Just the sight of it turned her off.

"Come on, suck it for me," Brick said in a low voice.

Ten minutes of this shit and then I can leave, Abie thought. Pulling off her jean shorts and kicking off her gladiator sandals, she got on her knees facing Brick, leaned over, and took his dick in her mouth.

"Yeah, that's it, baby, suck it," Brick moaned. Abie didn't even have to use her hand; she could fit his entire shaft in her mouth. Other than Brick's moans, the only other sound that could be heard was her lips smacking against his balls while saliva served as her lubrication.

Brick's breathing got heavy, and sweat was forming on his brow. Abie sucked and sucked until he could barely contain himself. When his dick was at full formation, Abie sat facing him, opened her legs in a V-shape, and lay back so Brick could enter her valley. He snatched off her G-string, an indication that he wouldn't be able to hold out much longer.

"Be careful," Abie said, referring to the small ring on her clit. Brick tried to position himself inside Abie, but with each thrust his small dick slipped out.

"Wait, let me do this." Abie pushed him over onto his back and got on top of him. She bounced up and down on him to create friction and speed up the entire process, which was boring her to death. Brick was in a world of his own, slapping Abie's ass with each plunge.

"Whose pussy is this? I said, whose is it?" he panted.

"Yours, baby, all yours," Abie faked. As she had thought, Brick was about to climax. He put his hands on her waist, guiding her up and down until he exploded. Then Abie jumped up abruptly.

"What's wrong? Did I hurt the baby?"

"No. I have to go. I forgot I have a client this afternoon."

"No, you don't. I saw the schedules for today, and you're free all evening."

"This came up last minute. One of my regulars called and wants to see me."

"So you're just gonna keep fucking all those men while you're pregnant?"

Abie rushed to the bathroom, which was adjacent to the bedroom, and turned on the water in the sink. The pricey ceramic tile floor was cold. Ignoring Brick, she grabbed a washcloth from the linen closet and washed up before putting her clothes back on.

"Abie, did you hear me?" Brick asked.

"I have to work, Brick. This is my job. The baby is about the size of a pea. I feel sure he or she won't feel a thing," Abie said. She sat on the edge of the bed and fastened her sandals while Brick adjusted his pants. She noticed he was sulking, so she moved closer to him.

"Listen, the sooner I get my transition package, the sooner I can let this job go, okay?"

Brick's face lit up.

"I'll make it happen for you today. Don't worry about a thing."

Abie stood up and kissed Brick on the cheek.

"I'll see you later." Abie looked out the window cautiously before hurrying out the front door. She didn't want anyone to see her leaving. When she thought the coast was clear, she darted out the door down the concrete walkway, crossed the driveway, and made her way to the walkway of the main house. Little did she know that Rachida had been watching from the moment Abie went to Brick's apartment. Rachida was concerned because none of the women were supposed to be there—no exceptions. If Brick needed to speak to them, he was supposed to do it at the main house. That was one of the rules set by Madam. Furthermore, Rachida's theory about Uncle Brick beating Abie was shattered based on Abie's demeanor. If Uncle Brick was responsible for the black eye, Rachida was sure Abie would stay as far away from him as possible. The Abie she'd seen earlier was detached and cold. The Abie leaving Uncle Brick's apartment was in good spirits. What was obvious was that Abie and he had something going on, and Rachida was going to get to the bottom of it.

Who's Fooling Whom?

Abie pulled her 2008 Infiniti G37 two-door coupe from the three-car garage and slowly maneuvered around the three cars parked in the driveway. It was two a.m.—her normal business hours. She tried to be discreet so she wouldn't wake Uncle Brick. Abie had already serviced all her clients for the night and was on her way to meet Scoot. The gravel beneath her car wheels churned like rocks tumbling down a hill, and tonight the sound seemed thunderous. She looked through her rearview mirror at Uncle Brick's apartment to detect any movement but the dust from the rocks blocked her view. She followed the long driveway until it met the main road. She loved the quiet and peacefulness of the small town, which had fallen asleep hours earlier. She passed very few houses since each house sat on numerous acres of land. The winding road was dark, and an occasional deer or two could be seen grazing on the side of the road. She rolled down her windows since the summer air was still a bit stuffy. The inside of the car lit up from Abie's cell phone, an indication that she had an incoming call. She grabbed the phone from the passenger seat while concentrating on the road.

"Hey, baby. Wassup?" she answered.

"Yo, where you at?"

"On the way to you. I should be there in about twenty minutes. I had to wait for Brick to go to sleep. That nigga is clocking my every move."

"That nigga lucky he still breathing right now, yo. I should've sent some of my niggas from Bunche Place over there to take care of his swole ass," Scoot said.

"You can do whatever you want when we get our money. Just calm down."

"Calm down? That nigga almost broke my fuckin' jaw. I still don't understand why you told him I did that shit to you."

"Scoot, we need to get this money, right? The bruises were a decoy to make him think I'm afraid of you and need him more than ever. Just go with the flow. I'll show you what I found when I get there."

"All right. I'ma let you handle it," Scoot said.

"Be there in a few."

Subdivisions started to appear, as Abie neared the city. She merged onto I-295 and headed east. Scoot lived in a small brick rancher in the east end of Richmond, an older neighborhood where most of his neighbors were retirement age. He'd bought his rancher at an estate sale after an elderly widower had passed away. In the year since Scoot had moved in, several neighbors had called the police based on the amount of traffic that went in and out of his house. It was obvious to those who lived around him that he was a drug dealer, and they despised his presence in their neighborhood.

Abie pulled her car into the driveway behind Scoot's Escalade. She popped her trunk and grabbed a large manila envelope before using her key on the side entrance of the house. The sound of Scoot's Bose sound system was so loud the glass panes shook in the door. The entrance took her straight into the eat-in kitchen, where dishes were piled high in the sink and Pizza Hut boxes were stacked on the stove. She was perturbed because she'd just cleaned his kitchen the day before and he'd let his friends come over and dirty everything up again. Based on the smoke that hung in the air and the bottle on the kitchen table, Abie knew Scoot and his friend Link were in the living room smoking blunts and drinking Hennessey. They didn't notice her when she entered since the music was so loud. They were both just lying back in the chairs, bobbing their heads to the music. She kicked her way through the clutter on the floor—numerous pairs of Air Jordans, Timberland boots, and empty Xbox 360 video game cases—to the bookshelf that housed all Scoot's music equipment. By that time, Scoot and Link had both seen her.

"Yo, what you doing, shawty?" Link asked.

"Turning down the music. Do y'all want Henrico County to come around here tonight? I can hear the music all the way outside. Y'all are just asking for trouble." Link, a short dark-skinned brother with thick dreadlocks and gold fronts, sat up on the sofa, then leaned over the coffee table to try to hide his weed and other drug paraphernalia.

"Link, I didn't say I brought Henrico County in here with me. I just said the music is so loud you're lucky no one's called them yet. Ain't nobody checking for your stash. Scoot, can we go in your room and talk about this for a minute?" Abie asked, pointing to the envelope in her hand.

"Oh, yeah, we can do that. Yo, Link, nigga, don't try and smoke up all the shit either," Scoot said. He watched Link cut down the middle of a couple of vanilla Dutch Masters cigars with a razor blade, then empty the contents on a paper towel before sprinkling weed in its place.

"Nigga, I got you. Go 'head and do what you need to," Link responded without looking up from his operation.

Scoot followed Abie down a small hallway to his bedroom, which was nothing to write home about. With all the money he made, he refused to buy a decent comforter and curtains for the bedroom, and his black lacquer furniture was outdated. Piles of clothes were tossed in the corner on a compact weight bench that Scoot hadn't used since moving into the house. The only thing on the wall was a small flat-screen TV mounted above a portable fireplace that didn't match any of the furniture. More shoes were scattered around the floor, and the dresser was lined with various bottles of cologne, some of Scoot's jewelry, and empty Hennessey and beer bottles.

"Scoot, you need to call Molly Maids or something. This place is disgusting."

"What's wrong with it?" Scoot held out his arms and turned several degrees to scan the room for the mess that Abie could see but he obviously couldn't. Abie just shook her head before pushing the clothes piled on the bed to one side so she could sit.

"Okay, so his real name is Bernard Jefferson. I went online and looked for every Bernard Jefferson I could find in Atlanta. Only two of them have a sister. Only one of them has a sister living in Atlanta. I think this is him, Scoot. Actually, I'm pretty sure it's him, and this is his sister." Abie pulled out a sheet of paper and gave it to Scoot, who stared at the paper intently, reading every word silently. When he got to the last line, a look of bewilderment crossed his face.

"You mean to tell me she's a—"

"Yes, Scoot, it's got to be her. As a matter of fact, I found something in his apartment with her name on it, so I feel ninety-nine percent positive they're one and the same."

"So now what?"

"What do you mean 'Now what?' It's time to get paid. If I blow the lid on this entire operation, imagine what's at stake. She won't let that happen. I guarantee she'll pay the $250,000 we demand once she sees that I know about her."

"What do you need me to do?" Scoot asked.

"Well, you need to make the call. Set everything up. She doesn't know you or your voice, so you'll be perfect. Just read the script I wrote and tell her she has twenty-four hours to respond. Give her the number to the TracFone to call you back. Make sure you tell her that if you don't hear from her in twenty-four hours, the whole thing will be exposed." Abie handed Scoot a brand-new prepackaged TracFone.

"Tomorrow, Scoot. Do it tomorrow at two p.m. Don't fuck this up."

"Man, I told you about talking to me like I'm a fuckin' kid, yo. I can handle this."

"I'm sorry, baby. I know you can handle it. I just want to get it done so I, I mean so *we* can make our move, okay?" Abie leaned over, kissed Scoot, and put her hand between his legs. No matter what was going on, she always knew what tool to use to get a man to see things her way. Most of the time it actually worked too.

"What? You wanna fuck me now? Naw, not tonight," Scoot said, pushing Abie's hand away. She leaned back and inspected him.

"Oh, I see. You've been fucking some bitch tonight, haven't you? Tell the truth, Scoot."

Scoot smacked his teeth and stood up, his Levi's sagging, exposing his Calvin Klein boxers. Abie grabbed him by the front of his jeans and pulled him to her.

"What the fuck you doin', Abie?" Scoot said, caught off guard.

"Let me smell you! You think I'm stupid? Who the fuck is she?" Abie yelled while struggling to pull Scoot's jeans and underwear down. He tried pushing her away but her anger fueled her strength while Scoot's high fueled his weakness.

"Abie, go 'head with that shit. Stop playing, damn!" They continued to tussle until Abie was able to pull Scoot down on the bed. She rolled him over, pulled his dick out of his pants, and smelled it.

"You a nasty motherfucker!" Abie yelled, punching Scoot in the chest. He looked puzzled because he'd just taken a shower about thirty minutes before Abie got there so he knew his dick still smelled like Irish Spring.

"What the fuck is wrong with you?" he yelled before he stood up and adjusted his jeans.

"You just took a shower? Why you just take a shower, Scoot?" Abie asked.

"Because I been ballin' today and I needed a shower. I knew if you came over here and I was still musty and shit from playin' ball you'd have something to say."

"No, you had a fuckin' girl over here and you had to shower before I came over to get her funky-ass pussy smell off your dick. I'm not stupid!" It didn't matter that Abie had just fucked Uncle Brick because that was different. Uncle Brick and every other man was business for Abie. Scoot was supposed to be her man.

Scoot grabbed Abie by both arms and pinned her down on the bed. "Why the fuck you like playing these games with me, huh? I told you, you the only one for me, Abie. You the only one I want. Link in there about to smoke up all my shit, and right now my high is coming down fucking with you. I'ma do what you need me to tomorrow. We gone get this money, then shit will be aight between us, so just chill."

"You promise?" Abie said.

"Yes. Now go home and I'll call you later, aight?" Scoot released her arms so she could get up. The music was still loud even though she'd turned it down when she came in. Link must've turned it back up while they were in the bedroom. Abie smirked as she followed Scoot back to the living room. Missions one and two were both accomplished—Uncle Brick had received her transition package and had given it to Madam Celecia earlier that day, and now Scoot was going to handle the important business Abie had entrusted him with. As a plume of smoke formed around Link's head, she made a quick exit so the smell wouldn't get into her clothes.

The Big Payback

"**Y**es, I need to make an airline reservation leaving Richmond, Virginia, going to Acapulco, Mexico."

"How many in your party?" the reservationist asked.

"Just one. Oh, and I need a one-way ticket." Abie held the phone to her ear with one hand while scribbling notes with the other. Everything was falling into place, and pretty soon she'd be on a plane to Mexico with the madam's money, on top of her savings, which included some of the money she'd skimmed from Scoot. Since getting her transition package, she was ready to make her move and collect her $250,000, which was scheduled to happen in a few hours. Once she got that money, she'd head straight to the airport, hop on a plane to Mexico, and never look back.

Abie was tired. She was tired of being used by men, tired of being pimped by women, just tired. After receiving one of those pop-ups on her computer about taking a luxury trip to a resort in

Acapulco, she'd started dreaming. She dreamed of a life full of turquoise water, palm trees, and sandy beaches. The more she researched Acapulco, the more she realized that it was where she wanted to be. Then, reality set in. What would she do in Mexico? Be a whore to survive? That was all she knew how to do. She was still about ten credits shy of the college degree that Madam was pushing her and the rest of the girls to get, but Abie was done with that too. So, in an effort to move on to a new life, she'd be the one using men and the one woman who'd been pimping her for the past few years—Madam Celecia. Abie knew she had to have enough money to survive for a while wherever she decided to go, so she'd cracked the code on Madam's identity and conjured up a blackmail scheme. Her surfing the Net for everything she could find about Acapulco, Mexico, had turned into a search for Madam. If her identity was revealed, all hell would break loose.

Abie was so engrossed in making her reservations, she didn't hear Rachida come into their room.

"Yes, I'll pick up my ticket electronically at the airport. Thank you very much."

"Airport? Where are you going, Abie?"

"'Chida, damn! You scared me. Why are you spying on me?"

"Spying on you? All I heard was that you're picking up a ticket at the airport. So where are you going?"

"The less you know the better, okay?" Abie avoided eye contact with Rachida. She hated lying to her best friend, and she wished she could take her with her, but she didn't want her to be a part of the scheme. Abie grabbed clothes from her dresser and threw them into her suitcase in an unorganized fashion. She could feel Rachida behind her but she ignored her. She only had a few hours before everything went down, and very soon after that she'd be boarding an airplane, getting as far from Richmond as possible. Once she reached her destination, she'd call Scoot to let him know where she was.

"Abie, where are you going? And didn't you hear? We have an emergency meeting with the madam today." Abie perked up and stopped packing.

"What?"

"We have an emergency meeting. Uncle Brick just came over and said we need to be downstairs in the parlor in an hour. That's why I came up here to get you."

"Shit. Emergency meeting about what, did he say?"

"Nope, only that it was mandatory."

Abie turned to face her friend. "I need you to cover for me. I have somewhere to be, and it's very important. I need you to tell Uncle Brick I was never here. I'm going to sneak out the back door, and as soon as I see Uncle Brick come over for the meeting, I'm going to jump in my car and leave."

"Abie, what the hell is going on with you? First the black eye, then I see you leaving Uncle Brick's apartment, now you're packing a suitcase heading who knows where."

"You saw me leaving Uncle Brick's apartment? What the fuck, 'Chida, now you following me?"

"No, Abie, I'm concerned about you. Something's going on with you and you won't tell me what. Is it Scoot? Are you running from him?"

"'Chida, please, don't ask me questions. Just leave it alone." Abie turned back to her suitcase and took a few more items from her dresser. Rachida grabbed her arm.

"Abie, tell me what's going on right now or I'm going downstairs and telling Madam everything and I mean it. If you're in danger, she needs to know."

"No! Damn, 'Chida, I told you, this doesn't concern you. And I don't appreciate you following me around. The only reason I went to Uncle Brick's was for help getting my transition package. I needed to get it expedited, that's all. I got my package, I got my money, so I'm ready to get away from here. Maybe that's what the meeting is about."

"Abie, you said one-way ticket. That means you're not coming back. What are you running from? Something else is going on."

Abie paused, breathed heavily, then addressed her friend.

"Okay, something's going on, but I can't tell you right now. But I promise, as soon as I get to my destination, I'll call you and tell you everything you need to know."

"You promise?"

"I promise, 'Chida. But right now, I really have to go. Please, promise me that you'll keep all this to yourself. I really have to leave, though."

Rachida hugged Abie. "Okay, I promise. But you better call me as soon as you get wherever you're going. I can't believe you're leaving me."

"I'm only leaving for a little while. When everything blows over, you'll see me again. Now go downstairs and distract Uncle Brick for me."

Rachida did as her friend asked, looking down the hall to ensure that no one saw her leaving the room. Abie zipped her black rolling suitcase and set it by the door beside the matching bigger one. She checked her cell phone, and moved to the window to see if Uncle Brick had come over yet. Her nervous energy took over and she paced the floor several times before returning to the window. When she saw the door to Uncle Brick's apartment open, her heart started beating really quickly. She hoped Rachida could keep him downstairs in the parlor long enough for Abie to get down the back stairwell and out the back door. She'd parked her car on the main road, so she'd go through the woods to get to it. The footsteps and voices in the hallway told her the other women were heading downstairs to the parlor. She grabbed her suitcases and hid in the closet until the coast was clear. When all the voices had trailed off, she slowly opened the sliding doors to the walk-in closet, grabbed her purse from the bed, and opened the door to her room. The women's voices could all be heard in the parlor, as well as Uncle Brick's. That was Abie's cue to get off the premises quickly. She headed down the long hallway, past the other bedrooms toward a bay window that provided a fair amount of sunlight. The hardwood floors in the hallway creaked in certain spots, so she tried to be careful getting to the stairs. The winding stairs led to the oversized kitchen, which was located in the back of the house. Abie's heart raced as she got closer to the door, and she almost panicked when she realized that as soon as she opened the door, the alarm sensor would beep, causing Uncle Brick to investigate. "Fuck!" she said softly. How was she going to get out the door without it beeping? She sent Rachida a text to come to the kitchen. She stood in the pantry and waited for her. She entered the kitchen, looking around for Abie.

"Abie?" she whispered so Uncle Brick and the others couldn't hear her. Then she noticed her and rushed over.

"What is it? The meeting's about to start in like two minutes."

"I know." Abie pointed to the alarm panel box on the wall beside the door.

"It's gonna beep when I open the door. So I need you to act like you opened the door so I can get out of here."

"Okay. Be careful, Abie. Whatever you're doing, just be careful."

"I will. I promise, I'll call you. Bye, sis." They hugged and then Abie opened the door, and with both pieces of luggage in her hands, and her purse on her shoulder, she ran down the wooden plank steps and disappeared into the woods. Rachida closed the door behind her and rushed back to the parlor.

"Did someone come in the back door?" Uncle Brick asked.

"No, I was double-checking it because it wasn't closed all the way." Rachida took a seat beside one of the other women and watched as Uncle Brick dialed Madam's phone number. The women all waited attentively for her to pick up.

"Good afternoon, Madam."

"Hello, Brick. Are all the ladies there?" A noise in the background made it hard for them to hear her.

"What was that, Madam? We can't hear you."

Madam paused for a moment before speaking.

"I'm sorry, I'm not in my office. I asked if all the ladies were there."

"Everyone except Abie. I couldn't get in touch with her. I believe she had a last-minute client who wanted to see her," Uncle Brick lied. He knew everyone's schedule from morning until night.

"Is that right?"

"Yes." Uncle Brick really had no idea where Abie was. Even though she'd been given her transition package, she was still on the payroll for two more weeks.

"Well, good afternoon, ladies," Madam Celecia said to the group.

"Good afternoon, Madam," they all said in unison, almost sounding like a classroom full of students.

"I called this meeting because I was just notified that a conference is being held at the Richmond Convention Center tonight for Gamma Alpha Psi fraternity. The president phoned me to see if I could have a few ladies available this evening. I figured I'd give him everyone, since nobody was scheduled to work today. Rachida, have you talked to Abie this afternoon?" All eyes turned to Rachida.

"Uh, no, Madam, not this afternoon. I spoke with her earlier this morning," Rachida lied.

"Okay, no worries. I was going to give her the president of the Virginia chapter as a client, but since she's not there, you can have the honors. The men will be finishing their meeting at the Convention Center around seven p.m., after which they plan to have dinner. They'd like you all to meet them at the Doubletree Hotel near the airport at ten p.m. for drinks. Brick will give you your assignments. These men pay very well, and they're gentlemen, so I want you all to treat them as such. I know a few of them will be flying out early in the morning, so you may not have to do a long shift. Since you're all going to the same location, you can carpool. Keep an eye out for each other, and make sure you touch base with me throughout the evening via text. Any questions?"

"Madam, what if Abie shows up? Do you want me to send her over there or does she just take it as a loss?" Uncle Brick asked.

"She'll have to sit this one out, Brick. Any more questions?"

The women whispered to one another about being able to work together. They always felt safer when they worked in the same location. Besides, they'd be able to drink and socialize together too.

"Okay, I'll take that as a no. Brick has your packages. Have fun tonight, ladies."

Uncle Brick pressed the END button on the speakerphone, then handed out manila folders. Rachida hoped Uncle Brick would call her name early so she could escape without being left alone with him. As luck would have it, though, he called her name last.

"Rachida, let me holler at you for a minute."

Rachida tried hard to keep her composure and not give anything away. She knew what Uncle Brick was going to ask her.

"Tell me the truth. Where's Abie?"

"I don't know where Abie is."

"Rachida, you and Abie are best friends, roommates, as close as they come. You mean to tell me she didn't mention to you where she might be going today?"

Rachida shook her head. She couldn't stop looking down at the

manila folder she was holding, constantly tearing at the corner
out of nervousness.

"If I find out you're lying to me, you know I could get you kicked
out, don't you?" He stood there, giving Rachida a chance to con-
fess, but she wouldn't take it.

She looked up at him. She didn't like his threat, but she
wouldn't give up her friend, no matter what. "I told you, I don't
know where she is." Her heart was beating so hard she was sure he
could hear it.

"Well, if you hear from Abie anytime soon, have her call me,
okay?"

"Okay," Rachida answered. She turned on her heel so fast she
almost knocked over a plant that sat on a table in the foyer. She
took the steps two at a time up to the second floor, passing several
closed doors until she reached the room she shared with Abie.
Out of habit, she locked the door behind her and pulled her cell
phone from her pocket. She sent a text message to Abie.

Hey. Where r u? They r looking for u. R u still leaving town?

Yes, in a few hours. I had to make a few stops first to collect
some money but I'll be leaving later tonight. Thanks for
covering for me. I promise I'll call you as soon as I get to my
destination. I'll explain it all to you then.

OK, be careful. Luv u, sis.

Ly2.

Rachida erased the text messages and relaxed a bit since it
seemed like Abie had gotten where she needed to be and would be
on her way to her destination soon. What she couldn't understand
was why Abie was running away from everything. She took her
mind off Abie for a moment and concentrated on getting ready
for her client.

Golden Showers

"Just stand right there. I want to look at you," Mr. Gamma Alpha Psi President, aka Eric Bosh, told Rachida. He'd had his share of Courvoisier, just as Rachida had had her share of apple martinis at the bar in the lobby. Now she stood naked in the doorway that connected the bathroom to the bedroom of Eric's hotel room at the Doubletree. He was lying on his side staring at her while stroking his dick.

"Now turn around and bend over so I can look at your ass." Rachida did as she was told, bending over and wiggling her ass at the same time. She was still wearing her stilettos, and with her legs spread apart, she grabbed both ankles so her ass was up in the air and Eric had a full back view of her pussy. He got even more excited and stroked his dick harder and faster. Rachida had been there for almost an hour and they still hadn't fucked. Everything with him was visual. This was probably the first time she'd ever had a customer who got excited just by looking at and touching her body. Eric moaned from his own touch and gave Rachida more demands, which she followed with no problem. To her it felt more like a game than work, so she was happy to oblige.

"Rub your clit. Play with it. Yeah, that's it, keep playing with it." The more Rachida stroked her clit, the more Eric stroked himself. Her hair hung on the floor and she looked back through her open legs at his arousal. He turned over on his back but never let go of his dick. Rachida figured he was ready for her to jump on him like a stallion so she stood up, smoothed her hair back, and seductively pranced over to the bed.

"Do you need my help with that?" Rachida asked, putting one hand around Eric's dick. She put the tip of the head in her mouth to get it wet, but before she could start sucking him, he told her to stand on the bed. She slid off her stilettos and did as directed. She figured he wanted to see her valley from another angle for more visual stimulation.

"Golden shower. Go ahead, give me one." For a minute, Rachida had to think about what he was asking. She'd heard about these from the other women, but had never had any of her customers ask for one before. She didn't really feel comfortable peeing anywhere other than a toilet, but if Eric wanted to pay $500 to get peed on, so be it. She hoped he wouldn't then want her to lie down on a pissy-ass bed. She took a deep breath and tried like hell to make a golden shower look sexy. Straddling his body, she released slowly so that the liquid drizzled down her leg versus shooting out like a water fountain.

"Yeah, girl, that's it, give it to me, yeah, on my body, yeah, keep on, yeah, yeah, yeah!" Eric's moans heightened the more Rachida peed on him. She couldn't figure out what got him off about this, but within a matter of minutes, he was exploding all over his chest. She stood there for a moment, not sure what her next move should be. Eric lay there with his eyes closed for a moment before saying a word. The cold from the air conditioner was causing chill bumps to pop up all over her body. But the last thing she wanted to do was get in that bed after peeing in it.

"So, what do you want to do now? You want to go for round two inside me or what?"

"No, I can't do that. I'm married, so I can't, like, fuck you or anything. What about toys, you got any?"

"Sure." Rachida hopped down off the bed and grabbed her duffel bag from the chair in the corner. She had several tricks in her bag. Vibrators, bunnies, beads. She was always prepared for whatever a customer wanted. She held up a pink two-headed vibrator designed to stroke her G-spot and penetrate her at the same time.

"What about this?" she asked.

"Oh, yeah. Let me see you work that."

"You want to see me put it in my pussy, huh?"

"Oh, yeah!" Eric yelled. Rachida took a seat in the chair and opened her legs wide. She propped her left leg up on the bed, giving Eric full view of her pussy. The vibrator hummed softly and she eased to the edge of her seat and fulfilled herself, since Eric wasn't going to do it for her.

When it was all over, she'd fondled and fucked herself, along with peeing on herself, and Eric was completely satisfied.

"Damn, I'm starving. You want to grab something to eat before you leave? I saw a Waffle House across the street from the airport."

"Sure. Let me jump in the shower first." They both got cleaned up, carrying on small talk with each other to fill the awkwardness of two strangers. They rode in Eric's rental car. While Rachida waited for her waffle and eggs and he waited for his steak, eggs, toast, and grits, she learned that he was originally from Alabama but was living in Maryland. He tried hard not to discuss his wife and kids, so he focused on talking about the fraternity instead. Rachida learned everything she'd ever wanted to learn about Gamma Alpha Psi. The entire conversation bored her, and she couldn't wait until the heavyset blond waitress with a missing front tooth and dirty apron set their plates down in front of them. The Waffle House had a minimal crowd of people leaving the nightclubs who wanted a bite to eat before going home. There were also a few street hustlers in there who were probably finishing up shifts of their own and had the munchies after smoking weed. Besides, they served the best waffles and eggs one could buy at two a.m.

Eric and Rachida ate their food quietly, and before long she could hear police sirens in the distance. The sound got closer and closer, and it was hard not to notice the group of police cars speeding into the parking lot of the Red Roof Inn across the street. Everyone in the Waffle House looked through the windows trying to get a peek at the event. The sight of the officers made Eric nervous, since he was out in public with a woman who wasn't his wife.

"You ready?" he asked abruptly. She gulped down the last of her orange juice.

"Sure." By the time they'd walked outside, a crowd had started to form on the Waffle House side of the street, and the cop cars were coming from all directions.

Before they could reach Eric's car, Rachida heard someone calling her name.

She squinted and noticed a woman in a burgundy uniform coming toward her. She realized it was Tandy, a friend who worked at the Red Roof Inn. Tandy ran across Williamsburg Road to where Rachida and Eric were standing.

"Rachida! You have to come quick. My coworker Jenny said she saw the body and it's Abie," Tandy said, trying to catch her breath.

"What?"

"Abie, she got shot. You need to come now." Tandy grabbed Rachida by the arm.

"I'm sorry, but I have to see what's going on. I think my best friend may be in trouble. I'll get a ride back to the hotel. Don't worry about me." Eric jumped into his car so quickly it was a wonder he let Rachida finish her sentence. Tandy pulled Rachida across the street through the crowd and up a back stairwell so they could bypass the police perimeter. Since Tandy worked at the hotel, she had access to the rooms so she was able to get into the room next to the one where Abie had been killed. The police were still gathering in the parking lot waiting for the crime-scene investigators to arrive so this gave Tandy a window of opportunity to sneak Rachida in. Tandy opened the door slowly and they entered the room. It looked like a massacre had occurred there. Blood splatters were on the walls, the bedspread, even the dresser and TV. Abie's lifeless body was on the floor naked right by the entrance, between the dresser and the bed. Rachida almost fainted at the sight of her friend.

"Abie? Oh, my God, Abie! Abie, what happened? Oh, my God! Tandy, what happened to her? Who did this?" Rachida went to kneel down beside Abie but Tandy pulled her back.

"You can't go over there, Rachida. You might contaminate the crime scene. I just wanted to make sure that was her. I'm so sorry. Come on, we have to go before the police come back in."

"Tandy, who did this? Why? Why? Oh, God, why? Abie, noooo!" The sound of the door opening sent Tandy running through the access door to the adjacent hotel room. Rachida just stood there, frozen, screaming.

"Hey, what are you doing in here? You're not supposed to be in here. Who are you and how'd you get in here?" Rachida was numb. All she could do was stand there and scream uncontrollably. What was Abie doing here? She was supposed to be on an airplane long gone by now. Who did this to her? And why?

Whodunit?

The days after Abie's funeral were a blur to Rachida but somehow she made it through without breaking down. She'd become a bit of a recluse since Abie's death, and working was the last thing on her mind. Madam gave her two weeks off to get herself together, and she used those weeks to find the strength to start her own search for Abie's killer. Initially Scoot had been questioned by the police as a possible suspect, but they'd had to let him go because he had an ironclad alibi. They told Rachida that there were no leads in the case and no witnesses. No one saw Abie go into the hotel room. The room was not registered to anyone. Abie's car was found at a park 'n' ride at the airport. None of it made sense. What they *could* tell her was that it seemed like Abie had met her killer at the airport and was abducted there. There was evidence that supported this theory that the police weren't able to disclose to Rachida.

Rachida was ready to find Abie's killer. The first thing she had to do was talk to Scoot to see what he knew about what Abie might've been involved in that day. It was still hot outside even though the sun was just setting, putting a haze over the city. Rachida jumped into her car, opened the sunroof, and let the farmhouse get farther and farther behind her. It didn't take long for her to reach the city, but by the time she reached Scoot's house, the sun had completely set. Scoot's Cadillac was parked in the driveway and music was blaring from inside. Rachida parked her car and walked through a shabby, chain-link fence down an uneven paved walkway. When she walked up the porch steps to the screen door, she noticed that the front door wasn't closed all the way. She didn't see any more cars in the driveway, so she assumed Scoot was there alone. The door squeaked as she slowly pushed it open. She peeked inside and scanned the living room. The music was so loud it felt like the bass was coming from inside her head.

"Scoot!" Rachida yelled but she knew it was impossible to hear over the music. She waited a minute or so to see if he'd come out but he didn't, so she went in and turned the music down. The living room was a mess with empty fast-food containers, Styrofoam cups, and other trash strewn about. It smelled bad too, probably from the trash in the kitchen. The house didn't look like it had been cleaned in days, maybe even weeks.

"Scoot!" Rachida yelled again, this time walking down the hallway toward the bedroom. When she reached his bedroom door, it was closed, so she knocked.

"Scoot?" she said again. No response. She turned the knob and opened the door. Her eyes got as big as lemons. He was lying in a pool of blood on his bed, faceup, his wife beater stained with blood, and several bullet holes in his chest. She inched away slowly, not sure if she should call the police or run like hell out of the house.

"What the fuck is going on?" Rachida paced and rubbed her forehead to stop herself from throwing up. She'd cried so many tears for Abie that she didn't have any more left, and quite frankly, she didn't care that Scoot was dead. All she cared about was that she hadn't gotten a chance to talk to him before he was murdered. As she stood there, confused and a bit numb, she gathered her composure and decided to search Scoot's room to find any evidence that could prove whether he'd killed Abie. Rachida hurried to the front door and locked it. She looked through the tattered miniblinds to make sure no one was outside. Then she went back to Scoot's bedroom and tried to avoid looking at him. She rummaged through his drawers, his closets, and even under his bed looking for anything that might prove guilt. The room was already in shambles, so it probably didn't make much difference that Rachida was searching it. She kicked through several piles of clothes on the floor looking for anything that would help her. One of the piles covered a small plastic trash can, inside of which was a Trac-Fone and some sheets of paper with pictures and personal data on someone named Karen Jefferson-Duvall. Jefferson-Duvall was the pastor of Missions of Faith Baptist Church, a megachurch in Atlanta, Georgia. Rachida had heard about the church from its Sunday TV broadcasts, and the pastor of the church was a spiritual advisor to a lot of celebrities. *Why did Scoot have information on her?* Rachida wondered. It didn't make sense, especially because Scoot was far from spiritual. The TracFone looked brand-new. Rachida turned it on and hit the MENU button, looking through the call history. Only two outgoing calls had been made, both to a number with a "678" area code. Rachida dialed the number to see who answered.

"Thank you for calling Missions of Faith Baptist Church. This is Pastor Karen Jefferson-Duvall. I'm unavailable at the moment, but your call is very important to me. Please leave a detailed message and I'll call you back at my earliest convenience. Thank you for calling and have a blessed day."

Rachida's legs almost buckled. That voice. She knew it anywhere. That same southern drawl, oozing with sweetness. It was the madam's. Rachida was 100 percent sure of it. *Pastor* Karen Jefferson-Duvall? Madam Celecia was a pastor? That just didn't make any sense. How was that possible?

"Come on, Scoot. I know you're dead, but you have to give me more here. I need more." Rachida spoke to the corpse as if it would answer her. Then she dug through the rest of the papers from the trash can and read each to see if there was anything else that might help her with the puzzle. Then she saw it, the very last page—the script Abie had written and given to Scoot. It all started to make sense.

Pastor Duvall, if you want to keep your identity as a madam a secret, I suggest that you meet my associate at the park 'n' ride at Richmond International Airport with $250,000 cash tomorrow at 4 p.m. This will give you plenty of time to make travel arrangements to get from Atlanta to Richmond. Don't tell me you don't have that kind of money, because I've been privy to information stating that you do, thanks to your brother, Bernard Jefferson, or should I call him Brick? Two hundred fifty thousand dollars cash. No questions asked. You'll see a white Infiniti G37 in Parking Lot G6, Space #15. If you don't show up with the money, my associate will go straight to the authorities and share how you've been spending government money running a prostitution ring. Oh, by the

way, your husband, the famous Bishop Cleo Duvall, might not
like the idea either.

So that's what Abie had been up to. She'd tried to extort money
from the madam, who just happened to be a pastor. What kind of
twisted mind could have been living such a double life? But did
the pastor kill Abie or hire someone else to do it for her? Then it
hit her—the emergency meeting the day Abie was killed. The
background noise on the phone call could have been from the airport. Could the madam be so cold, though? Was she capable of
brutally murdering Abie? Rachida couldn't believe it. She shook
her head over and over again, tears rolling down her cheeks. With
all she knew, the evidence was clear, so Rachida decided it was the
right time to call the police. She called Detective Wilson, who'd
been working on Abie's case.

Rest in Peace

It was all over the news about Pastor Karen Jefferson-Duvall.
They called her everything from the "Anonymous Madam" to the
"Perverse Pastor." When Rachida broke the story to the detective,
he didn't believe her initially. But as she handed over the evidence (after he promised he wouldn't bust her for prostitution)
and told him everything she knew, he worked out a deal that would
put her into a witness-protection program and prevent her from
doing any jail time.

Jefferson-Duvall's duty at the church was to minister to battered and homeless women by taking them off the street and giving them a roof over their head, food to eat, and access to
programs and classes that would help them get on their feet. That

was supposed to be the extent of her ministry. But somewhere along the line, it had turned into something criminal and sinister, all because of greed. Jefferson-Duvall had used her husband's power and celebrity to build up a clientele for the prostitution ring.

At first she thought she hadn't done anything wrong. She told the cops she was just trying to help these women by getting them off the streets. They didn't have anywhere to go, and she gave them classes, taught them social skills, provided good doctors for them, and gave them twenty-four-hour security. They had the freedom to leave whenever they wanted, so why was she being charged with a crime? The women had willingly been prostitutes. Her calling was to minister to women and help them better themselves, and that's what she'd been doing.

Well, just like everyone else who heard the story, the Atlanta Police Department didn't buy it. In fact, while Jefferson-Duvall was in a small session ministering to a few battered women, Atlanta PD burst into the church and arrested her in front of her husband and parishioners. After she was read her rights, Jefferson-Duvall asked what she was being charged with. The officer said two counts of first-degree murder and twenty counts of solicitation for prostitution. They also told her she'd be extradited to Richmond as soon as possible. Even though she didn't pull the trigger, she'd hired the man who did and she'd witnessed the execution.

Around the same time Jefferson-Duvall was arrested, the farmhouse was raided and the women there were charged with prostitution, while Uncle Brick, aka Bernard Jefferson, was charged with one count of first-degree murder for Scoot's death and one count of being an accessory after the fact for Abie's murder. It turned out that he'd murdered Scoot in a rage over his involvement in the extortion scheme involving his sister. He hated the fact that Abie had used him, and he wasn't sorry she was dead.

It wasn't hard for him to pump those bullets into Scoot's chest and watch him die. Jefferson-Duvall refused to name the triggerman who'd actually killed Abie, but there was enough evidence to nail her as the mastermind behind the murder.

When the news broke, Councilman Sullivan was forced to step down after he was named as a client of the Southern Girls' Escort Service. And he wasn't the only one revealed. The press was given a list of all the clients, which caused even more turmoil in the community.

Rachida changed her name and moved to an undisclosed location. Since Jefferson-Duvall never named her accomplices, Rachida was sure there was probably someone out there who'd been paid to finish her off. It didn't matter to her, though. She realized that Abie had been looking for a way out of a life that had become too much for her to bear. Abie had grown tired of being used by everyone she knew, and she just wanted to go away somewhere to get away from it all. Rachida was just happy that justice had been served for her best friend and that Abie was finally at peace.

MONIQUE S. HALL

Ms. G-Stacks

How It All Went Down

"**Y**ou have a call from Stacks at the Fulton County Jail. Do not use three-way or conference calling or your call will be terminated. To accept the call, press 1. To decline, press 2," the automated message stated.

Damn, I thought. *What the hell has happened now?* I had that fucked-up feeling deep in the pit of my stomach, the one where you know something is wrong but you can't quite put your finger on it.

I quickly pressed 1 and waited for the operator to connect the call. I hadn't seen or heard from Stacks, my live-in boyfriend of the last four years, all day, which was totally out of character for us. Although he was a hustler who worked on the streets, we always communicated and knew each other's whereabouts.

Earlier that day, I'd texted him more than ten times, and the messages had gone unanswered. That had bothered the hell out of me and made me feel queasy.

"Babe, it's me. I'm at the County on Bankhead!" he shouted through the phone.

"What for? Babe, what happened?" I asked.

"Some niggas from Decatur set me up. Jetta and me were over there handling bid'ness with some major cats. Before we had a chance to make good on the drop, the po-pos stepped in." He sounded defeated and exhausted.

I braced myself before I asked the next question. "How long until you get a bond?" I already knew the answer but I asked anyway.

"There ain't gonna be a bond. I violated my parole. Even if I beat the drug rap, they caught us red-handed with the guns. I'm gonna get an automatic five years. There ain't no way to beat it— not even if Johnnie Cochran came back from the dead. They caught me dead in the wrong on this one."

My stomach went from queasiness to a simmering boil. Everything stood at a standstill. Stacks was my man, my lover, my every-fucking-thing. He had been holding us down for years.

Not only was Stacks a bona fide hustler, he was also a hell of a provider. The world was ours, and he made sure to serve it to me on a silver platter. We had it all: Benzes in every color, iced-out jewelry, condos, and various waterfront properties. If money could buy it, we had it.

My baby had so much money, the streets called him G-Stacks. He had truly earned his moniker and lived up to it, although he'd moved beyond the G-marks to millionaire status. He kept it real and he kept it gangsta.

"T, I'ma need you more now than evah to keep shit tight for me. I can't say much over the phone, but come down to visitation tomorrow and see me. I'll explain everything. I need to see you face-to-face. Now ain't the time for tears. I need you to man up," he said.

"Okay, baby, I got you," I said. I know I had to be strong. My nigga needed me to be mentally right for the task at hand. Whatever it was he needed, I was prepared to do it. I was his "Ride or Die Chick." Him being behind bars was not going to change that.

I took a deep breath, gathered my thoughts, and put my psyche in check. My man was a boss, and I was a boss bitch. Whatever he needed, I was prepared to handle. Knowing Stacks, it was not going to be anything simple. The truth is, there ain't nothing simple about him, or me either, for that matter.

Thinking of a Master Plan

"Taylor Dixon, you may go back and see Felix Martin. He will be brought in momentarily by one of the guards," the corrections officer stated. I hated jails, almost as much as I hated the police. I know they're supposed to protect and serve but most of the time, the only thing those motherfuckers do is harass people and lock up our black men. To me, there ain't nothing noble about that.

I sat at the visitation booth and waited for Stacks to be brought in. When I saw him, my heart almost stopped beating. My baby had a black eye, a bruised lip, and a swollen face. "What the fuck happened to you?" I asked.

"Nothing I can't handle. Detective Morgan, one of the po-pos, got upset because I wouldn't talk their language. So since he couldn't get me to narc on my connect, he took it out on my face. He's a fucked-up nigga anyway. You know me, baby, I'm gonna make him earn that badge."

I was steaming. I made a note to find Detective Morgan and pay him a visit later. I wasn't going for that shit—no way, no how. "So what is it you need me to do? I called your mom and she sends her love. She'll be down to visit later today," I spat out without a breath in between. I hate visits because after you leave, you always realize there was something you forgot to say.

"Taylor, I need you to take over the operation," he began. I thought I was hearing things but I knew I wasn't. Whenever Stacks is serious, he calls me by my government name.

"I know you've been off the streets for a few years now, but you still know the ropes. I'ma be down for at least five years. I got too much product out there to collect on. Niggas need to know that while I'm down doing this li'l bid, my crew can handle bid'ness. I ain't trying to come back to the block and rebuild," he said, looking at me more seriously than I'd ever seen him do in a long time.

"Why can't we just stack what we have and work legit from here on out?" I asked. "We have enough cash to live comfortably. The boutique is pulling in enough to cover the mortgage. The car wash is holding its own, and our restaurant ain't hurting at all. It's a cash cow all by itself." The truth of the matter was, I was proud of our businesses. Even though they started from illegal money, they had become legit.

"T, haven't you realized that once you're in the game, you can't just walk away? This empire I built ain't about to crumble just 'cause I gotta lay down behind the walls. Niggas are depending on me out there. Families eat because of me. Li'l niggas who ain't got no daddy and got crackheads for mommas are enrolled in colleges 'cause I pay for that shit. This shit goes deeper than the little boutique money that you make for a hobby. The reason you can do the things you do is because of the moves I made for us in dem damn streets. Now I'm not asking you to do no more for me than what I'd do for you." I could tell by his tone that he meant it. I thought for a moment. I knew that if the shoe was on the other foot, Stacks would do whatever I asked with no hesitation. My mind flashed back to our first encounter.

It wasn't like I was new to the shit he was asking me to do. Hell, I met Stacks on the block. Back then I was an eighteen-year-old wayward teen trying to make a dollar out of fifteen cents. My mom had passed away because of a drug overdose and I never knew my father. How I managed to complete high school was a mystery all in itself being that I was practically from pillar to post. My mother,

God bless her soul, could never keep a steady roof over our heads due to her addiction, so I quickly learned that I could do one of two things: starve or survive. I chose the latter and learned how to sell drugs. Stacks was a mid-level-weight man who was known to have a good heart. Although he made his money selling drugs, he was one of those who gave back to the community. It wasn't unusual to see him throwing a barbecue for the neighborhood, paying someone's rent who would be facing eviction, or taking the less-fortunate kids of welfare mothers on shopping sprees. I guess he tried to karma all the bad shit he did. He was a little sweet on me and I knew it but never used it to my advantage. I bought my first fifty-cent pack from him. I flipped it, came back, and got a hundred-dollar slab. Once I flipped that, I copped an eight ball. I eventually moved up from an ounce to an ounce and a half. The next thing I knew, I had worked my way up to a bird. Stacks was impressed by my hustle and took me under his wing.

I won't lie and say that I wasn't attracted to him. Hell, Stacks was finer than a motherfucker. I'd have been a fool not to be interested in him. I was actually a nice piece myself. I stand 5'6" with caramel-colored skin, long beautiful wavy hair, and a body to die for. I'm a showstopper by any man's standards, but I learned early in life that beauty can only get you so far. Stacks would constantly tell me that I needed a real thoroughbred to help me man these streets. I took what he said in stride until one night a drug deal gone bad almost cost me my life. I'd been serving this customer, Tate, for about six months. By this time, I'd moved up to the majors. I was purchasing ten keys a week. Tate would buy two keys at a time and was never short. But this particular night he seemed different. He normally just cops his product and bounces. This night he was a little extra friendly, but I paid it no mind. That was my first mistake. After making our normal exchange, he started grabbing me and fondling one of my breasts.

"T, you a fine-ass bitch. Let me get a piece of dat ass," he said.

I could smell alcohol and weed on his breath. Normally I pack my "Nina," but since I'd been dealing with him on a regular basis, I saw no need. I should've known better than to get caught slipping. The streets like to call our gun of choice Ninas, short for nine-millimeter Glock.

"Look, Tate, you need to back the fuck off. I ain't trying to deal with you like that. You're drunk and you're high. I'ma act like this shit ain't happen," I said in my hardest try-a-bitch-if-you-wanna voice. But he wasn't trying to hear that shit. "No" was a word he wasn't used to. As we began to wrestle, he got more belligerent. I managed to scream but then he slapped me so hard he knocked the taste out of my mouth. I had just about given up hope of winning the struggle when Stacks appeared out of nowhere with a gun to Tate's head. He cocked the trigger and said, "The lady said no, nigga. Ain't you ever heard 'no means no'? What are you, some kind of rapist?" Stacks asked the question not really expecting an answer.

"What the fuck you doing at my house?" Tate asked. I knew that he was crazy because no one in their right mind would question a man who's holding a gun to their head.

"Dude, you got a lot of nerve talking shit right now," Stacks said. He uncocked the gun and hit Tate upside the head, knocking him unconscious.

Realizing I was free, I quickly pushed Tate off me. I glanced at him lying on the ground. I couldn't control the anger that had erupted inside me. I started kicking him and punching him. He didn't budge. Then I spit on him. Stacks gently took me in his arms and held me. I was trembling and out of control. "Thank you for saving me. How did you know I was here?" I asked.

"Something about ole boy didn't sit too well with me ever since you started dealing with him. I normally check on you and your drops from time to time. I told you I had my eye on you and I meant that. You're still a woman, meaning you're vulnerable just like any other female, as you learned today."

"Well, this is one time I can say that I appreciate you being all up in my bid'ness," I said, trying to muster a smile.

"Let's get out of here before he wakes up and I have to put a cap in his ass," Stacks said. "I already don't feel right leaving him breathing, but now ain't the time or place to handle this nigga. He has too many nosy neighbors. If shit gets out of hand, I'll pay him another visit. The next time, he won't be so fortunate." As we walked out the door, I stopped dead in my tracks.

"What you waiting on? Come on, Taylor. Let's get the fuck out this nigga's house. What are you lollygagging around for?" he said. I didn't say a word. I went to the coffee table and picked up the two keys Tate had bought from me earlier.

"He won't be needing this product. I have a strict 'right to refuse customer service policy.' This nigga stepped out of pocket, and he might as well find a new vendor," I said. I was dead ass serious. I had the dope and the money.

Stacks laughed out loud. "Girl, you crazy. Let's roll up out this joint." We left Tate's spot and I followed Stacks back to his crib. From that day, we've been inseparable. He had won my heart, and there was nothing I wouldn't do for him.

I quickly came out of my daydream and popped back into reality. I turned my attention to Stacks and listened to him as he laid down the details of the master plan he'd devised. I was all ears. My baby's livelihood depended on me keeping shit in check. There was no way I was going to let him down.

Down Like Four Flat Tires

After leaving the county, I made arrangements to meet Jetta at our restaurant. Jetta was Stacks's right-hand man, also known as his street lieutenant. Since Jetta wasn't on parole, he had a bond and would be my assistant, so to speak. I had picked up Stacks's phone from his impounded property. Every contact I needed to run the bid'ness properly was stored inside it. Our restaurant, located in southwest Atlanta, was named "Big Mamma's," which is what people in the neighborhood called Stacks's grandmother. She was a strong, sturdy woman who knew her way around a kitchen. Although she was pushing eighty-three, she was still light on her feet. Everyone from the mayor to diplomats frequented the restaurant to get a taste of her cooking.

When we bought the restaurant, grandma took charge and organized things. She knew about Stacks and me running the streets. She was the main reason I left hustlin' alone and went legit altogether. "Them streets is mean and ain't safe for no womenfolks," she used to continuously say to Stacks and me. We ignored her as much as we could but she didn't let up. "If you care about that girl, you'll make her settle down. Your grandpa, God bless him, would have never allowed me to carry on like you let Taylor," she would say to Stacks. Tired of her constant complaints, Stacks finally made me leave the game altogether. Instead of hustlin' the streets, I enrolled in community college and took some business classes. Then I opened our boutique, helped run the car wash, and made sure things ran smoothly at the restaurant. Grandma stopped complaining and, to be honest, I was happy and content. Stacks and I had plans to get married, but we were still young and in no rush.

I sat in a booth in the back of the restaurant and waited for Jetta. I spotted him walking in the door and waved him over to where I was sitting. As he approached me, I could see that he had been beaten up pretty badly too. He was a redbone, so if you looked at him too hard, he'd bruise. He had a black eye that he sported proudly. "I see Detective Morgan fucked you up too," I said, not really expecting an answer.

"Yeah, that's one fucked-up-ass cop. He ain't shit without that badge," he said.

"I feel you. Listen, are you hungry? I was waiting for you before I ordered anything. I'm hungry as hell."

"Shit, a nigga starvin' like Marvin. I didn't get out until five o'clock this morning. Stacks sent me a message to come straight over once I made bond. By the way, thanks for posting that for me," Jetta said with sincerity. That was one of the reasons I had so much love for him.

"Not a problem," I said. Stacks wouldn't have it any other way. After we placed our orders, I started filling him in.

"Stacks is going to be out of commission for a while. But we ain't taking no shorts. Y'all still gotta eat. With that being said, I'm coming out of retirement. I'll be heading the operation, and you'll be assisting me. I got to have a strong hand out there to make sure niggas don't take me lightly. That's where you come in. I plan on running this shit with an iron fist 'cause I don't want niggas to think that just 'cause I'm a bitch, I won't peel their cap back. I got to represent for my man, and I won't have it any other way. I need you to ride with me on all the pickups so they can get used to seeing my face again. I know Carlos from Fourth Ward is always late with payments. I need to make sure he don't try to game me out of our change. Since he's the one most likely to try me, he'll be the first one I'll make an example of if he don't come correct," I said with authority.

We were briefly interrupted when the waitress brought our

food. Since Jetta was starving, he wasted no time digging in. "Ain't no nigga gonna try you or get the drop while I'm around. You can bet your pretty ass on that. Stacks is my man, and since you're his family, you're my family. We're down like four flat tires plus the fifth wheel on a caddy, feel me, ma."

"I'm glad you feel that way 'cause I consider you a brother. In these streets I need to feel like I can count on somebody. Go ahead and enjoy your breakfast. I have a few things to handle, and then let's meet at the car wash tonight at six-thirty. I plan on letting everyone know what the deal is so there won't be any misunderstandings. Gather up everyone on the squad and let them know there's a mandatory meeting. I want everyone there." Jetta could tell I meant business and nodded, letting me know he understood exactly what I meant.

I got up from the table, said my goodbyes to my restaurant staff, and walked out the door. As I moved toward the parking lot, I took out my keys and pushed the automatic unlock button to my 600 Mercedes Benz. It was the "S" class, white on white, surround sound, and a navigational system. It was one of the luxuries Stacks had provided. There was no way I was going to give up "the good life." I was going to handle the business as if my man were out there doing it himself.

In the meantime, I had other things to deal with. Detective Morgan was at the top of my list. Word had it that he was a sucker for a big butt and a smile. Since I had both, he might as well consider me "poison," as Bell, Biv, Devoe put it so eloquently. I was going to make this silly-ass Dick Tracy putty in my hands. If Stacks knew what I was planning, he would be totally against it. But that wasn't my concern now. Since I'm the head nigga in charge, I'm going to do this my way.

Planning the Double Cross

I was sitting in the zone three precinct waiting for Detective Morgan to come out of a meeting. It was very busy inside. The secretary was aggravated because the phones were ringing off the hook and she was alone at the desk. Officers were jockeying for position at the coffee machine. The line there was about as long as the line at a good club on Saturday night. There were several boxes of doughnuts on the table by the vending machine. Everyone stopped and helped themselves to them. Some of them took more than their share. *Now I know why them motherfuckers so damn overweight. That's why they can't catch nobody unless they're in a high-speed chase,* I thought to myself and laughed out loud. Suddenly a dark-skinned man, approximately 6'3", with sparkling white teeth, beautiful skin, and features as handsome as those of the singer Tyrese appeared in front of me. For a moment, I was in a trance. The nigga was a stunner, but I had to remind myself that he was a pig and therefore also the enemy.

I was happy that when, not if, this nigga took the bait, it wouldn't be as dreadful as I'd thought. Since he was good-looking, that meant he had his share of women throwing themselves at him. Luckily for me, I'm a bad bitch. I ain't Halle Berry but I'd give that chick Gabrielle Union a run for her money. I ain't never had a problem getting and keeping a man. I don't take no for an answer, and if I so much as bat these pretty eyes, I'll get my prey.

"Ms. Dixon?" he asked.

"Yes, that's me, but call me Taylor," I said in a flirtatious and friendly tone. I noticed him giving me an approving once-over.

Got 'im, I thought to myself. I knew this nigga couldn't resist me. I was hell on wheels and I knew it.

"Well, Taylor," he paused before he spoke, "how can I be of service to you?"

"Well, Detective Morgan, I'd love to speak to you about Stacks—I mean Felix Martin," I said. He looked at me, unsure of the reason for my visit. I lowered my voice before I spoke again. "It's somewhat of a personal matter but I think I can be of great help to you."

"Come back to my office," he said. "It's a little more private and a bit more comfortable."

I followed him to the back where his makeshift office was. It looked like a scene from *Law & Order*. The desk was old but sturdy. Nothing stood out. Even the phone was old as hell, only one step above a rotary phone. Several awards and plaques were on the wall. On his desk was a photo of a beautiful woman who could have easily been mistaken for a model. I assumed it was his lady. But Detective Morgan didn't seem like the faithful type. I still had a chance. Not even a bitch could stand in my way. I took a seat in the vacant chair in front of him.

"As I was saying, Stacks, my ex, was arrested last night. As much as I hate to say this, I'm not surprised you whipped his ass during interrogation. I'm actually glad you did. That nigga used to beat my ass night and day. I had to buy so much makeup from MAC to cover the black eyes and bruises he used to give me, I could have owned the company," I babbled. I wanted him to relax and let his guard down.

"So you say Felix is your ex? You don't seem like the type who'd deal with a filthy low-down Negro like him. And speaking of the whipping, he and his crony Jetta deserved it. I plan on taking him down. I've been trying to nail his ass to the cross for years. I got his ass on a humbug," he said braggingly.

"A humbug? How so?" I asked. It was easy playing this nigga.

"Well, I'd been staking out a well-known drug dealer named Bulldog who runs Decatur. We'd been waiting to catch the thug dirty coming off I-20. We knew the make and model of the car he was driving and the time and place where everything was going down. The only thing we didn't know was who the supplier was. So imagine my luck when your ole boy, Stacks, shows up on the scene. But then we had one fuckup that we hadn't accounted for.

"What was that?" My anticipation of his answers was getting the best of me.

"Bulldog got away with the dope, so I have no product to put with the bust. All we could get Stacks on was a gun charge. Since he's a convicted felon, that's an automatic charge," he continued. "I couldn't let all our investigation hours go to waste. I tried to rough him and his partner up to find out who their supplier was, but that nigga wouldn't roll. So I had to settle for the illegal firearm charge. One less knucklehead on the streets."

I was fuming inside but I played it cool. My years of living in the streets had enhanced my acting skills. You couldn't tell the difference between me and Angela Bassett. I was worthy of an Oscar. I opened my legs briefly to let him get a glance at my nicely trimmed pussy. I noticed that I had his eyes looking exactly where I wanted, so I shifted in my chair, a move I took directly out of Sharon Stone's *Basic Instinct* handbook. She would have been proud. That nigga took the bait. He might have been a cop, but he wasn't immune to pussy. His eyes perked up and his dick stood at attention.

"Listen, Taylor, maybe we can help each other. I'm not sure how busy your schedule is this evening, but I'd like to talk to you in a more comfortable setting."

"Sure, no problem. I know a lot about Stacks. Maybe my info can help you nail him," I said. I had no intention of helping this nigga. I just wanted to string him along.

"I have a meeting at six-thirty, but it shouldn't last too long. If you like, we could meet around, say, ten-thirty," I said, feeling like I'd achieved my goal. He was panting like a lapdog. This shit was too easy.

"Uh, I'd like that a lot. Judging from our encounter, you seem very intriguing," he said.

"Well, I guess you'll soon find out." I got up and noticed his eyes traveling from my long legs to my breasts. *Yeah, I got this motherfucka.* I love it when a plan comes together. I walked out of the precinct feeling on top of the world. I reached into my jacket and turned off my tape recorder.

The Meeting

Our car wash was downtown on Peachtree Street. It used to belong to the rapper Erick Sermon. He made it a known hot spot because he used to sell rims out of it. Everyone who knew anyone frequented the spot. When he put the word out that he was selling it, Stacks didn't hesitate. He had a vision of turning it into a car wash. There were no black-owned high-end car washes, but Stacks saw no reason he couldn't be the first. I felt like we were the Jeffersons because we really moved on up. Once word got out that Stacks had converted the shop, money started coming in hand over fist. You know how niggas like to show off their cars. What better way for a baller to front than to profile his ride at a black establishment on Peachtree Street? Niggas was in there so deep, it was like Black Hollywood, only we were in the "A."

As I pulled into the lot, I noticed everyone's cars. It looked like a scene from an old classic gangsta movie. Frog, Rick, and Delano loved to drive fixed-up hoopties. Frog drove a candy-apple-red '62 Impala. Rick profiled an all-white-on-white '72 Caprice. Delano drove his heavy Chevy. Since I didn't see Zoot's ride, I figured he rode shotgun with one of them. I noticed several other cars on the front street. Jetta, Carlos, Sweet Meat, and Jake were parked on the side. I parked and quickly stepped inside the building. There was a lot of commotion but when they saw me, the room grew silent. "Gentlemen, I'm glad to see that everyone could make it on such short notice," I began.

"Hey, T," everyone said in unison.

I walked toward the small conference room, and everyone followed and took a seat. Stacks had had this room specifically built so he could conduct business. Even though he was a dope boy, he ran his operation like a Fortune 500 company. There was no half-stepping allowed. I took my seat at the front of the room where Stacks would normally be seated.

"As you all know, my man, your leader, has caught a case. He's going to be down for a minute. That ain't stopping shit 'cause business will run as usual. Actually a little stricter because, well, you know how niggas try to get over," I said.

"Question?" said Zoot, who'd been listening attentively.

"Yes, Zoot," I said.

"We already heard you'd be handling business in Stacks's absence. I mean, I mean no disrespect, but you his bitch. You ain't sold no dope in years. Niggas ain't gonna respect no bitch," he said. Everyone nodded in agreement except Jetta. I knew I had to do something drastic to make these Negros not only respect me but become believers. I reached back as far as I could and pimp-slapped him. It shocked the shit out of him. He wanted to hit me back but he looked at Jetta, who had a look on his face like, *Try it if you wanna.* He looked back at me, saw that I had my hand firmly placed on my Glock, and changed his mind.

"Now if you see a bitch, bitch nigga, handle your business," I said. "I'm the same bitch who fronted your ass your first eight ball when you and your little crew was still beating the block. I'm the same bitch who put you up on my man Stacks, and I'm the same bitch who'll take your ass out if you don't cooperate! Stacks put me in charge. I know the game, and I have his best interests at heart. I won't cheat you 'cause cheating you would be cheating myself. Now y'all niggas are either in or out," I said and didn't blink.

Carlos was the first to speak, which surprised me because he was the one I thought I'd have the most trouble with. "T, we all understand and we're down with the movement. Please excuse Zoot. He's been a little uptight since he heard about Stacks. We all think you're more than capable of handling things." He sounded convincing. I looked at Jetta and he gave me a nod, letting me know it was cool to pipe down for a second.

"All right, listen up," I said. "Frog and Rick, I need you to go out and collect on all your tickets in the Bluff. I don't want you extending any credit for a while. Carlos, I need you to continue to hold things down on Boulevard in Fourth Ward, but you need to be on time with your shit. You're generally late but I want you caught up to speed. Delano, Sweet Meat, and Jake, continue with your BI on the east, west, and Fulton Industrial side. Everything should be lovely if you follow my rules. This shit ain't about me. It's about us. We're family, ain't nothing changing. We all got to eat, so let's get this money so we can break bread. Any questions, concerns, or feedback?" I asked. No one said a word. "Well, in that case, this meeting is adjourned." As everyone left the room, they gave me hugs and goodbyes. Zoot stayed back. I could tell he wanted to speak in private, so I waited until everyone was out of earshot before I spoke. "What is it? Is there something you needed to say?" I wasn't concerned about him thinking I was soft. I knew I'd bruised his ego.

"Look, I apologize. I didn't mean to get out of pocket earlier. It's just that I've been real loyal to Stacks. I've always looked up to him, and you, for that matter. I respect everything y'all are doing. I ain't trying to cause no waves, but you gave everyone a job but me. Why is that?" he asked.

"'Cause you're gonna roll like I roll. You're rolling with me. I need eyes and ears, so you're going to be my direct connect," I said.

"So that's what's up," he said. "I got you, Momma. I'll hold it down with you. I always knew being with Stacks would pay off." He was so excited. He said his goodbyes and rushed off to meet his partners. It's too bad he didn't have a clue. You have to keep your friends close and your enemies closer. Zoot had already proved he wasn't family by questioning my fitness to lead the crew but I wasn't going to let him know any different. As long as he thought he had the upper hand, he'd continue to do what he does best. Fuck up. He was known to screw up from time to time. Stacks had let that shit slide. He blamed it on youth, but I wasn't feeling that shit at all. I already knew I had to watch everyone closely. Now that the order of business was out of the way, I could plan for the remainder of the evening.

Detective Morgan was meeting me at a place in Midtown. The condo actually belongs to my girl, Moet, who dances at Magic City, a strip joint. She uses it as a spot to entertain tricks. Since Morgan was the ultimate trick, he'd feel right at home.

Two Can Play the Fool

Moet had purchased the condo in Atlantic Station, a prominent area in the heart of Midtown, which was a sight for sore eyes. The name of the complex was Twelve, and it was a modern-style building with high-end décor and loft-style living. Moet had truly outdone herself. When niggas stepped into this place, they knew they had to empty their pockets. I had chosen this spot because I knew better than to have Morgan in my own place. If Stacks caught wind of my activities, he'd kill me. Plus I didn't want anyone on the streets to get the wrong idea seeing me talking to the po-po. At this point, there was no turning back. I knew it was risky business, but I couldn't let Stacks go to prison without a fight.

When I arrived at the condo, I quickly set the atmosphere for the evening. I lit candles throughout and put on light jazz. Kenny G was my shit. On the way over, I stopped at Publix and bought some precooked food from the deli. I quickly took it out of its containers and put it in pots and pans. I wanted him to think I'd spent some time in the kitchen. Then I set the table. I made sure to have my hidden camera set up. And the batteries were charged in my tape recorder.

Morgan rang the doorbell at exactly 10:30. I took a deep breath and prepared to play the role of my life. "Lights, camera, action," I said to myself.

Opening the door, I put on my biggest Colgate smile. Even though he was the police, he had a street swagger. He had his role all together. Had I not been with Stacks and had he not been a pig, I might have been enthused. But that wasn't the case. "Nice place, real nice," he said. He looked around the place like the true Dick Tracy he was.

"Thanks, I aim to please. After Stacks and I split, I needed something a little more me, I guess. It's not as big as our mini-mansion but it's mine," I said, trying to sound meek.

"It's certainly impressive, and so is the scent coming from those pots in there. Girl, tell me you didn't come straight from the precinct and start throwing down?"

"Yeah, I guess I did. I realized that after a hard day's work, you might have an appetite. I decided to cook you a li'l something something," I teased, noticing that he was definitely impressed.

"Well, damn, Taylor, you're a woman of many talents, aren't you? Not only are you beautiful but you can cook too. Now that's what I'm talking about. I'm glad you're a real woman. I'm so tired of these new-millennium wannabe Beyoncé bitches who want to be independent yet still dig in a man's pocket asking them to pay their damn bills," he whined.

"Honey, I've been cooking since I was six. I had no choice. My momma didn't have no money for restaurants or shit like that. We were poor but somehow we made it. Sometimes all we could make was a wish sandwich," I said.

"A wish sandwich? I never heard that one. How do you make it?" he asked.

"You take two pieces of bread, mash them together, and wish you had some meat."

He got quiet for a moment and looked sad. "Damn, girl, you were poor, huh?" he asked.

"Yeah, we were, but look at me now. I made it out in one piece," I said, changing the subject. "Come on, let's have dinner. Go ahead and have a seat. I've already set the table."

When he saw the setup, he was impressed again. I could tell by his gestures that he hadn't expected all this. He probably thought he was going to come over, hit this ass, and bounce. Well, it ain't gonna happen, Cap'n. But I was going to let him think whatever he wanted to. It didn't take him long to gobble down the fried chicken, canned glory greens, candied yams, and macaroni and cheese. "This shit is delicious. It's so good, it makes you wanna slap your momma!" he raved.

I giggled silently to myself. He was a simple-ass mark. There was no way in hell I could've gotten away with disguising a Publix meal as homemade with Stacks. He could tell the difference between frozen, canned, and fresh vegetables on the spot. I had tried that once and he'd damn near lost his mind.

"Let's go in the living room, where we can make ourselves more comfortable," I suggested. He was so eager he damn near hopped and skipped there. I followed him to make him feel like he was in control. He sat on the sofa and patted the empty space next to him, prompting me to take my place beside him.

"So tell me how you got involved with a loser like Stacks," he said.

"Well, I didn't know he was a loser when I met him. He was suave, cool, and seemed to have his shit together," I said.

"Oh, I'm quite sure he did have it somewhat together. Hell, I've been trying to catch him for years, but no matter what, he always got away. However, I busted one of his crew members a few months back. I thought I was going to have to rough him up in the interrogation room. Boy, was I wrong. As soon as we got his scary ass in the room, he damn near pissed on himself." He laughed out loud. The alcohol seemed to have loosened his tongue. I pretended to be amused and laughed along with him.

"I never thought Stacks would have a leak in his inner circle." I coaxed him so he'd keep talking.

"Oh, he sure does. His name is Zoot. What kind of name is that? These guys kill me trying to be hard. Get 'em in a six-by-nine cell with a bunch of hardheads and they turn soft as butter. Most of these dudes don't stand a chance alone. Zoot was a weak motherfucka. He gave me some info on Stacks that seemed to check out. So I cut the nigga loose 'cause I knew I could use his ass later on down the line if need be." He was in the zone now. He couldn't shut up. He'd confirmed for me what I'd already suspected. Zoot was the talkbox of our clique. He had to be dealt with accordingly, but everything would happen in its proper time.

"Well, Detective Morgan, I hope you got his ass. Stacks has been getting away with shit for as long as I can remember. He got a slap on the wrist for that aggravated assault charge. It's time for him to be put away. He tried to dog me and take my kindness for weakness," I spoke clearly and distinctly. I wanted the recorder to pick everything up.

"Taylor, call me Derrick. I'd like to think we could get beyond the bullshit. After all, we're getting to know each other better."

"Sure, I can feel you on that. Anyway, how do you plan on getting Stacks? I mean, if you have nothing solid, how will you put him away?" Here he was, Mr. Big-Time detective, and he couldn't even see that he was being played. He thought he was playing on my broken heart, but all along I was playing on his ego.

"Babe, I'm tired of low-life thugs getting away with breaking the law. I'm fed up with the little sentences the judges keep giving these repeat offenders. Every day I go out and fight crime only to see these scumbags make more money than I've got saved up for my pension. Well, I got your boy Stacks. His gig is up. Fuck the rules. Hell, ain't nobody playin' by 'em anyway. I planted the guns on his ass. He already had one in the car, but his boy Jetta was willing to take that rap. He outright claimed it but I wasn't going out like that. I planted my trusty throwaway on him too. Imagine his surprise. Do you know that his partner was willing to take that rap too? Unbelievable, the power he has over these dudes." Morgan was really irritated, but I was ecstatic. I could hardly contain myself. I'd gotten him to admit to setting up my man.

"So, Detective Morgan, you set Stacks up? Damn, I bet he's in there shitting himself. You know he's on parole. That's a five-year minimum for a convicted felon."

"Well, if you ask me, five years ain't long enough. Enough about him. Let's talk about you," he remarked as he moved closer. He started rubbing one of my breasts and kissing my neck. I could smell his hot drunken breath. The thought of a pig this close to me was more than I could stand.

"Baby, don't you have a girlfriend?" I asked between gasps. Morgan was horny as hell, and he'd let his guard all the way down. There was no shame in his game. He was all over me like white on rice.

"No, what I have is a nagging-ass wife. She's a royal pain. If it wasn't for my kids, I'd have left. Enough about her. Let's concentrate on me and you." He thought he was kicking game. *Typical nigga,* I thought. Right on cue, I realized he'd given me a way out of this mess. I had to bring my A-game skills to the table.

"Derrick, I thought you had a girlfriend. I didn't realize you had a wife. I don't do married men. Especially men with children. I'm not a home wrecker. I could never live with myself if I broke up your home, even if your marriage is on shaky ground. I refuse to be the straw that broke the camel's back. There's no good karma in something like that."

"Damn, man, you mean to tell me you got my dick harder than a motherfucka and all of a sudden you get a case of morals? You've got to be kidding me," he mumbled under his breath.

"Look, Derrick, I'm sorry. I really mean that. I'm not one of those females who tries to work a man up and leaves him hanging. Seriously, Stacks had my mind all fucked up. It took me a while to get back to a place in my life where I felt normal. If shit is really bad like you say at home, maybe you guys should get some counseling. I know it helped me." I sounded like some wounded, pathetic, weak ho.

"Hey, it's cool. I need to get out of here before I change my mind and jump your bones. For the record, do yourself a favor and don't go near Stacks. Leave those street-life thugs alone. You seem to be a decent young woman with a good head on your shoulders. Be more selective when choosing the next time," he said before getting up. He picked up his keys and walked toward the door.

"Detective Morgan?" I called out. I had to at least put the icing on the cake.

"Yes, Taylor, what is it? Have you changed your mind?" He sounded hopeful.

My next statement dashed his hopes. "No, I haven't. But I wanted to say thank you for everything even though we can't be intimate. You revealed so much today through your candid conversation. You've been very enlightening, and I appreciate it," I said. He had no idea how true my statement was.

"Well, I'm glad I could help. I'm going to go ahead and get out of here. If you need anything or have any second thoughts, just give me a call." He walked out, closing the door softly behind him. I quickly got up and locked it before letting out a sigh of relief.

Without missing a beat, I walked over to the sofa and reached under the pillow. I pulled out the recorder I'd hidden prior to Morgan's visit. It was still recording. I pushed the STOP button and rewound. I played back the conversation; everything he'd said was loud and clear. I went to the TV stand and pressed its POWER button. The TV was actually a high-definition camera that had filmed the whole scene. I was impressed by the electronic gadget. The sales rep had bragged about how great it was, and he'd been right. Now I had to see my baby Stacks. I knew he was worried about me. First thing in the morning, I'd head down to County.

What's the 411?

I sat at the visitation booth waiting to see my man. Although he'd only been in jail for three days, it seemed like a year. We'd never been apart for any real length of time since we'd been living to-gether. Visitation at County was the worst because they had a thick Plexiglas partition that kept us from touching each other. They made visitors feel like they were seeing an animal instead of a loved one. When they brought Stacks in, my face lit up like a kid with a bag of candy. "Hey, baby, how are you holding up?" I asked.

"Babe, I'm good. I'm in here maintaining. I hate that I'm not out there taking care of you. You know I love you, right?" he asked. He already knew the answer.

"Of course I know you love me," I said. "Don't be stressing yourself about things out here. I did like you asked. I called the meeting, gave everyone their expected post, and laid out the things to be handled."

"I heard that, li'l momma. I also heard you had to pimp-slap Zoot. What was that all about? I never expected him to go against the grain. When I get out, I'm going to have a word with him," he stated.

I decided to switch the conversation. I could sense him getting angry and wanted him to stay focused. "Baby, I got Zoot in check. He knows his place with me. The money is coming in real nicely. Before I came here, I collected what was out. Every last penny was accounted for. I'm going by today to retain your lawyer. I have an appointment with your parole officer this afternoon at two. I'm trying to get her to agree that if the judge grants you a bond, she'll lift the parole hold. You might be out by next week. If you agree to go home on the monitor, I think they'll grant you house arrest." I was hoping this little bit of news would cheer him up.

"What did I do to deserve you? You've always had my back, even when times got rough. I can always count on you. I'm lucky to have you in my life." As he spoke those words, I could see tears forming in his eyes. Now Stacks ain't no punk. I'd only seen him cry twice in my life. The first time was when his grandpa, Mason, died. Mason was the only father he'd known. The other time was when his best friend, Steelo, Jetta's big brother, was shot and killed. Some say the bullet was meant for Stacks. No one knows if that was true or not. What I do know is, Stacks took his death really hard. It was almost two years ago, and anytime anyone mentions Steelo, Stacks's whole demeanor changes.

"Why are you getting all sad on me?" I asked. "We deserve each other. Of course I got your back, and you got mine. You took me off those cold lonely streets and showed me nothing but love. You've been a provider, a protector, and the love of my life. Now, I know you're feeling like your back is against the wall. But I want you to remember this, ain't nothing too hard for God. We might not be perfect and I know we ain't living all the way right. But God takes care of his own. I might have lost my momma but you gave me more family. He gave me you. I'm not gonna lose you to the streets, jail, or no bitch. You feel me?" I asked him. I wanted to make sure he understood me.

He looked at me in amazement. "Baby, you gotta believe I ain't fuckin' around with no females. Yeah, I'm a G but I'm not stupid." He was pleading his case.

"Stacks, don't you think I know that already? You're a man. And a powerful one at that. Yeah, I know females try to sway you. I don't blame them, not one bit. I got your phone. I see the text messages. I'm not concerned about all that. I know you know where home is. If you forget, trust me, I know how to remind your ass." I put my fist up to the glass and smiled to let him know that although I meant it, I was still being lighthearted.

"Girl, you are so feisty. That's what I love about you. Ain't nobody going nowhere. If I have to do these five years—" I cut him off abruptly.

"I just told you you ain't doin' no five years. Now you better get some faith. Don't punk out on me now. That ain't the man I know and love. Like you told me, 'Man up, motherfucka.' " He laughed so hard the tears in his eyes fell. I knew he loved me more than life itself. I also knew he was worried about everyone but himself.

"Time's up," the jailer announced. He seemed pleased to break up our happy moment. I looked at the fat motherfucka and rolled my eyes. He had a bad case of the "Booty Do." That's when your stomach sticks out more than your booty do.

Stacks noticed the change in my expression and burst out laughing. "Behave, Li'l Momma," he said.

"Okay, I'll behave, Daddy," I said. I blew him a kiss and left the county lockup feeling a hell of a lot better than I had a few days ago. I had a new pep in my step. I knew my baby was coming home. I stopped by the Best Buy and found the sales clerk who'd helped me with my camera. He was ecstatic when I gave him a two-hundred-dollar tip. It was only a drop in the bucket for me, but for a seventeen-year-old, it meant a pair of Jordan's, a new handheld PSP, or a PlayStation. I also made sure to write a great letter of recommendation to his general manager. I knew it was the highlight of his day.

I drove over to the Fulton Industrial Parole Office and waited for Stacks's parole officer. An attractive woman appeared and motioned for me to enter her office. Unlike the precinct, it had a little glam and flair. Of course it had that corny Georgia State seal on the wall, letting you know you were in a government building. However, the people in this branch seemed like they wanted to be at work. From the outside looking in, they all seemed attentive. "Ms. Dixon, you're here about Mr. Martin, correct?" she asked. Her tone was stern but very gentle. I felt very comfortable.

"Yes, ma'am, I am. You see, my fiancé has been abiding by the conditions of his parole for the last six years. His records show no trouble, not even dirty urine." I wasn't sure exactly how he'd passed. Stacks smoked more weed than Shabba Ranks and Bob Marley combined. We teased him that he wasn't just black, he was a Jamaican.

"Well, unfortunately, Mr. Martin is locked up on a gun charge. He's a convicted felon, which is an automatic five-year sentence. Judging by the police report, he's the guilty party. That actually surprised me, he seemed to be following all the rules and regulations of parole," she said.

"Listen, you and I both know that he hasn't broken any rules. Why would he actually commit a felony? Don't you find that odd?" I asked.

Up to this point, we were both standing in her office. "Forgive my manners, Ms. Dixon. Have a seat."

I sat down, and instead of sitting behind her desk, she sat next to me. She made me feel at ease.

"Ma'am, I have some pertinent information that could free Felix immediately. I haven't shown it to anyone because I wasn't sure who to disclose it to first."

"Ms. Dixon, please call me Carol. I'm much too young to be a 'ma'am.' At least I'd like to think I am," she said in a lighthearted and calm voice.

"Of course you are. It's just that my mother always taught me manners. I guess it's that southern hospitality that's embedded in me. Anyway, I have a tape and video that will show that Felix is not only innocent but that there are some people on the force who need to be brought to justice."

Carol was all ears now. I played the tape recording first. She not only listened, she took out a pen and started taking notes. When I played the video footage, she turned bright red. She was a sister; we don't wear our feelings on our sleeve. I could tell she was really angry.

"Ms. Dixon, is that you in the video?" she asked.

"Yeah, it's me."

"I'm shocked that you put yourself in that situation. You must really love him. Mr. Martin is a lucky man," she said.

"You're right. I do love him very much, but I must correct you. I'm the lucky one."

"Well, in light of this recent discovery, I can't see why we won't have Mr. Martin out by his next hearing. This tape is evidence that he was clearly set up. Not only will he get off, but Detective Morgan might be taking his place."

Carol was upset for three reasons. First, she disliked crooked policemen. Second, she hated when people didn't believe in giving others second chances because she felt that once a person had served their time, they were free to live their life. Last but not least, she despised cheating husbands. As it turned out, Detective Morgan was her brother-in-law. She explained to me that her sister had married him eight years ago. No one in the family trusted or liked him. She'd had her suspicions that he was screwing around on her sister. Now she had valid proof. I definitely didn't want to be in his shoes. She was a boss bitch on the right side of the law. I could tell she wasn't bullshitting. After giving her duplicate copies of the tape and video, we discussed the strategy for nailing Morgan.

I knew that Morgan would have hell to pay. I'd done my duty for the day. Both Stacks and his parole officer had all the 411 they needed.

My next order of business was to see Zoot. I hit Jetta on his cell and made arrangements for him to meet me at my boutique. Once I gave him the formal update, I figured we'd pay our respects to Zoot. It was time for him to pay the piper.

We arrived at Spondivitz in Hapeville at approximately eight o'clock. That's a spot where all the D-boyz and ballers hang out. The food was banging. Spondivitz is on Virginia Avenue, not far from the Hartsfield International Airport, the largest airport in the world. At first glance, one would think it was some ole bullshit. But as they say, never judge a book by its cover. It's one of the best, if not the best, seafood restaurants this side of the Mississippi River. It's known for strong drinks, delicious food, and high-ass prices. Ballers took their best bitches there when they wanted to impress. Hos knew that if they were there for a date, it was definitely going on their pussy tab. Stacks and I love Spondivitz. He'd gotten so cool with the owner, we'd come and have him open during off-hours. That, of course, would set us back a pretty penny but we had it to spare.

Zoot was sitting at the bar drinking a strawberry daiquiri. To me, that's a bitch drink. Real niggas drink cognac, bourbon, and vodka. I knew this nigga was a pussy.

"What's poppin', Zoot?" I asked in a cheerful voice. Everything was going as planned, and he was the final piece of the puzzle.

"Ain't too much shaking. I'm sitting back sipping this drink and checking out some of the lovely ladies," he said.

"You call that a drink? That's a bitch drink. Real niggas don't drink syrup and whipped cream unless they about to eat some pussy," I teased. "Bartender, bring us three shots of Patron, chilled and with salt." The bartender hurried away and came back with the shots.

"Damn, baby girl, you doin' it like that? Okay, I'm with you, let's get these shots out of the way." His voice was unsure. He wasn't a drinker, he was a smoker. I knew that but I didn't give a shit. I wanted him to get real toasted. We threw our shots back and I motioned for the bartender to bring us another round. I knew Jetta could hold his own, and I wasn't worried about myself. I can drink the average man under the table. Patron was one of my favorite beverages. I knew Zoot wouldn't be able to handle his liquor, but I didn't give a damn. We placed our food order and I quickly checked on Zoot. The two shots of Patron had him tipsy as hell. He was trying to be hard and maintain his cool. Jetta and I had to hide our amusement. Little did he know, he had a long night ahead of him. Then his weed hunger must have kicked in, because he completely cleaned his plate. I guess he was trying to soak up some of the liquor he'd been slurping. Unfortunately, I wasn't letting him off the hook. I kept the drinks coming. His sick ass was going to pay. Toward the end of dinner, I could tell he'd entered the twilight zone.

My iPhone was beeping, letting me know the second phase of the plan was about to occur. I texted Moet back to let her know I was at the back of the restaurant. When she approached our table, Zoot's eyes lit up. He'd secretly had a crush on Moet for years. Sometimes he'd stop by Magic City on a slow night just to make it rain on her. He thought that would impress her, but she wasn't fazed in the least. For her, it was always money over niggas. She knew that as long as she was stripping in the club, she'd never have a serious relationship. She considered Zoot a loser who was trying to hang with the big boys. When I'd told her about the situation with Stacks and how Zoot had become a snitch, she didn't hesitate to be part of my deceitful plan. I'd offered her a pretty penny for her help, but out of loyalty and obligation to Stacks and me, she refused it.

"Hey, Taylor. What's up, Jetta and Zoot? Nice to see y'all here. Especially you, Zoot," she said seductively. Moet has a way with men. Jetta and Zoot had been locked at attention since she'd approached the table. Like I said earlier, I'm pretty easy on the eyes, but Moet puts me to shame. She has a rosy complexion, with beautiful, almond-shaped hazel eyes. Her lashes are long, thick, and full. Her body is shaped like a Coke bottle. That bitch is bad. She's 5'10", bowlegged, with long, natural, sandy-brown wavy locks. I could see why dudes spent their money on her. She was the truth. I kicked Jetta to bring his ass out of his daze. Noticing the stern look on my face, he popped back. It's funny how men can be so weak. Pussy is powerful, and we women know it.

Locking in on our prey, Moet went in for the kill. "Zoot, I've been admiring you for quite some time now. It's just that with work and all, I never really get a chance to kick it and let my hair down. But tonight is my day off and I'm looking to have a good time."

Zoot acted like he'd just hit the lottery. Drunk or not, he definitely wasn't turning down the chance to be with the likes of Moet. She was his dream, and now he had his golden opportunity. T-Pain said it best. Zoot was in *love* with a stripper. "Excuse my manners, baby. Have a seat," he said as he scooted over to make room in the booth. Moet took a seat so close to Zoot you'd have thought they were Siamese twins. Moet, being the party girl that she is, was ready to bring on the festivities. "Whatcha sippin' on, girl?" Zoot asked. He had his big-boy demeanor on now. I couldn't believe it. Earlier when we were doing shots, he'd seemed hesitant. Now, in front of Moet, this dude went from Clark Kent to

Superman. The funny part about it was, this nigga never went into a phone booth. He changed right in front of our eyes. "I want you to feel like you're dating TI. You can have whatever you like," he boasted. I had to admit, he brought out his swag.

"Bring me some Patron and, hell, let's chase it with Rosé." Moet said it like it was the everyday norm, which in her case it was. She was used to that type of lifestyle. Eager to please, Zoot put his order in. There seemed to be no limit to how far he'd go to please her. That included buying out the bar.

I wanted to stay and watch how everything would unfold, but for things to run their course, I knew I had to flee. Moet and I had already discussed how things would go down. I was more than confident in her skills. I made up an excuse about having to be at the boutique for a staff meeting and left the restaurant. On the way out, I spotted Tate. I think my presence startled the hell out of him. Neither of us said a word. I dared that loser to even blink. I had my Nina strapped to my thigh, and as much as I loved Spondivitz, I wouldn't have minded taking his ass out on the spot.

Sensing that I wasn't someone to fuck with, he turned and got lost in the crowd. I looked at Jetta, who was standing right next to me like the CIA. He was armed and ready to blast a nigga. "That dude is nothing but trouble waiting to happen," he mumbled. Jetta disliked him almost as much as I did, but for his own reasons. I turned and looked back in Spondivitz and noticed Tate at the table talking to Zoot. I texted Moet a brief message and started walking toward my ride. I read her return text and took a breath of air.

"You want me to go back in there and handle both of them marks?" asked Jetta, who was ready like Freddie.

"No," I said. I was smiling inside. I knew that with Moet listening in on their conversation, it was just as good as me being there with front-row seats. "I got this, Jetta, trust me. There's more than one way to skin a cat."

Playing Pussy and Getting Fucked

I hid in the walk-in closet of Moet's condo. Originally, we'd only planned on having to deal with Zoot. However, when Tate had showed up unexpectedly, I had to get two for the price of one. I could hear Moet giggling as she came down the hall. She'd initially agreed to bring Zoot back but when I texted her about luring Tate to come too, I knew she was game. She was my closest girlfriend, and I'd confided in her about how he'd tried to rape me. We'd said that if we ever caught that nigga slippin', we'd toast his ass. Well, tonight was his night.

They thought she was going to have a ménage à trois with them. Zoot was so fucked up he didn't care if he got the pussy or not. Just being in the same room with Moet was good enough for him. Tate, on the other hand, was a true hard leg. He was all about trying to beat some pussy to sleep. I'd already warned Moet to be extra-careful when handling him. Both of us were packing our Ninas with hollow points and silencers. I'd nicknamed my Nina "Justice" because when I pull her out, it's just like being a judge; niggas was getting the life sentence.

Tate tried to be aggressive and set the tone for what he thought was about to be a magnificent evening. "Moet, baby, go to the back and put on one of those sexy-ass outfits that you wear onstage. You so damn fine, you have me in the corner screaming like a bitch," he teased. Moet giggled and excused herself to go get dressed. While she was changing, I could hear Tate and Zoot whispering. "Yo, I thought you said your boy Stacks was out of commission and you'd be handling things. What happened? Before this shit went down, I was getting my keys for the low-low. Now your boy Carlos acts like he don't know our situation. He ain't even trying to front no yayo," he said. I couldn't believe my ears. Zoot had been supplying the enemy with our own product. Here I was thinking Carlos would be the weak link, and it was Zoot who was not only snitching but double-crossing. Hell, naw, this lame ass had to be dealt with.

"Listen, man, I've been trying to earn my position back. Unfortunately for me, Taylor's been made chairman of the street team. She's changed my post, making me hang with both her and Jetta. I couldn't stand his brother, Steelo, which is why I marked his ass. Being around him is like being with Steelo's ghost. He's a walking replica of that fool."

Did I just hear what I thought I did? Had he truly set up Steelo's murder? He'd just signed his death certificate. I hoped his mother had insurance, 'cause she was about to need it.

Moet returned to the room barely wearing a sexy two-piece ensemble. She had her portable stripper pole in her hands. She twisted it into its place and gave the guys a million-dollar smile. "Hey, boys, let's role-play. I'll play the stripper and y'all be my big ballers," she said.

"Fo'sho," Tate said as he began taking out his roll and throwing money at her. Not to be outdone, Zoot took out two rolls of money and started throwing bills her way too. Moet was enjoying the attention. She stepped over to the stereo system, turned on some seductive music, and dimmed the lights.

"Hey, Mo, you're turning me the fuck on. I gotta get a piece of that good-good. I want to tap it first," said Tate.

"I got first dibs, nigga. It wasn't my idea to invite you anyway," Zoot said, crying like a baby.

"Oh, suga, two is company and three's a blast. I'm a bottle of bubbly, remember? Now bring that dick over to Momma," she crooned in a sultry voice.

Zoot trotted over to Moet, while Tate started taking off his clothes. I swear he was butt-naked before Zoot could even make it over to Moet. Zoot started fondling her, kissing one breast, and going down to her secret garden. Moet sighed with glee. She was either enjoying the attention or she was putting on a hell of an act. She looked toward the closet and winked at me, letting me know it was all a game. My girl was damn good. Tate joined the party and started kissing every place that Zoot wasn't.

"Damn, baby, you got the sweetest-tasting pussy," Zoot said. He was smacking like it was a pastry.

"Let me taste some of dat." Without waiting his turn, Tate just dug in. He literally pushed Zoot out of the way and staked his claim.

"Boys, I got a surprise for you," Moet said, giving me my signal.

"What's the surprise?" they said in unison.

"Remember I said we were going to role-play? Well, I have a new character for you guys. I want you both to try out for the part. The winner gets a special treat," she teased.

"What's the part? I've been told I could've been the next Denzel or Jamie Foxx if I'd stuck with it in high school." Zoot was really laying it on thick. He was not going down without a fight.

Quietly I appeared out of the closet. I took Justice out and pointed at my target.

That's when I said, "The character she wants you to play is pussy, and you're both about to get fucked." My voice scared the shit out of them.

"What the fuck is going on?" Tate said.

"Uh, T, why you playin' and shit? Put that gun down before you hurt somebody," Zoot pleaded.

"I know you don't think I'm playing with your ass 'cause I'm not."

"T, why you holding that gun like that? We're family and supposed to be as one," Zoot was stuttering.

"One? Are you kidding me? Family? Nigga, please, you are bad

blood." I was fighting both anger and tears. I thought of everything Zoot had done. He'd not only set Stacks up, he'd had Steelo
killed. Oh, this nigga was about to get it. "Fuck, nigga, you got a lot
of nerve. I heard every fuckin' thing you said. You a fuckin' snitch
and a murderer. There's no need to explain, motherfucka. You
about to die."

I heard a strange noise from across the hall and briefly took
my eyes off Zoot. Taking full advantage of the distraction, he
jumped up and tried to take the gun from me, catching me completely off guard. We were suddenly in a tug-of-war with the gun.
I wasn't a weak bitch by any means, but this dude was really over-
powering me. Somehow, while we were fighting for the gun I
tripped, knocked over the coffee table, and fell to the floor.

Trying to gain control, Zoot maneuvered his weight and rolled
on top of me. He was prying my legs open like he was going to rape
me. I was still hanging on to the gun. I wasn't about to let up. It
was him against me. We were both fighting for our lives. There
was no way I was going to die. I began to fight with everything I
had.

I could see Moet out of the corner of one eye, and noticed her
going for her gun. I knew my bitch had my back. I wasn't worried.

Tate seemed shocked by the events taking place. He was about
to go for the gun he had hidden in one boot, but Moet beat him by
a millisecond.

"Not, so fast, nigga. You a little too slow on the draw. Raise
your hands in the air where I can see them," she said. He followed
her order to the letter. He wasn't about to test her. He knew she
wouldn't hestitate to shoot him. Without taking her gun off her
target, Moet took his gun.

Meanwhile, Zoot and I were still scuffling over my gun. I suddenly saw a way out. I kicked him in the groin with all my might
and he doubled over in the fetal position. I'd gained full control of
my weapon.

I gathered myself off the floor and stood over him. I was out of breath, but my eyes told him what was what.

Without another word, I popped him two in the head.

Tate started crying and trying to plead his case. "Look, Taylor, I know I ain't perfect or nothin'. That little shit that happened back then was a misunderstanding." He looked at Moet, hoping to get some help.

Moet wasn't willing to be his cheerleader. "Bitch, I know you ain't looking at me to save yo ass," she said. She was staring him down, not budging or considering his whining.

"Look, I know I was wrong, but two negatives don't make a positive. You ain't got to kill me. I ain't gonna tell nobody that y'all murked that man. I didn't like him no way." He was crying now. What a sellout.

"You're right, you ain't gonna tell nobody 'cause you ain't gonna live to tell it, nigga. You stand to be corrected. Two negatives do make a positive, at least in the world of math." I had talked enough. I pulled that nigga's skull back and gave him three to the head. I shot him once for me, once for Stacks, and once for good measure. BAM! BAM! BAM!

Moet and I stood there a second and looked at the two corpses lying on the ground. Then she quickly got dressed. True to her nature, she checked both their pockets, took all their money, and swiped every piece of jewelry. "They won't be needing this where they're going. I hope they burn in hell," she said.

While she was doing her sweep, I called Jetta and let him know that the deed was done. "Come through and take care of this. You're going to need the cleanup crew."

I didn't say another word. I looked at Moet and gave her a nod, letting her know everything was complete. Just like two boss bitches, we popped our collars and walked out the door.

It Ain't Over Until the Fat Lady Sings

That night when my head finally hit the pillow, I was out like a light. Stacks's parole officer called me the next morning to let me know that she'd be in court that day. I was ecstatic. Stacks had no idea that she was going to push to reinstate his parole. I had hired a great lawyer, David Wolf, the Perry Mason of Atlanta, to make sure Stacks would have the best counsel possible. I quickly dressed to the nines and headed to the Fulton County Courthouse. I looked like a black Erica Kane. When Stacks's legal team noticed me, they beckoned me over. Once they let me know the motions they had before the judge, I took my seat. In twenty minutes, the courtroom was filled to capacity. I looked around and saw Detective Morgan strut into the room. He had a confidence that bordered on arrogance. He just knew his shit didn't stink.

"Order in the court," the bailiff announced. "This is the Honorable Jacob Means's courtroom, District Four, Circuit Thirteen. This is a criminal court docket. There will be no cell phones, pagers, or electronic devices used. If you have them, please turn them off now. There will be no conversations or interruptions while court is in session."

The jailer brought in the inmates from the jail. They were handcuffed and shackled at the ankles as if they were on a chain gang. Stacks glanced around the courtroom and noticed me. He gave me a nod and a slight smile. I waved at him and smiled, showing all thirty-two teeth. He knew I was his number-one cheerleader.

Shortly after all the inmates were escorted in and seated, the judge entered. "All rise," the bailiff said in his deep baritone voice. Everyone stood and the judge explained how he ran his courtroom. We all listened attentively. He turned to his court clerk and asked for the court docket, which listed the order he would call the defendants. Fortunately, Stacks was up first. All paid attorneys have the first at bat in Judge Means's courtroom.

"Is there any special order that needs to come forth before I begin with the court proceedings?" the judge asked. None of the lawyers made a move, letting the judge know that business could continue.

"Okay, let's get going with today's docket. Mr. Felix Martin, please stand with your attorney of record and approach the podium."

The judge seemed to be in a good mood, which was unusual, since he's known as "mean as Hell."

"Mr. Martin is charged with violation of parole and possession of a firearm while being a convicted felon. State, let's hear your case."

Robert Jenkins, the Assistant District Attorney for the state, approached the judge to give his detailed opening remarks. "Your Honor, Mr. Felix Martin is a known thug and drug dealer. He's accused of violating his parole by carrying a gun. In addition to possession of a firearm, he was also in the process of completing a major drug deal that would have taken place had the authorities not learned of the crime and foiled it."

"Your Honor, that's speculation," said David Wolf, Stacks's attorney. "The state can't prove that my client was at the location in question to buy drugs. In fact, the state can't even prove that there *was* a drug deal. No drugs were found at the scene of the supposed crime."

Judge Means looked at both attorneys and spoke sternly. "This is a court of law. What we will do today is try the facts, and only the facts. I don't want to hear about circumstantial evidence. I don't want to hear a lot of what-ifs, what could have beens, or what may bes. Do I make myself clear?" It was more like a statement than a question.

Both attorneys nodded in unison.

"Now, Mr. Jenkins, can you call your first witness?" Judge Means asked.

"Your honor, I'd like to call Detective Morgan to the stand."

Morgan approached the witness box like a true professional. He looked like a picture cut out of *Law & Order.* He looked very clean-cut. Little did anyone know he was as muddy as the Mississippi River.

After being sworn in, he took a seat.

"Detective Morgan, are you the arresting officer of the defendant Felix Martin?"

"Yes, sir."

"Could you give me a little background about the arrest and what you and your partner uncovered at the scene of the crime?" the ADA asked.

"Of course I can. On the night in question, my task force and I were doing surveillance on a known drug dealer. We were told by some confidential informants that a big drop was going to be made. We joined the DEA and the local Red Dogs to make the biggest drug bust to date. While we were doing surveillance, we noticed Martin and an accomplice enter the gas station store with a duffel bag. We had just seen our mark enter the store a few minutes prior, so we knew the drop had been made.

"One of our officers reacted too quickly and jumped before the command. In the middle of this fiasco, we believe Martin was able to dump the drugs. When we arrested him, no drugs were found. However, we did find two weapons. Martin's accomplice claimed the first one, but we found the second gun directly on Martin. Since he's a convicted felon, we booked him on the weapons charge. Ballistics were run to see if the gun had been used in a crime. So far, nothing's come back, but we're running it through the NIC system too," he said, full of confidence.

Mr. Jenkins felt like he'd already won his case. He was so sure of it, in fact, that not only did he call no other witnesses, he was ready to rest his case.

The defense was up next. David Wolf was a pro, and just like his namesake, he was ready to pounce. The courtroom was his territory, and he ruled it proudly.

He approached the witness stand. "Detective Morgan, you're a decorated officer, correct?" The detective nodded.

"I mean, you've had one hell of a career," Wolf continued. "You were awarded the Purple Heart, you've been named Detective of the Year for the State of Georgia, and you're the head of the task force for Zone Three. I must say, I'm impressed. You took those words 'To serve and protect' to heart." Morgan looked a little uncomfortable, not sure where Wolf was going.

"Your Honor, can he get to the point?" Jenkins said. "We all know about Detective Morgan's achievements. Where is this line of questioning going? In fact, I haven't heard a question at all."

Judge Means looked at Wolf and said, "Mr. Wolf, how do Detective Morgan's achievements relate to your client?"

"I'm glad you asked, Your Honor," Wolf replied. "Detective Morgan is what we call the scum of the earth. Instead of fighting for the law, he's taken the law into his own hands. He's used his badge for his own selfish ends. He's setting up innocent people, putting them in jail for crimes they didn't commit, and stepping on them like dirt to climb the ladder of success." He didn't give the ADA a chance to get a word in.

"Objection, Your Honor. This is pure speculation. This is defamation of character. This is unethical. I demand that he recant those statements." The ADA was fuming.

"First of all," the judge said, "no one demands anything in this courtroom except for me. I'm shocked, Mr. Wolf, at your statements. You better have some proof to back up these statements, or not only will you be fined, but I'll have the State Bar review this case. Now, what proof do you have of such allegations?"

"Your Honor, may I enter exhibit A? It's a tape recording of Detective Morgan admitting to not only setting Mr. Martin up but also to beating him and his accomplice." Wolf was in rare form.

Detective Morgan looked angry. "I'm not the scumbag here. Those drug-dealing fools are, and this—this—thuggish, cold-hearted bastard is trash!" He couldn't control his temper. The ADA tried to keep Morgan from speaking, but it seemed he'd gone into a zone.

This was a spectacle, and I was surprised that Judge Means let it go on. I'm pretty sure I even saw him smirk.

"Yeah, I may have planted something on him," Morgan said. "Why not? They've been getting away with shit for so long. Some-body had to stop them. But instead of going after them, you want to go after me. I'm a taxpayer, for God's sake. I keep your ass safe. Every night I go out there and fight crimes while you sleep in your comfortable beds. Then when we do bust these thugs, they go hire these high-price attorneys who get them off. So, yeah, I planted a gun, because I couldn't catch him with the dope. I had to account for something; I had forty hours of manpower I had to explain to my superiors. If I didn't get a bust, it was my ass. And, yeah, I roughed him up a bit. Who gives a damn? It's better than the bul-lets he dodges every day. You people kill me. I mean, whose side of the law are you really on?" Morgan had clearly lost it.

The courtroom was silent. As Wolf entered the evidence, he asked the judge if he could play the tape for the courtroom. Under normal circumstances it wouldn't have been allowed. I mean, I wasn't a police officer, and Morgan wasn't aware that I'd taped him. But since he'd incriminated himself, it was fair game.

After hearing the tape, we knew it was a win. I looked at Stacks and winked. I knew he'd be furious when he found out that I'd put myself in danger to keep him from going to prison, but I'd deal with that after he was free.

After closing arguments, we sat on pins and needles waiting on the judge's verdict.

"In light of everything that has occurred, I'm really amazed. The law is supposed to serve and protect. But in this case it seems that *some* people took the law into their own hands. I'm here to make judgments based on the facts presented to me. It's clearly an injustice to the people and the system I serve when one of our own believes himself to be above the law. I first of all demand the release of Mr. Felix Martin immediately. We apologize for the inconvenience.

"I'd also like to demand an investigation of department standards and regulations by Internal Affairs, and I'm calling for Detective Morgan's badge to be turned in until a full-fledged investigation is completed. Court is dismissed."

I ran over to Stacks and gave him a huge hug and kiss. He smelled like jail, but I didn't give a damn.

"Baby, I told you I had your back. I knew you were coming home. I'm so happy." I was smiling from ear to ear.

"Yeah, baby, you definitely put your work in on that one. I'm so happy to have you in my life. You're a trouper, just like TI and Tiny. You had a nigga's back. But, baby, I ain't going to trip now, but if you ever put your life in jeopardy again, I'm going to be real upset, you hear me?" I knew he was serious and I understood.

As we walked out of the courthouse hand in hand, I turned and whispered in his ear, "I love you so much, Stacks."

We paused for a moment, then he looked me in the eye and said, "I love you too, Ms. G-Stacks. You are one hell of a woman." I smiled. I knew I was engaged to a boss, and he knew he had a real boss bitch on his side. With that, we popped our collars and headed to the car. Hell, that was just one episode of many. We had money to make and a life to live.

Acknowledgments

Keisha Starr

First and foremost, I would like to thank God for not only creating me but instilling such a wonderful passion for the art of writing. I would like to thank Nikki Turner for giving me this opportunity and for being a mentor. In addition, I would like to thank my amazing family and close friends for believing in me and always pushing me to follow my dreams. Dawn Lamb and Elon "Nick" Wizzart, thank you for being the greatest parents in the world! Gary, the father of the family, I thank you for being the best cousin a girl could ever have. You stand a million men strong! Also, I would like to thank Gene for giving me tough love when I need it and for always encouraging and supporting me. Last but certainly not least, I want to thank the three people who make me get up and strive for success every day: John, Barbara, and Rallin (JBR). Your legacy will forever live on!

Tysha

I, first and foremost, thank God for all he continues to bless me with. I thank my sons, Je'Vohn and Reese for their unconditional love and support. We have an unbreakable bond. My brother, J.J., thanks for your help on the storyline. I love you baby brother! To my sister Tracey, my godsister Jenna, and my cousin Keedee, I thank you for being consistent with always encouraging and pushing me to share my ability to tell a story to the world.

LaKesa Cox

First, foremost, and always, I have to thank God for keeping me, taking care of me, and always being there for me. To my daughters who are both growing into beautiful young ladies: Continue to strive to be the best in everything you aspire to do. Don't take any shorts. To my baby boy who keeps this woman working hard at motherhood: Thanks for keeping me on my toes! To my husband: Thanks for your never-ending support and for always having my back. Seeing that this book is all about "women's work," I'd like to give a special thanks to two of the hardest-working hustlers in the single-mother business: my mother Patricia Crossin and mother-in-law Joan Roots. Thank you both for working hard to raise your children by yourselves. I realize now that it had to be hard work! Mom, you sure made it look easy! And finally, to Ms. Nikki Turner: my diva friend, homegirl, and all around sister in print, thank you so much for giving me the opportunity to do this thing again and represent for the ladies. You are the best at what you do, and I appreciate your continued support.

Monique S. Hall

First of all, I would like to thank my Heavenly Father, for allowing me to accomplish my goals and always watching over me, your lost sheep. For you truly left the ninety-nine to save this little one. I also want to thank my mom and dad, Thomas and Marylin Hall, for all their support; my sister, Teresa Rogers; my brother-in-law, Rev. Michael Rogers; and my niece, Michaela. Family is so important.

There are two young ladies who have been more than family: Dana Robinson and Nachelle Hemphill. You are my rock. Travian Williams, thank you for all your help on this project. I would like to give a special shout-out and dedication to Nikki Turner, who has been a sister, a friend, and a confidante. Thank you for allowing me to be a part of your vision and for allowing me to spread my wings.

About the Authors

Born Keisha Wizzart in Baltimore, MD, KEISHA STARR has always had a passion for creative writing. Early on, she traveled and performed with her family's band, The Determination Band, one of Baltimore's first reggae collectives, and began writing songs, school plays, cheers, and poetry, becoming a published author at just thirteen years old. And by age eighteen, she'd recorded her first CD, *True Confessions*. Keisha has gone on to write music for local artists and major powerhouses like Island Def Jam and Universal Records. She also writes for print publications including *Iconography* and *Ezo Magazine*. Keisha Starr has written her first urban novel, *Jamaican Me Go Crazy,* which she plans to release with a musical soundtrack.

TYSHA is the author of *The Boss*, the story of a female hustler. She is also a contributor to multiple anthologies including *Street Chronicles: Girls in the Game,* which is where Bossy and Aisha were first introduced to fans of urban fiction. Tysha is the mother of two adult sons. She was born and raised in Youngstown, Ohio, and currently resides in Columbus, Ohio. She is hard at work on multiple literary projects. Look for new titles coming soon.

LaKesa Cox, dubbed the Countess of Urban Drama by Nikki Turner, is the author of two novels, *After the Storm* and *Water in My Eyes*. She also wrote the short story "Power," which was published in Nikki Turner's *Street Chronicles: Girls in the Game*. Currently seeking a literary agent for representation, LaKesa recently completed her third novel, *Fetish for a Blue Skyy*. She resides in the suburbs of Richmond, Virginia, with her husband and three children. Feel free to hit her up on Facebook or email her at lakesacox@comcast.net.

Monique S. Hall's captivating debut novel, *Two Tears in a Bucket*, has received great reviews from *Library Journal*, BookExpo America attendees, and several book clubs nationwide. Her creative abilities extend beyond writing urban literature. She also hosts a talk radio show on WXYB, Tampa Bay, 1520 AM, serves as the editor-in-chief of the *Hawkeye* newspaper, and is a featured columnist for *Street Elements* magazine. She is also a liaison and advisor for The Real Freeway Rick Ross, and one of the contributing writers to his autobiography and upcoming biopic. Look for more to come from this extremely talented author.